The day

Is a day you give up on yourself ~
author unknown

Trust Me
By
Amii Maguire

Dedication

To the one person who has always been there, we might have been young when we married but I wouldn't change a thing with all the ups and downs. You complete me.

Love you Steve! Always and forever ♥

Acknowledgements;

Firstly, I would like to say a massive thank you to my beautiful husband, you've always supported anything and everything I've wanted to achieve, with you I always feel anything is possible. You are my heart and soul. ♡☆♡

To my children: You make us proud every day. You have never been a moments trouble and I'm proud to be your mum. My eldest Will for being such a good example of what a human being is about, for always leading by example and setting the standards for others. My daughter Grace for being you! Don't ever change and continue to chase your dreams of joining the police. My baby Alfie for always making us smile and the purity in which you view the world, that's what makes you special. I love you all equally ♡

To my mum and dad: Thank you for everything you have done for your four children. You've always shown us that with hard work you can achieve our dreams and always been there when you knew we needed it ♡

To my nan: Because of you, I found my love of the written word and I am doing the one thing I have always dreamed of doing. I was grateful we had the same love of reading and would share our books. Though you're no longer with us, you will always be in my thoughts ♡

To my BFF: Holly, aka: Beverley, I never really had a best friend until you. I thank God that we met and I have you in my corner. You truly are an angel. You don't know how much you keep me going woman, love you always ♡

To my other BFF: Vera Fowler, we are soul sisters, woman. We are so alike it's uncanny. You make me smile daily and everyone needs that in their life, so I thank you for being you, don't ever change missis. Love you ♡

To my special Ladies: S. J. Batsford, Sallyanne Johnson, Tammy Bendix Pierce PA, Kelly Graham, Stacy Stewart, Clare Bentley & Sandra Hearn PA, I really appreciate all your support and encouragement. You help to keep me focused and show me with the right support you can achieve your dreams. Remember I will always have your back ♡

To the members of my reading group: Amii's Bootylicious Ladies, you make me smile daily. Thank you for being a part of my journey ♡

To Sally Orchard for editing my first baby, I really appreciate your help sweetheart ♡

To my Aunts Diane & San: Thank you for setting the right example for us all to learn from and for being there for mum and dad when they needed you the most ♡

And of course, Liam Reagan, I am so glad I met you at the start of this journey because you keep me on track with our sprints and daily catch ups. You are one of life's true angels and I wish you every success with your writing journey, Mister ♡

And finally, you! I would like to say, thank you for taking a chance on me and buying my book. You will never truly understand how much your support means to me and I wish you every success in your life.

Love

Amii

Prologue

I run my fingers through my hair. Before I realise I'm doing it. I glance back at all the bills piled up on the kitchen table in front of me.

How has my life come to this? We were happy, we were in love or so I thought?

I close my eyes again. I don't know how I'm going to come back from this.

The house, the boys, and the food shopping, how am I going to clear his debts.

Fuck! I drop my hands on top of the table and stare at my wedding rings. He promised me the world, for better for worse, for richer or poorer, in sickness and in health, to love and to cherish, till death us do part, well from where I am sitting, I'm not dead yet, but I might as well be. There's no way I can come up with the amount of money he owes.

I hear the bed creek above, and I hold my breath. I don't want the boys to see me in this mess. They think he's working late; they think he'll come back. How do you tell a six- and nine-year-old, their hero of a father fucked off?

No goodbye, no I love you.

Just silence.

Just an empty wardrobe, a missing car and a mobile phone sitting on the hall table. Oh, and the empty bank account. In hindsight I should have known, I knew something was not right, he hid all the bank statements and when I asked, he'd say they hadn't arrived, then get annoyed.

Ian had been distant for a while; he'd been short tempered with me and then over time he was the same with the boys. If I tried to talk to him, he would tell me nothing was wrong or that he was stressed at work, which I found strange as he only worked as a mechanic.

I thought if I loved him harder, he'd remember what we had, but the more I tried, the more he pulled away. And now I'm sitting here, and he's gone; no note, no nothing.

Just a deathly silence.

I wipe away the tears running down my cheeks, as I take a deep breath and hold it. I just need some time to think about what I need to do next.

I listen for any sound of the boys getting up but there's nothing but silence, one of them must have turned over.

I stand up and I lean on the table, staring down at all the final demands, mortgage arrears. I shake my head in defeat, I want to give up, I'm baffled at how we got here.

I turn and walk over to the kettle, I could do with a big glass of wine and as I have no alcohol, a coffee will have to suffice, then I can try to think how to get out of this mess.

I look out of the kitchen window, over the front garden as I wait for the water to boil. I try to clear my thoughts, as our life together plays in my mind. I knew as soon as I stepped in through the front door, something was off. There was an eerie atmosphere. The boys and I had just got back from swimming and Ian would normally greet us and would have already started to cook dinner by the time we reached home, but not tonight.

As Thomas and Elliott rushed out into the garden to play football, I paused as I glanced at the telephone table with Ian's phone on it. While I listened to the silence, trying to catch any sign of him upstairs but nothing.

2

I made my way upstairs to our room but as I paused at the door, an uneasiness settled over me. I pushed the door open; I glanced inside and caught my breath.

Our bedding was all over the floor, the drawers were open and empty, while the wardrobes on Ian's side were open and empty with all the coat hangers all over the floor.

I stepped further into the mess, looking at all the devastation left in his wake. Spinning on the spot with tears in my eyes, I noticed Ian's wedding ring on my side of the bed, right next to my pillow. If I hadn't been so alert, I would have missed it. I perched on the side of the bed, as I picked up the last remembrance of my marriage in my fingers, I felt the pressure on my chest, and I fought to control my breath as I felt the first tears fall.

As I sat there, I sobbed for my heartache, my boys and our life together.

I met Ian when I was sixteen, he was seventeen. We fell in love fast; he was all I could see. I spent every spare second with him. Everyone around us said it was puppy love and we wouldn't last but we fought to prove them wrong. I gave up everything for him. My friends, my dreams, and my education. I always dreamed as a little girl of becoming a nurse, just like my grandma, but I became pregnant instead.

My family disowned me, or should I say my father disowned me; my mum never had much choice. He couldn't accept my love for Ian. He thought he wasn't good enough, but as far as I was concerned, he was enough for me. I loved him more than life. Ian worked for his father in the garage, his father, Stanley owned. We quickly got married after I found out about the baby and moved into a small two-bedroom house with a courtyard and a toilet outside.

3

We lived a simple life with simple tastes, I never needed anything more, Ian's love was enough.

I was happy, I felt safe. We had Thomas and then three years later Elliott arrived. I had the dream life, we had each other, we built our life together, we were happy, I know we were.

I remember the long nights where we would lie in each other's arms and talk for hours. The way his touch set me on fire. The looks across the kitchen, where his eyes would be a light with desire. The way we'd climb into bed at the end of an exhausting day and make love for hours.

The click from the kettle brings me back to the moment. I pull a mug from the cupboard before adding the coffee, boiling water and milk. I just can't get my head around everything. We were married for ten years.

Ten years of complete bliss. We very rarely argued and now, nothing; he walked away from me, from the boys without so much as a backwards glance.

I feel completely crushed. After grabbing my coffee, I sit back down at the table and just stare into space, frozen in the nightmare of my life.

How can I go on? How can I survive without him?

As I sit here everything comes crashing down around me all at once, the realisation that my world has fallen apart.

I know I need to be strong for the boys, but I feel like I'm dying inside. I thought we were enough. How stupid am I?

I can feel the rage building inside me. That bastard! That fucking bastard has left us with nothing.

I stand up, shaking, I completely lose my head and upturn the table with a loud bang. The bills, letters and last demands end up flying up into the air as I drop to my knees before falling on my back as the tears flow down my cheeks.

4

I don't know how long I lie there for, but I feel my body tingling from lying in a foetal position most of the night on the cold kitchen floor. I look up to the window and see the sun starting to break through the dark clouds to signal the start of a new day, a day I don't know how to survive. I've never been on my own, I have never had to support myself. What am I going to do?

So, I do the only thing I can do. I pull myself up from the floor and stand there looking at the mess I created and sigh. I know I don't have long before the boys will be up.

I take a long deep breath, blowing it back out and start to pick up the mail, wishing the red letters were junk mail not a weight around my neck.

I place them all back into the kitchen drawer as I put back the table and chairs, then head back upstairs to shower before the boys get up and want food.

While I'm standing under the hot water, I start to think of how I'm going to get us out of this. I know now I'm going to need a job or two. Ignoring the ache in my heart, I turn off the water and grab a towel.

I wrap the towel around myself as I walk into my bedroom, I stand on the threshold as I look at the mess. It's still in, the state Ian left it.

I quickly grab my underwear, leggings, and vest top before turning on the spot, staying in here is only adding to my anxiety. I leave the room to get dressed, then get ready to face the day.

I don't want to look at the mess anymore and I certainly don't have the energy to clean it up. I need to concentrate on sorting the bills, I don't want to have to clean anymore of his mess.

While I'm getting the boys breakfast ready, I pick up my phone and text Livvy aka Olivia Thomas, my best friend. We've been friends most of our lives and she has been my friend since primary school. I know she'll know what to do to try and sort this mess out. She's the one person I can count on.

"Morning Livvy, are you busy this morning? I could do with some Livvy time after I drop the boys at school. Love ya."

I had just put the boys' bowls down on the table, as Thomas and Elliott came running down the stairs and jumped onto their chairs.

"Morning, Mummy," Elliott says, cheerfully, too young to understand what's going on.

"Morning, monkey," I rub his hair and kiss his forehead as I turn to kiss Thomas too, and I notice he looks sad.

"What's up buddy,"

"Where's Dad, Mum?"

"Oh, he went to work early, baby. I'm sure he'll be back later." I hated lying to him, but I wasn't ready to see any more hurt or sadness on his beautiful face.

I turn away from the boy's as I feel the tears building, so I busy myself from my dark thoughts. Just as I turn to flick the kettle on, my phone bleeps with a message. My heart instantly begins to race as I think Ian had decided to text me, not that I really wanted to hear from him, but just a small text to explain everything would have been nice. Then I remember he had left his phone behind. I flick open my screen and sighed a breath of relief.

"Morning Beautiful. Of course, we can, I'm in all day sweets, come around after you've dropped the boys and I'll have the kettle on. Love you too, Angel xx"

6

I smile as I finish making myself a drink and I stare out over the front garden as I see the dark rain clouds roll over in the distance. I glance at my watch and realise I need to get the boys ready for school before they are late and I fall completely apart, that's something I want to save them from.

They shouldn't have to see me fall apart; they are too young to handle all this. I rush around getting them dressed, coats on and lunch bags in the car as we make our way to the school gates. I genuinely love my boys but today I need them safe in school before I fall into a breakdown. As I watch them walk in, I feel a little bit of the ten-ton weight lift off my chest.

As I pull up outside Livvy's, I feel like I've been holding my breath since yesterday. My heart feels like it is beating out of my chest, my head's pounding and I feel physically sick to my stomach.

I sit in the car trying to stop my racing thoughts. I hear a tap on the car window and look up, as soon as I see my best friend, the banks burst, and I sob uncontrollably. I struggle to catch my breath as Livvy pulls the door open before helping me out of the car, lifting my arm around her shoulder as she tries to help me into the house.

As I stumble into the hallway, I lose my footing and crash to the floor. I gasp, trying to catch my breath, but it all becomes too much, and my world goes black.

Chapter One

Hannah

~ Two Years Later~

"You've lost weight."

I hear from behind me and realise the words are coming from my best friend, Livvy's mouth. I gasp, turning on the spot as I feel my eyes fill with unshed tears as I look at my beautiful friend.

We haven't seen each other since Elliott's last birthday because Liv's been working on a cruise ship in the Mediterranean. She always wanted to travel the world but never got around to doing it, so when the opportunity came up to work on a cruise ship, traveling the Mediterranean, while getting paid, she dived at it, not that I could blame her.

"You're back!" I smile.

"Of course, I'm back. I told you we planned to be back at some point this month. We docked early, so I came straight here but honestly, Hannah, what are you doing working in this dump?" She purses her lips.

I pause and I drop my eyes to the greasy cafés floor and sigh. For the last two years since Ian walked out on us, I've had to take any job I could find while trying to support the boys and put myself through an online, night course.

Working here was not the most glamorous job but it pays the rent and food for the boys, so it's better than no job at all. At nearly twenty-eight I needed to gain extra qualifications to get a better job. Due to my lack of experience since leaving school as I was a stay-at-home parent. It's hard to find a decent job or one that pays enough to keep me and the boys afloat.

Since Ian left I've had to make some tough decisions. Like giving up our family home, the only place we had lived in since the day we got married and the only place the boys could call home from birth. It had been particularly hard on the boys as they not only lost their dad, but they also lost their home and we had to move across town to a small, terraced house. I did think about moving away all together but decided to stay close in Uckfield a small town on the edge of East Sussex.

"It's just a bridge job, Livvy. I only have a couple of months left and if I work extra hard, I might be able to finish earlier." I whisper, hoping my supervisor doesn't hear.

My supervisor can be a complete bitch at the best of times without her hearing what Liv had just said. As soon as I get this Secretary & PA Diploma finished, I will be looking to leave.

I reach for Livvy's hand, and I pull her to the booth at the back of the café. As she sits down, I look up at the clock, hanging above the counter and notice I have ten minutes before I have my break.

"Do you want a drink? I've got my break in ten minutes, I'll come and join you."

"Yeah. The usual, please." She replies.

With a nod, I make my way back towards the kitchen. I quickly put the dirty plates in the dishwasher, then put the order in for table five. Once I'm finished, I move around the counter and make our coffee then carry them back to the booth and slide in.

"So, what's new with you? What have you been up to, Han?"

"Me? Oh, you know, work, work, sorting the boys and trying to fit in my assignments. Not much." I laugh aloud.

Livvy's eyebrows dip.

"Has Ian been helping out? You can't do it all on your own."

"He's got a younger model or so I'm being told by his daddy dearest. He hasn't made any contact with us or made any time for the boys but that's okay, he'll regret it when they're older," I shrug.

"Well, I'm back now, so I'll help, you know that." Livvy smiles as she reaches across and gives my hand a tender squeeze.

"Thanks, Liv. I've really missed you. What are you going to do now though? Are you going back on the cruise?"

"I've decided not to do anymore cruises, Hannah. I miss home too much and you and the boys too. I spoke with Lenny, and he has a job in his accountancy firm, so I'm going to do that. It's not much, answering phones and making appointments but it's here, close to you and my favourite duo, so I'm happy."

I grin like a Cheshire cat. I love that she wants to be back home, and I get to see her more. I hadn't realised how much I had missed her while she's been away, until she was sitting there in front of me. I make a mental note to thank her brother, Lenny, when I see him next. Lenny pops around to see the boys often and if I have an assignment I need to do, he'll take them out for me so I can work in peace. I don't know how I would have managed without his support. I love him like a big brother, and he's really good with the boys. They need a positive male role model especially with their dad not around.

"You've made my day, I'm so happy Livvy, I've missed you so much."

"I missed you too, Han. And the boys." She smiles as she watches me intently. "But by the looks of it I think we need a girl's night out, missis. You look like you could do with a night on the town to let your hair down."

My face drops. I would love a night out to let my hair down but I've no one to have the boys. Martha, the next-door neighbour who has the boys after school sometimes, is in her seventies and I can't ask her to watch them until the early hours. Also, I can't justify spending money on drinks and not on the bills or the boys. I drop my eyes to the saltshaker sitting on the table; I really need some time to myself, but it's not justified.

"I'd love to Liv but I've no one to watch the boys and I can't spend money on drinks when there's things the boys need, sorry." I sigh defeated.

"Hey, I'll sort the boys and this night out is for me, so I'm paying, woman. No arguments, understand." She pouts with a raised eyebrow.

Livvy knows I could never say no to her, even though it usually meant getting into a load of trouble when we were teenagers.

I glance across the diner and the time catches my eye.

"Shite, I better get back to work before Grotbags realises I'm still not back from my break," I jump up.

"I must be going too, anyway. I'll text you tomorrow to arrange Friday night."

"Okay, I look forward to it Livvy,"

I pulled her into a long hard hug. I had totally forgotten what it was like to have my girl just around the corner. I lean back and place a kiss on each cheek, before I rush off as I need to finish my shift so I can collect the boys from school.

I blast across the playground, puffing like I've smoked twenty cigarettes. Grotbags has been in a foul mood since yesterday, making me work harder than any of the other staff and snapping any time I spoke to her. I'm hoping she didn't hear my conversation with Livvy about me only staying there while I finished my online course, when she came to the café Wednesday. It wouldn't have surprised me if she had or one of the other staff told her because she tends to make everything her business within those walls but there's nothing, I can do about it now but keep my head down and my mouth shut.

I glance at my watch as I see the classes start to come out from the classrooms, I need to get moving. Livvy texted earlier to say she was picking me up at eight thirty tonight and Lenny was going to have the boys for me, which I didn't mind, I really appreciated all his support since Ian walked out. The boys adored him and thought he was the best thing since sliced bread.

As I glance across the playground, I see Thomas holding Elliott's hand as they walk in my direction. It's hard to believe that in six more months my big boy is going to be in high school. I just don't know where the years have gone.

"Hey boys, everything okay?" I ask as I glance at the scowl on Elliott's face.

"No, I want to go to Adam's house to play but I can't because you're going out and we have to say with Aunt Martha,"

"Elliott, yes I am going out with Aunt Livvy, but Uncle Lenny is going to watch you and I'm sure he has lots of man stuff planned." As soon as I mention Uncle Lenny, both of their faces light up.

12

They love to spend 'men time' as they call it with Lenny, he's been a positive influence on their lives and God knows they have needed it.

"Yay! What are we waiting for? The sooner we are home, the sooner Uncle Lenny will be here."

"Way to make me feel appreciated, boys," I laugh.

I stand in front of the mirror, with my hair flowing down my back, my makeup light and a towel around my body. I've tried on four pairs of jeans and three tops, and nothing looks right.

I feel horrible.

I think it's a sign that I shouldn't be leaving the boys to go on girl's night out, my guilt is gnawing at my confidence.

I sigh and decide I need to text Livvy and say I've changed my mind, that maybe we can have a girl's night in with boys and Lenny, instead. Just as I'm about to pick my phone up, the doorbell rings and I hear Thomas and Elliott charging for the door. After a few seconds, I hear them cheering, so I know I'm too late to text to put it off.

I hear Livvy making her way up the stairs as Lenny's trying to calm the boys down.

I turn as my bedroom door opens, and I look at Livvy. She looks amazing in a thigh length crimson shoulder less dress. I've always felt ordinary when next to Liv, even more so tonight and I feel deflated. I know I could never look good in anything like that.

If I were struggling with my confidence before, I have now hit rock bottom. As I'm lost in thought Liv walks closer.

"Hey, you, you're supposed to be ready by now, missis."

"I'm not going, Livvy, I have nothing to wear, I look awful in everything I have tried on and I just feel like shit," I ramble.

"Stop right now!" Livvy exclaims. "You are the most beautiful person I know. You could look good in a black bag, woman." I watch Livvy step back and walk to the door, as she reaches it, she picks up a holdall that she must have brought with her.

"Now, I knew we'd have the whole, I've nothing to wear crap, so I brought some of my going out dresses for you," Livvy smiled.

I signed; I knew there was no way of getting out of it now. In one way I was looking forward to it, but it had been such a long time since I'd had just adult company, I was worried I'll make a fool out of myself. I don't know what to talk about or how to behave when you're out. It's been so long since I've been out I have forgotten what to do.

I see Livvy open the bag on the bed as she starts pulling dresses in all colours out. It's like she's pulling a rainbow out of her holdall.

"Wow! How many dresses do I need for one night?" I laugh.

"I know what you're like Hannah, so I brought several for you to try but you need to hurry up, the cab will be here in fifteen."

I glance across all the dresses and see a black slim fitted one with a see-through lace top and I reach for it. I hold it up in front of me and walk towards the mirror, it's gorgeous; not that I could ever pull something this stunning off.

"That dress will look beautiful on you, go and get it on." Livvy demands as she chucks me a black lace thong from my chest of drawers.

Once I'm in the bathroom I make quick work of my scrap of material thong and shimmy into the dress. As the material slowly drifts down my body, I start to feel different; I feel sexy and confident. I pause as I open the bathroom door, taking a deep breath, then walk into the bedroom. Livvy had just finished pouring some vodka and cranberry juice into some tumblers when she lifted her head and her mouth hit the floor.

"I'll change, I know I look ridiculous,"

"You will do no such thing, my friend. You look absolutely fabulous!"

"Really?"

"Really! Now come and have this drink before we have to leave."

I take a swig of the cranberry vodka and nearly choke.

"Oh my god! How much vodka did you put in this thing?"

"Enough." She shrugs her shoulders with a smirk. "Enough to loosen you up so you will enjoy tonight."

After I downed the first drink, Liv pours me another and hands the glass to me.

"Bottoms up," Liv winks as I down my second drink. My head starts to feel a little light as the alcohol travels around my body.

Great, I was going to be pissed before we made it to Scarlett's.

I hear the doorbell ring, so I chug down a third drink as I grab my red heels and we make our way down the stairs.

When we reach the bottom, Lenny is standing at the open door, and as he turns around his eyes widen once he sees me.

"Fuck me, Hannah. You are breath-taking! Make sure you are careful tonight, looking like sin, you'll have all the men chasing you."

15

"I will, and thanks for watching the boys Lenny".

"Any time Hannah. Now go and have some fun but not too much huh!" He winks.

I don't live far from the club, so it only takes us five minutes before the taxi is pulling up in front of the main doors. My nerves are starting to get the better of me as I watch Livvy climb from the cab as she pays the driver, I take a moment to compose myself.

"Come on Hannah, the line to get in is only small if we rush now,"

I get out and follow Liv to the line of people excited to get inside, we are about ten groups back from the front door. I take a look around as the alcohol buzzes through my veins. Livvy nudges my shoulder to catch my attention. I look up at her face, as she nods her head in the direction of a gorgeous man, who's leaning up against the streetlight, looking down at his phone.

"Are you waiting for someone handsome?" Livvy shouts.

I step back into the shadows as my cheeks burn with embarrassment. I can't believe she's called out to a complete stranger.

As the stranger lifts his head in our direction, I step back further into the wall, trying not to draw attention to myself. I see his face light up as he takes in Liv in her dress.

"I am actually, Beautiful. I'm waiting for my best friend to arrive."

"Well, you could come and stand with us if you like, you can keep me warm while we wait to get in". She flutters her eyelashes at him.

"Nothing would give me greater pleasure, sweet cheeks."

Now, I knew how our night was going to proceed, I was just going to be the third wheel. I watched him walk with swagger towards us, and I could see from the way he walked he was a player and that was the type Liv went for, I stood silently watching the two of them snuggling up and laughing with each other.

I would have loved to be so free and confident in myself to call a man out and openly flirt, but that would never happen. I hear the man all over Livvy say something about his friend had just arrived, so I lift my eyes and scan up and down the line, but when they connect with the tall dark stranger, I nearly swallow my tongue as my eyes bulge, he's like a walking God.

Men never really catch my attention, but this man is something else.

I am in so much trouble with this stranger, I have never felt this type of attraction before and I'm not sure how I am going to survive tonight.

Chapter Two

David

"Remember drinks tonight,"

I heard as I was pulled from my thoughts while trying to read the same sentence for the past half hour. I've been distracted all day.

As I looked up, I saw Shawn leaning against the doorframe with a smirk in place. I'd forgotten I had agreed to be his wingman tonight.

I don't know why I keep agreeing to go out with him, I always feel so guilty, but he's been my best friend since we were six and he's been with me throughout all my life events.

"What time? I need to pop home to change and check on Gaynor," I really don't need this tonight I think to myself.

"Eight thirty at Scarlett's,"

I lift my eyes from the contract I have been struggling to comprehend and glance at the clock, I notice it's half seven already.

I sigh, I work later and later every day, I wish I didn't feel so trapped, but it is what it is.

"Okay, I'll meet you outside. See you soon."

I stand, reaching over to turn my computer off and I leave everything on my desk. Maybe letting my hair down for a bit will be good, but in the end, I always end up feeling like shit. I'm out having a good night while Gaynor's at home, trapped in a wheelchair with no way out.

Even though she constantly tells me to do what I want. She has never really been interested in anything I do, we have always lived separate lives, even though I tried in the beginning. This isn't how I saw our life.

I know we didn't exactly start out in love, or even in any kind of lust, but I was hoping after the 'I Do' bit we would eventually connect on some level. But the more I tried the more it felt fraudulent.

I had the most beautiful bride ever, but all I could see was chains, chains that my father had tied around my neck.

I never met my father until I was fourteen. I was HIS dirty secret, my mum, Estelle, was the one he wanted but he couldn't marry. It's just a shame that he couldn't let go of her either. He used her as a release and would turn up three or four times a week, always when I was in bed or out with friends.

She doted on him, worshipped the ground he walked on, but always knew she'd never be his wife or his equal half. She was from a working-class background and my father was an upper-class snob, with expectations and the expectations where he'd marry someone from money and father a litter of snobs.

Unfortunately for them, the woman he married couldn't have the litter he needed to carry on the family business, but my mum had me, much to my grandfather's dismay.

I rub my tired eyes as I grab my keys and jacket. I hate thinking of my past; it shouldn't have been this way. My mum was a big believer that love would find a way, unfortunately it was only in the books she read that it ever happened, but she liked to live with her head in the clouds.

I smile as I remember how she always wore rose tinted glasses, even after everything she went through.

When she died, I was fourteen and it destroyed my world, but not as much as when I was packed up and hauled into my father's universe. I hated him from the beginning.

He was everything I wanted nothing to do with, but I really didn't have much choice. I hated that he could dictate my life so much but in a shitty kind of way. Still, I also longed to be someone he could be proud of, just a shame it came with so many conditions.

I spent most of my time with Joyce, my dad's P.A. She was like my grandmother, always there when I needed someone.

I left school top of my class and achieved all that I wanted without having to put much work in. I went straight into the construction industry and worked my way up until I became the owner of Shepard's Construction Limited with the help of Joyce and her husband Albert.

My father wanted me to follow him into the family business, but it wasn't for me. I never wanted to be a part of my grandfather's scheme and I would never have fitted in. I was too opinionated.

There was no way I wanted to end up becoming like him, heartless and disloyal.

I might not be the most loving husband, but I did always put Gaynor first or at least I did at the start. Now I have gone past trying. I might feel trapped. But I always made sure she had a roof over her head and food in her stomach.

As I pull my car into the drive, I sit quietly and gaze up at the house. This was my dream home, I had the bungalow built, I had such high hopes, with stupid young dreams and now, I'm fully aware of how life works. It seems things are meant to be loved and people are meant to be used, somehow the dynamics have changed; but I will never be happy using people and that is why I will never work for my father or grandfather.

When I come home, I don't feel excitement and content, I feel heavy, agitated, and empty; like I have most of my life. I know as soon as I walk through the door, I will hear nothing but silence. I glare at the front window and see the light of the lamp glowing out.

I dread walking in to see the look on Gaynor's face again. Sometimes the guilt is unbearable, I feel like I'm drowning in self-hate. I sigh and jump from the car. I know I need to get a move on.

As I open the door, I glance towards the first door in the hallway which is the bedroom that Gaynor lives in. I used to share the room too for the first year or so, not that we did anything marital in there, but since the accident Gaynor decided she needed her own space. So, to make her happy I was shoved into the second bedroom.

I could count on one hand the number of times we've had sex and I still wouldn't use all my fingers. She was either tired, busy or watching a movie. If I was honest, she didn't really do it for me anyway, but I kept up the pretence up for everyone else.

I move down the hall towards the kitchen, but I decide to go back and check to see if she's okay before I get ready to meet Shawn.

After a second, I tap on her door and slowly open it in case she's already asleep, but I have no such luck. As I walked in, I noticed Gaynor had dropped her phone onto the bedside table, like she had been texting someone.

"Oh, you're home?" Gaynor glances my way.

"Yeah, sorry I'm late. Things were hectic at work." I lied. "How was your day?"

Surprisingly, I can't remember the last time we had a conversation. All we have is pleasantries. In fact, we've never had the relationship where we'd sit for hours talking, our marriage was

21

a means to an end, well it was for her anyway. I had always hoped it would become more but it wasn't to be.

"Mum popped in; you know how fun that is." She frowned, "I'm just getting ready for bed, and I might put a film on."

"Sounds good. I'm just going to grab a shower before I meet Shawn. Do you want anything?"

"No, go and enjoy yourself. I don't need babysitting David." She sighs.

"I wasn't suggesting you did Gaynor. I just simply asked if you needed anything." I grunted back.

I slip from the doorway and head straight for my room before I quickly strip off and jump in the shower.

Standing under the spray I let the heat of the water release the tension of the day, as I massage in my shampoo. I instantly feel my muscles relax.

I don't know about going out. I could happily jump into bed. But going out and sitting in a different setting isn't such a bad idea, either.

꧁꧂

The noise coming from the club can be heard through the window of my uber as I pull myself from the car. I glance down the street towards Scarlett's trying to see if I can catch a glimpse of Shawn.

As I move closer to the line, I see that Shawn has already attracted the attention of a few ladies. Great, just what I need, he usually waits until we are in the club before the flirting starts and usually by then, I'm peacefully sitting in the corner reading work emails or looking at files stored on my phone.

While I'm approaching, I see that one lady's not paying any attention to Shawn or who I presume is her friend hanging off each other. I slow my pace as I see the beautiful brown-haired woman, she is not overly tall and has curves to die for.

From where I am, she seems a little shy. I see her lift her eyes and look around, but as soon as she notices me her eyes widen. She is dressed in a fitted black dress that sits just above her knee, and skin-tight. She was made for sinning, and I wanted to be the one to sin with her.

I struggled to pull my eyes from her glorious body. Once I reach them, Shawn smiles and introduces me to the lady hanging all over his body.

"David my man, about time. I thought you'd gone to bed with your slippers and pipe."

"Nope, no bed or pipe, Shawn. Just a hot shower and change of clothes."

"Ladies, let me introduce to you my best bud, David Shepard. David this gorgeous thing is Livvy, and her quiet as a mouse friend is Hannah,"

I drag my eyes from Hannah and glanced at Livvy, she was sexy in that obvious kind of way, and not my idea of sexy at all. Her friend on the other hand, now she really was stunning, she is the first person to ever catch my attention.

I knew when I married Gaynor that I would live by my vows, so while Shawn was off getting his rocks off, I would be the one to settle bills and toddle off back home to my lonely double bed with my wife down the hall. Not once had I ever looked at another woman or dreamed of a different life. Not until now.

I smile at them both and turn back to Hannah to catch her eyeing me.

"Hi ladies, the pleasure is all mine,"

Hannah just drops her head, as her eyes hit the floor and Livvy drapes her arms across my shoulders and whispers.

"You'll have to excuse Hannah, it's the first time in years she's been out, and she's not used to having normal people to converse with," she giggles, throwing Hannah a teasing smile.

I can tell that Livvy's had a few before she came out, but I can't tell if Hannah has, that was until she tried to walk in a straight line into the club.

Shawn grabs Livvy's hand and drags her through the entrance as I slowly follow closely behind the beautiful Hannah, trying my hardest to keep my eyes from her gorgeous arse. I'm so distracted that I nearly bump into her once we reach the bar. I blush, as Hannah glances back at me and she probably thinks I'm a complete dick for nearly knocking her over.

I'm struggling to tear my eyes from this beautiful lady peering at us all from beneath her lashes, when Shawn declares we need to get some drinks, and I just smile.

I look over to Shawn to see he's watching me with a surprised stare. I shrug my shoulders and try to play it off.

Shawn orders a round of shots, two beers and two Sex on the beach cocktails. He knows I can't do shots; it makes me ill. I'm not really a drinker on a whole, so I have no idea what he's playing at. I don't say anything as we all stand lined up against the bar ready to down the After Shock, I gag and laugh. I feel Hannah giggling beside me, as I watch the colour of her cheeks bloom pink. I'm glad I'm not the only light weight in this group. For the first time in years, I feel myself starting to relax and let my hair down.

I feel alive.

I can sense Hannah's body drawing closer to mine, I feel us being pulled together, especially as the alcohol flows. I've never felt this magnetic pull before, I am drawn to her on another level. I look into her eyes and feel the vulnerability in them. I see myself reflecting back.

At one point, I had lost count of the number of shots, beers and cocktails for the girls we'd had. Livvy and Shawn disappear just after midnight, which left me with Hannah, and I'm struggling to hold the burning desire I have for this woman.

We have spent the last hour laughing over all the things our best friends have done while drunk. I have never laughed as much as I have tonight. My stomach muscles ache from the constant laughing. I don't think we've drawn breath, all night.

We have so many things in common, music, films and she while she talks, I watch her mannerisms and she reminds me of my mum. Especially as she talks about her favourite romance novels.

When Hannah whispers in my ear, asking me if I wanted to dance, I knew I should have said no, but I'm so desperate to feel her body close to mine. I don't think I could say no without dying on the spot.

I take Hannah's hand and lead her to the middle of the dance floor, but as she steps closer to me, I feel the sexual tension between us.

Once I feel her arms around my neck, I lose all sense of time and where we are. Everyone in the club just disappears, as this beautiful woman grinds her body along mine, my mind explodes with want and my desire erupts.

I feel her hips roll into me as she slowly turns on the spot, grinding her hips as her arse connects with my dick, while she moves with the beat of the song. I nearly come in my pants like a teenager on his first date. I don't know where this need has come from, nobody has affected me like this ever.

I feel my lips moving closer to her neck, they have a mind of their own. The first brush of my lips on her pulse and I know hundred per cent, I need this woman now.

As we sway to the beat of the song playing, I feel her hands in my hair as she loops her hands around my neck. Pushing her breast out, as I feel her tug at my locks, and I growl with want.

My breath catches in the back of my throat as I feel her teeth glide along my jaw. I can feel my cock hardening, I thrust my hips forward so she can feel my arousal. I hear Hannah's sharp intake of breath and know we are both in the same place.

I lift my arms until I reach her hands and grip them tightly, bringing them back down to her sides before twisting her around, and looking into her gorgeous chocolate eyes, asking for silent permission to take this further.

With a slight nod of her head, I know we both need to end this animalistic dance somewhere a little bit more private. It's a good job, I know this club like the back of my hand, I pull her towards the corridor at the back of the club. I've never felt this urgency to be with someone, it feels more vital than taking my next breath. I'm going to need a miracle to survive tonight.

I push on the door as we stumble, giggling and laughing, into the darkened corridor, all hands and mouth. I pull her close and then push her up against the wall. I let my hand glide up the inside of Hannah's thigh slowly, as I reach the apex of her legs, I feel her shudder with need.

As I continue, I feel the heat from her pussy and know I need a taste. I drop to my knees and trace the same journey with my tongue. The thump of the beat adds to the anticipation in the corridor. Just as my tongue reaches the lace containing her flesh, I see Hannah's breathing increase.

I slip my finger beneath the flimsy material containing her core and trace the outer lip of her pussy. I can feel the heat radiating beneath her thong and I'm too worked up to be gentle, so I yank on the material and rip it from her body.

I tried to focus on her face but being so dark made it impossible. I wanted eye contact before I proceeded. I needed to make sure she was okay before we carried on, she didn't seem like a one-night type of woman and that was all I could offer.

"Are you sure you want to do this?" I ask quietly.

"Yes," she pants.

Before she has time to take her next breath, I push my tongue into her core, and I feel her rock into my face.

My girl likes my tongue. I thought to myself.

Where had that come from?

I have no idea as she could never be 'my girl' no matter how much I wished that were true.

I slowly rubbed my index finger against her clit, and I could feel her orgasm starting to build.

I wanted all her orgasms and the thought of someone else seeing her in the throes of passion, made my blood boil. I lapped harder and moved my finger faster. I need her juices now, I needed to know that I could make someone feel so good that they couldn't hold back, I needed this to make me feel like a man.

I knew the moment Hannah lost control, her whole-body shook and her juices flowed down my chin. I slowly got up off my knees and took her face in my hands, to bring her lips to mine. I kissed her with so much passion that I thought I was going to suffocate her.

"I need to feel you," Hannah pants as she reaches for my jeans.

I want to step back and say no, to stop this now but I know I'd die if I do not know how she feels around my cock.

I grab hold of Hannah's hands and lift them above her head.

"Leave them there and do not move." I tell her.

I softly glide my hands down her arms. Once I reach the top of her breasts, I glide my fingers down until I reach the top of her breasts, I drop my head until I have her erect nipple in my mouth, over the top of the material of her dress.

I suckle and twist the nipple in my mouth with my tongue, while I tug and twist the other one with my fingers. I can feel Hannah's chest rising and falling with every breath she took.

I knew her desire was building again. I could feel it radiating from every inch of her glorious, sexy as sin body. I'm struggling to hold onto my desire.

I drop my right hand to undo the button and zip on my jeans; I withdraw my stiff cock and fist it in my hand. I'm not sure how long I'll last once I'm inside her core, it has been years since I felt the insides of a woman.

With a loud pop, I let her nipple drop from my mouth, I hear Hannah whimper so I know she can't be far. I drop my hands and lift her into my arms as I line myself up at her entrance. I feel the heat from her pussy on the tip of my cock and I know I need to feel her now, so I thrust forward and bury myself balls deep inside this beautiful woman.

I pause, enjoying the feel of the heat coming from her centre.

"Please David, I need more."

I pull back to the tip and forcefully push forward, I hear Hannah hiss as I connect with her core.

I am holding on by a thread, the need I feel to destroy this woman for all other men is strong. Without over thinking these feelings I have charging through my veins; I concentrate on finding my release.

I move with a fluid movement as I continue to push her towards her second release. I start to feel the tingle at the base of my spine and know I'm not going to last long. I drop my hand between us as I find Hannah's clit and circle it, trying to push her over the edge.

Just when I think I can't take anymore, I feel her start to milk my cock as I hear her scream my name. I feel my chest start to expand with pride as I feel her orgasm reach its height, with two more thrusts I'm coming harder than I've ever come before.

My heart feels like it could explode at any moment from my chest and I'm breathing like I've run a marathon.

I rest my forehead against hers with my eyes closed as I wait for our breathing to calm down. I'm frightened to open my eyes in case it has been a dream that I don't want to wake from. I feel Hannah run her hand across my cheek, I know I need to face my fears. I need to look at this woman.

I slowly open my eyes, lowering Hannah back down to the floor, and I hold on to her as she tries to gain the feeling back in her legs. I tighten my hold on this stunning lady, I'm not sure I want to let go of this feeling, I feel so exposed.

Once she is standing by herself, she moves back and out of my arms and I'm left with a feeling of bereft, like the connection we'd had was destroyed.

"I think we should find Livvy," she whispers.

I feel her pulling away from me, not just physically but emotionally, her wall has come back up and I feel her isolating herself again. I'm not sure what to make of this sensation of loss,

I've known this woman all of three hours and I have felt more in those three hours than I have in years, I'm not sure if I want this night to end or to lose this illusion.

It might be the beer goggles or the feeling of loneliness, but I want to get to know Hannah better, to learn about her life and her desires.

"There you both are."

I turn to see Shawn standing at the entrance of the corridor.

"Livvy was panicking that Hannah had left and gone home."

I shake my head, not sure whether it was to answer him or to tell him not now, but he didn't take the hint, he pushed the door open further as Liv storms in.

"Thank God, you're okay. I was worried and thought something had happened to you! Especially when I called Lenny and he said you hadn't made it home,"

Wait, what?

"You're married!!" I rage as I look Hannah in the eye from the lights coming through the door of the nightclub. I see her take a step back.

I can't believe I didn't think to ask, but who am I to judge? I've left Gaynor sitting at home. I needed to get out of here before I said something I shouldn't, I pushed past Shawn and headed for the outside. I know I've no right to be annoyed but the thought of another man touching her, night after night and being the one to share her life, sends my thoughts into a frenzy.

I feel the guilt of the situation crashing down on me and it feels like a ten-ton weight is sitting on my chest. I'm angry at myself for getting attached but also for overstepping the line, I will never be able to look Gaynor in the eye again.

Chapter Three

Hannah

"God, you look rough,"

"Shh don't shout Lenny," I groan as I roll over on the sofa and I nearly fell to the floor, but manage to right myself before I did. I felt like absolute crap, and I was pissed he woke me up from the amazing sex dream I was having. It felt so real, I could still almost feel the touch of his hands on my skin and how really it felt when I came all over his cock. It was the most action my vagina had seen in over two years, even if it was just a dream.

I didn't even make it to bed last night, I was still fully dressed, and as I wriggled my toes, I noticed I was still in my heels. I try to lift my head from the cushion, but the room begins to spin as a feeling of sickness rolls through me.

I lie there for a few moments trying to calm my uneasy stomach as I try to remember what happened the night before, but my mind is blank, it's like my memories have been wiped clean and all that is left is blackness.

As I keep my eyes closed, I see the flashes of lights and I can still hear the beat of the base from the club as my head pounds.

"I'll get you a coffee." I hear Lenny say. "Do you want something to eat before the boys wake up?"

Oh my god, the sound of food has my stomach rolling and not in a good way. I jump up off the sofa, kicking off my heels as I charge straight for the stairs.

I take them two at a time and head straight for the bathroom. Three steps in, and I'm on my knees with my head down the toilet as I empty the contents of my stomach into the bowl.

Oh fuck, I'm dying. I try to recall the last time I felt this hungover, but nothing comes to mind. I feel Lenny hovering by the bathroom door, and I groan.

I can officially say this is not my finest hour, but I feel so ill I cannot find it in myself to care.

Once I think I'm not going to be sick again, I lift my head, and I reach up to flush the remains of my stomach away. My mouth feels like a Sahara Desert, from the amount we drank last night, I feel dehydrated. I roll my head to the side as I try deciding if I have enough strength to pull myself up.

I slowly stagger to my feet and lift myself from the floor before I stand in front of the mirror, leaning against the sink as I reach for my toothbrush.

"How are you feeling?"

I lift my eyes to his in the reflection in the mirror, with a timid smile. I push the toothbrush into my mouth as I hold up one finger to signal to give me a minute to clean my mouth from this awful taste on my tongue.

I spit the toothpaste into the sink and my mouth starts to feel better.

"Like ten men," Lenny frowns at me.

"Nine dead and one dying; meaning like shite."

"Oh!" He laughs aloud, "Well, I guess it's a good job I've agreed to spend the day here with the boys then. So, you can go back to bed, and I'll sort them for you. If that's okay, of course?"

If I didn't have a distant memory of a chestnut-haired beauty, I would have kissed him, but my mind was racing to try and collect the memories from the events of last night.

"Thank you, Lenny, you are the best friend a girl could wish for." I smile as I step towards the door. "I'm just going to jump in the shower and then I'll go back to bed for a few hours. If you are sure, you don't mind taking them for a few hours?"

"Sleep as long as you need Hannah, you deserve a break,"

"Thank you."

I shut the door and lean the back of my head against the cold wood. I concentrate on my breathing as another wave of sickness overtakes my body and it's one thing, I really hated was being sick. After the sickness had subsided, I removed last night's outfit but wondered where my panties had gone. As I leaned in and switched on the shower, I tried to remember what I did last night but all I could remember were the loud music and flashing lights.

As I stand under the hot water, making it as hot as I could take it. I feel myself start to relax and I try to piece together last night's events. I vaguely remember arriving in the taxi, Livvy asking some guy if he wanted to wait for his friend with us. I remember Livvy hanging all over him, and I think his friend arrived, then I remember that the music was very loud and that there was so much alcohol, but after that, my mind was blank.

I try to rack my brains for details of…. Dean…. Or maybe David. Yes David! I think that was his name. I can barely remember either of the men, apart from one had amazing eyes, but that's it.

As I wash myself, I rub the shower puff over my skin, I try to wash all the sweat from last night off. As I reach the apex of my legs, I rub in the shower gel, and I feel a slight sting. And the dream I had last night came rushing back to the front of my mind, but I think it was more than a dream, I think I fucked that man in a dark corridor in the back of the club.

33

I bring my hands up and bury my face into them as devastation takes over, I've never done the one-night stand shit before.

Holy shit! Why can't I remember him?

As I try to steady my breathing, I remember the feel of his hands sliding up my thigh, as my skin prickled and my clit danced to the beat of his music, the way he paid attention to the way my body responded under his tender touch.

I remember how he lifted me into his arms as if I weighed nothing, I felt my body igniting at the thoughts of him as he lined up his cock at my entrance and thrust all the way in. I remember the feeling of my desire running through my veins and settling in my core, pretty much what is happening now, but this time alone with dirty thoughts of the sex god that held my body hostage. But for the life of me, I couldn't even remember his face.

I slide my fingers through my folds, as I remember the way he took control of my body. I gently glide my finger around my erect nub, as I slide my fingers down until they reach my entrance, replacing my finger with my thumb, while I push my finger deep into my core. Using my thumb, I apply a little pressure on my clit as I feel my walls start to tremble.

As I chase my orgasm, I slip two fingers into my core as one isn't enough. While I hook my fingers inside me, I massage my front wall and I feel the tremble start to build. I want this feeling to last forever, but the need to come is more urgent. I need to find my release more than I need my next breath, so I continuously pump my fingers and rub my clit as my orgasm crashes around me. I have to bite down on my bottom lip to stop myself screaming out in pleasure. I lean against the shower tiles as I try to come back down. I stand back under the shower spray and wash the remnants of the orgasm away as I suddenly remember Lenny is in the house somewhere and could have heard me in the throes of passion with my right hand. Oh, God. I hope I wasn't loud; I groan in my head.

Once I calm my breathing the reality of what happened hits me. I can't believe how stupid I was. I lift my hands up and run them down my face as humiliation takes over, I've never had sex with a one-night stand before, in fact I've only had sex with one man. How could I have been so stupid.

I can't even remember if we used protection and the last thing, I needed was an unplanned pregnancy, not to mention an STD. Fuck! I am going to have to get tested. I don't even know how to go about getting a test.

So, I shut off the water and step out onto the shower mat, dripping with water as I try to stand on my wobbly legs as I grab the towel and head to my room.

I run across the landing to my bedroom, I shut the door, and jump on my bed, before burying myself into the duvet and snuggle in. I stretch to release some of the aches in my tired muscles.

As I settle down, I decide to sort through my thoughts once I've had a sleep. For now, I drift off into a fretful sleep of dark corridors and a sexy blue-eyed man.

It's been a month since mine and Livvy's last night out, but it feels like a lifetime ago. I've worked so hard to get all my essays completed so I could graduate early. Though it hasn't been easy, I managed to hand in all my ten last assignments, and I got top marks for them all. It was really all thanks to Liv and Lenny helping Martha with the boys, I have managed to work around the clock and I'm qualified. I feel such relief knowing now I can start looking for a better job with better prospects and better pay.

To celebrate we are having a Chinese, a couple of bottles of wine and a movie with the boys, Liv, Lenny and Martha. I think it's perfect that I get to spend time with the people who mean the most to me. Livvy wanted us to go out on the town but after the last time I couldn't put myself out there again, I'm more a night in girl than a paint the town red, one.

I know Liv is desperate to go out again because she hasn't stopped sulking since she realised, a few days after that she had lost that Shawn guy's number.

I can only really remember David's eyes and maybe his hair, but I replay the encounter, over and over in bed at night. I can still feel the touch of his lips on my skin and the sound of his breathing as he entered my core.

I can honestly say, my B.O.B has had more action since that night than it had since Ian walked out. There was something about that man that had my body on fire.

I hear the doorbell ring, as I'm pulled from my fantasy, and I hear Thomas talking so I know it's either Livvy or Lenny that has arrived as Martha is already sitting in the living room watching a film with the boys while I get ready. I quickly rush to pull a brush through my hair and make my way into the hall.

I pause as I lean against the kitchen door frame, while I watch Thomas laughing and joking with Lenny. The boys really miss their dad, so I'm glad they have a male influence in their life.

Lenny glances up and sees me standing there, watching. I see the smile engulf his face as he ruffles Tom's hair and makes his way over to me.

"Don't tell me I'm the last one here."

36

I stand straight before I turn and walk back into the kitchen as Lenny pops his head around the door of the living room to say hi to Martha.

"No, you are second, but Martha lives next door so I'm not sure that counts." I call over my shoulder.

"Wow, I'm getting good at this being on time lark," he laughs as I start to pull the takeout menus out of the kitchen draw for tonight.

"You are. You just need to get Livvy to be so punctual," I laugh.

"Yeah, I somehow think that's not going to happen, Livvy would be late to her own funeral."

"Unless the vicar is hot," I laugh as Lenny gives me this strange look, and I suddenly feel a little self-conscious. "Then she'd be half an hour early." I smile.

Just as the takeout menus are all over the kitchen side, the doorbell rings again.

"I'll get it," I shouted, needing a minute to breathe. I really like Lenny but no more than I would have loved a brother, but recently I've been getting lots of mixed messages from him and most of them are pointing to him wanting more than friendship.

Elliott comes running down the stairs, and nearly misses the bottom two steps and landing in a lump at the bottom.

"Elliott, calm down mister before you break something."

"Is Uncle Lenny here?" He pants.

"He's in the kitchen, monster. Go and say hello, then wash your hands."

I notice the glue all over his fingers while he rushes towards the kitchen, he must have been gluing with Martha as they watch their film. Considering Martha's age, she is good with the boys and loves them as if they were her own flesh and blood.

Martha was only blessed with one child, and he doesn't live locally so she only sees him once or twice a year. He has two boys around the same as my two, so it's good when they come to stay in the holidays because they have Thomas and Elliott to play with.

I open the door to Livvy as a big bunch of yellow roses replaces her face.

"Congratulations, best friend!"

"Oh my god, Livvy. Those are absolutely beautiful!"

I feel the tears prick my eyes. It's been a long time since anyone brought me flowers. I grab Livvy and give her a big hug. I try so hard to stop the tears falling but my heart is filled with so much love for my best friend.

I take the flowers from her as we head towards where the others are. Martha is just walking out of the living room towards the kitchen ready to join the rest of us, she sees the beautiful bouquet.

"Oh, my. Those are gorgeous, Hannah." She smiles.

"Thank you, Martha. Liv bought them for me."

I see Lenny trying to organise the boy's food, as his head turns our way as we enter the room. He smiles but it doesn't quite reach his eyes. I place the flowers into some water, before I join them as Liv and the boys argue what's best to order as I take the only seat left next to Lenny.

"Beautiful flowers," I hear Lenny whisper in a hushed voice.

"Yeah, Livvy bought them," I smile.

"Oh, Livvy. That's great." He exclaimed, sounding a little happier about it.

As we wait for the take-out, everyone's talking about how their day's been and what they've been up to. Elliott tells us about his art project and how he needs to make a volcano from papier-mâché, Lenny offered to help him this weekend and volunteered Thomas to help too, much to his displeasure.

I loved having family time with everyone. Since my family disowned me, I didn't have many friends, only Livvy. Lenny only really started helping out once Ian had left and Livvy decided she wanted to work on the cruises.

As the doorbell rings, Lenny jumps up to collect our food. We aren't a conventional family and do things a little differently. We put all the food in the centre of the table, and everyone just helps themselves to what they fancy. While we sit and eat, we listen to stories of Martha's childhood and the boys are enthralled in all the tales she has to tell. She told the boys about one teacher she had at school that used to scare all the children. When they had Maths, he would get a different child every day to stand up and recite their times tables and if you got it wrong, he would throw his board rubber across the room and everyone would duck because if it caught you, it stung.

As we finished talking, I looked down at the table and saw everyone had devoured the food, along with a couple of bottles of wine and a bottle of lemonade for the boys.

We all moved to the front room, as Lenny took a tired looking Martha home and made sure she was settled. I did offer to take her myself, but he insisted as he hadn't had much to drink because he was driving. While the boys argue over what movie to watch, as we wait for Lenny to arrive back. I told Livvy all about the job I applied for and how the owner had asked me to go for an interview tomorrow at five-thirty. I had never expected to hear back from them, so I was really surprised when I had a reply back two hours later, offering me an interview the next day.

My nerves were shot as I hadn't had a proper interview ever. The job at the cafe I got was because Livvy was sleeping with the owner's son at the time, so he talked his dad into giving me some shifts until I got back on my feet.

Liv was over the moon for me and I, for once, felt like I could do this on my own. Since Ian left, I always felt that I wasn't doing well enough, the boys deserved better and that I was failing but tonight I felt like we had just hit gold and after all the struggles we had been through, hadn't been for nothing. Maybe they drove us to exactly where we needed to be.

We were going to be okay, at last, I knew it, I just need to get through tomorrow.

Chapter Four

David

I've been like a bear with a sore head since last month when I met Hannah and fucked her. She really did a number on me. I can still taste her on my tongue and hear her moans as I push balls deep into her core.

I know I need to forget her but God, she made my body sing and my heart leap.

When I got home after storming from the club, I went straight to my room and sat on the edge of my bed for what felt like forever. The guilt I felt was immense. How was I ever going to look Gaynor in the eyes after what I had done? Not that we have a conventional marriage, but she still wears my ring, and I did make promises that I planned to keep. Well, at least at the beginning.

If one thing came out of this, it has shown me that I was lonely, and I definitely wasn't happy. I tried to think of the last time that I truly felt happy, and realised it was before I was fourteen, before my mum was ripped away from me.

Still, just thinking about Hannah had my cock ready to explode so much, it nearly crippled me. No woman had ever affected me like that. I hated that I couldn't pursue her like a normal single man, not that really mattered as she was married too or at least that's what I had thought.

That night I went to sleep with her in my mind. I replayed every minute of our sexual encounter. She was hot and I was needy. I woke the next morning with a hard on and a hangover to end all hangovers. I jumped from my bed and headed straight for a cold shower, trying to calm my hardened cock, as I tried to wash away all last night's thoughts and memories.

Since that night, sleep hasn't come easy, and the guilt was constantly niggling at me. I barely come home and when I do I avoid Gaynor at all costs, not that she makes any effort anyway but still. I wished I could forget the brown-haired beauty and move on, but she's always there in the back of my mind.

It got even worse when the following Monday after ignoring his calls all weekend, Shawn walked into my office to find out what happened and why I stormed out of the club, leaving an upset Hannah behind.

When I tried to explain I didn't want to talk about it or Hannah, he dropped the bomb shell that the man Liv was talking about was actually Livvy's brother and not Hannah's husband. He went on to explain that she was in fact married, but her loser husband had walked out on her two years previous.

I felt like such a fool, but it didn't matter because I couldn't give her what she needed anyway. I was destined to be alone and unhappy; I chose my path, and I was going to walk it.

So, I did the only thing I could do, I threw myself into my work and tried to push Hannah from my thoughts. It was just a shame my brain hadn't got the message as the dreams of us together had become unbearable, every night was the same dream, the same touches and the same sounds. I was barely sleeping but I kept pushing on.

"What time do you call this?" My temp laughs as I walk into my office.

I glance up and see Jen sitting in my chair, with my mug in her hands. I don't know what made me angrier.

I take a deep breath because today of all days I do not want her snide remarks or flirty ways.

"It's called whatever time I fucking like as I own the business and do as I please." I raise my eyebrows. I see her slowly withdraw her breath as she stands from my desk. "I would appreciate it if you didn't sit at my desk, in my chair and use my mug."

"Sorry David, I didn't mean any offence, I was only joking,"

"Yeah, well I'm not in the mood for jokes." I grumble as she backs out of the door and into her small office next door.

I look at all the paperwork piled high on my desk and sigh. We currently have six projects going on; with extensions, remodels and new builds. I don't know whether I'm coming or going.

I think Jen needs to go, she's started to get a little too friendly and she really isn't pulling her weight. It wouldn't have shocked me if I walked in one day to find her naked in my chair with my mug. She flirts constantly and makes suggestive comments all the time. I swear she thinks I'm interested, but there's only enough room for one brown-haired woman in my head at a time.

I push my chair up to my desk and decide to advertise for a full time Office Manager and Assistant. I've had temporary workers on and off for about four years, but they are shit, none have lasted past three months because they think I come with the job.

I click on the local newspaper and post an advert.

Shepard's Construction Limited requires a full-time Office Manager and Assistant. Normal office hours, Monday – Friday. Pay Negotiable. Some experience preferred but not essential. Must be polite, good telephone manners, able to make appointments and must be able to type.

Please email; shepardsconstructionlimited@gmail.com
Immediate start needed. Thank you!

I read back the advert and pressed upload, I'm not too fussy who applies as long as they can do the basics.

I glance at the time and see its nearly lunchtime. I put the office manager situation out of my mind as I know I must finish some quotes and get back home for two because Gaynor has a hospital appointment that I'd said I would take her too.

Well, I say I agreed to, I haven't spoken to Gaynor since the weekend and then it was only in passing. She emailed me and asked if I was able to take her as her mom was going away and I assured her I would.

I power off the laptop as I stand and stretch from my desk. I grab my keys and make my way to my car. As I pass Jen's desk, I see her leaning forward in a provocative way with the top few buttons of her blouse open and I freeze.

"Oh David, can you just check this quote before I send it out, please." She leans further forward, and her breast nearly falls out.

I step around the desk and stand by the side of Jen; I look at the screen and make no eye contact with her at all.

"Yep, that's exactly right Jen. Now I need to take my wife to the hospital for an appointment, so please note I'm out of the office and any correspondence should be left on my desk. Thank you" I left the room before I lost my shit.

I need to keep her until I find a replacement and after that little performance it will be sooner rather than later.

I pull up in front of my prison and leave the car running as I get out and walk to the front door. I take a deep breath and try to calm my beating heart; this will be the first time I've spent any time with Gaynor since that night and I'm not sure if I can handle the guilt. I push my key into the lock and open the door before I change my mind. I walk to Gaynor's door and knock, while I wait for her reply.

"I'm coming." She shouts.

She pulls the door open, and she appears in her chair. Every time I see her in that bloody thing, the guilt eats me up. If I hadn't been too busy to pick my suit up that day, it would have been me sitting in that chair not her.

"Are you ready?"

"Of course!" she frowns. "No, I look pretty today? Or is that a new top?"

My breath stalls, normally when I try to complement her, she brushes it off and has since the well before we got married.

"Of course, you look pretty, I can't remember a time when you didn't."

She gave me a tight-lipped smile as she wheeled herself towards the front door.

"I'll help," I say as I go to step around her, but she turns and gives me a look to stop me dead.

"I'm not useless, David. I've been in this chair five years. I think I've worked out how to get to the car without killing myself yet."

I freeze. I don't know what to say or do, that won't make matters worse.

"Okay, sorry Gaynor I was just trying to help." I step back.

I watch her struggle into the car, I really want to offer to help her. We might not have the best relationship, but I do still care about her. In the end, I decide not to offer, I just take her chair and place it into the boot once she's situated in the car.

On the short drive to the hospital, the car is deadly silent, apart from the low hum of the radio, there was no sound but my heart beating.

You could cut the atmosphere with a knife. Gaynor stares straight ahead and makes no attempts to break the silence. I really don't know if I should try to start a conversation or leave things be. I need to face the situation; we can't keep going like this.

"So, what do you want to do after the hospital? Do you want to go for a bite to eat?" I ask hesitantly.

She turns her head in my direction, but I keep my eyes on the road.

"No."

That's it? Just no.

"We could try that new Indian in town."

"No, thanks."

Oh.

"If you don't want to go there, we could go somewhere else, maybe the old Italian you love,"

"I said, No, David. I went out yesterday with mom before she left, if you had bothered to ask, I would have told you,"

"Oh, okay. I'm sorry."

I see Gaynor look forward out of the corner of my eye. The silence has returned to the car and the atmosphere, well I wish I hadn't spoken. I pull the car into the parking space and climb from my seat.

I open the boot and place her chair by her door, I pull open her door and freeze. Do I offer to help, or do I let her do it herself? I look and see she is studying me.

I swallow hard, debating the best way forward but it's not in my nature to stand by and let someone struggle, so I swallow my pride and offer.

"Do you need me to help you, or have you got it?"

"I've got it."

I watch as she struggles into her chair, I want to help her, but I don't risk undermining her and her need for independence.

"You can wait in the car, I won't be long,"

"But I thought I was coming in with you?"

"I don't need a babysitter, David. I just needed a ride. I'm sure there's some work stuff you can be getting on with?" she rolls her eyes.

I don't reply. Instead, I just nod my head. I step back and let her continue to her appointment. I slip back into my seat and sigh. I lean my head back and close my eyes trying to fight off a terrible headache.

I don't know how long I sat there with my eyes shut but I need to do something because my thoughts are running rampant in my head. I reach for my phone and check my emails.

There are at least twenty emails regarding the job, I'm pleased to see that maybe by Friday I will be able to let Jen go and have a new one in place by Monday.

I glance down at the applicants and star a few that I will reply to tonight. One catches my attention and I open it.

Attention; Shepard's Construction Limited.

Please find attached my current C.V.

I may not have much experience, but I will always give you one hundred percent.

I look forward to hearing from you,

Best regards,

H. George.

I immediately replied asking if they are available for an interview tomorrow evening, I like that she hasn't tried to over sell herself and kept it real.

Dear Ms. George,

Thank you for replying to my advert for the position of Office Manager and Assistant.

Would you be available for an interview tomorrow evening at 5.30?

Best regards,

D. Shepard.

I attach my business card with the company address on it, as I'm not sure how long Gaynor will be.

I turn my emails off and open a file that Shawn had sent me this morning that I hadn't had time to look at but as I start to look at the plans. I glance up to see Gaynor wheeling herself out the main doors, towards the car but stops just outside the entrance; but she's not alone. There is a man that looks to be in his late thirties, laughing and talking to her.

I have never seen her this carefree and happy. I feel sad that I could never give her that feeling.

I drop my eyes back to my phone because I don't want her thinking I'm spying on her, but as I continue to stare at the black screen, I suddenly see that we are both trapped in this marriage but neither of us have the guts to end this nightmare.

I can't end it because I don't want to be the man who walked away from my disabled wife and she won't end it because she needs the security and, on some level, I think she wants to punish me for it being her in that wheelchair and not me.

I hear a tap on the window and see Gaynor's flat and dead eyes through the glass, if I hadn't just seen the joy on her face, I probably wouldn't have noticed the look in them now.

I rise from the car and come around to open her door. She pushes her chair beside the car and eases herself into the seat. I fold her chair and place it in the boot. I jump into my seat and

48

pause before I start the engine. I really want to reach out to her on some level but what do I say?

"Did everything go, okay?" I ask.

"The usual." Is her only reply.

I nod my head once and start the car. I pulled out of the space, as we drove past the entrance, I could see the man she was talking to, and he was watching us leave. I contemplate saying something, but I don't have the energy to argue once again, so I leave it unspoken. I zip my lips and leave the words where they need to stay.

"I just need to pick up some stuff from the supermarket. Do you want me to cook tonight?"

"I suppose."

I take a deep breath, I feel empty. How did we get here? I glance over towards Gaynor but she's staring out of the window, she looks as miserable as me.

"I've just remembered I need to go back to work, there's some plans I should have approved this morning and didn't get around to doing. Do you want me to drop you home?"

I feel like I can't breathe, I need to get away from the atmosphere and the hurt.

"Yep."

I don't even glance her way.

When I think back to the moment when she was outside that hospital with the man, it hurt. I can never make her look that way. Even on our wedding day she was always more worried about how she looked to everyone else than to me.

Do you think 'they' all loved my dress?

Do you think 'they' thought I was fat?

I was never in her thoughts; I was just a means to an end. We married because it was good for her father to be associated with my family name.

In a way, it was an arranged marriage that suited everyone but me. I had my reasons for going through with it, but it had nothing to do with the family name or business.

There was only one reason I went through with it and one reason alone, to please the man that was my sperm donor. He needed her dad to invest in his company or it would have gone under and one way to guarantee this was to get his only son to marry his only eligible daughter.

Why did I agree?

I remember being introduced to Gaynor at a family dinner. She acted sweet, shy and complacent. She had curves to die for and a gleam in her eyes that drew you in.

I was twenty-five, just starting out with my own business. She flirted, and she was cute, but I wasn't interested in her; she was too high maintenance for someone who was just trying to build his own empire.

Then one day I got a call from my father asking me to pop in and see him as he had something to discuss with me. I knew if he wanted to see me, then it wasn't anything good, but I went anyway. I needed to hear what he had to say.

I might have hated the man for what he did to my mum, but for some reason I also wanted to please him. I wanted him to make me feel like I was good enough.

When I reached his office, he called me in with a wave of his hand. I sat down on the big leather armchair in front of his desk while I waited for him to finish his call. I wished I hadn't bothered going, I wish I had told him I was too busy because from that day on my life was never the same again.

"Thank you for coming, David. I need to have a chat about a few things."

"Okay." I never gave him more than one-word answers unless he annoyed me.

"I see you've been getting on well with Gaynor and maybe enjoying that delicious body of hers."

I frown, not sure where he was going with it, but I didn't deny or agree. I had no interest in Gaynor what-so-ever, but I knew she was part of a bigger plan concerning my father, so I played along.

"I see. Keeping it on the down low, huh!" he smirks like a Cheshire cat.

"Well, I called you here because I've had a conversation with her father and he wants her to settle down and I think you'll be the most perfect match,"

My eyes bulge, as I try to take in what he's saying.

"I don't think so, I am not marrying Gaynor. She's nice and all that but not my type."

"Well make her your type, David! Look, I'm going to be straight with you. Her father wants her to settle down with a nice eligible unmarried man, I need his money to inject into the business. You get a wife and I get a boost to be able to improve the company. Win, win."

"Who's winning? Because it's not me. Look Dad, I would love to help you out on this one but I'm not. Gaynor isn't for me. So, the answer is no."

"David, I'm not asking you. Your mother's wishes were that I would make sure you're happy and that's what I'm doing. It's not like you have to stay married, five years tops and then you can get one of those divorce thingies and both move on."

I sigh. I couldn't believe what he was saying I should have known he would throw the mother card out at me, but I also know that I want to feel worthy and respected by my father.

So, six months later I was standing at the bottom of the aisle waiting for Gaynor to arrive at the altar with a chain around my neck.

I pull into the driveway and jump out to retrieve Gaynor's chair. I place it by the car door and open it, while I wait for her to lift herself into it.

"Do you want me to open the front door?" I ask.

"No, I'll manage." She grumbles.

I step back and watch her wheel herself into the house. I feel the relief leave my body as I retreat into my seat, just as the front door slams shut. I reverse backwards, backing out of the drive onto the road and head for the office.

I'm losing my mind trying to figure out how to change my life for the better, but I know deep down I'm stuck exactly where I deserve to be.

Chapter Five

Hannah

The sun was pouring into my bedroom through the gap in the curtains, as I slowly woke from my normal steamy dream. I rubbed my weary eyes and turned over as I tried to block the headache that was trying to form in my head. I couldn't believe how much wine I drank last night; a sign Liv was here she likes to drink a bottle or two.

I hear the boys stirring and I know that I need to get up and face the day. I have planned this morning to go shopping with Livvy and find something sophisticated for my interview later.

I have an interview.

I can't believe it; I would never have thought two years ago I would be in this position but it's nice to know that sometimes hard work does pay off.

I stretch and feel my back pull slightly. I sigh because I need to get moving but I am warm and cosy where I am.

I sit up and put my feet on the floor, and glance at the clock on the bedside table. It's seven-fifteen already, I only have just over an hour and half before the boys have to be in school.

I walk into the bathroom as I'm pulling on my dressing gown, I glance in the mirror and see the bags under my eyes. Great I'm going to my first ever interview with bags as big as suitcases.

I frown. I need to get a wriggle on. I brush my teeth and shout at the boys as I make my way downstairs. I head straight for the kettle and flick it on, before I grab the toaster.

Just as the toast pops up Thomas sits at the table with his hair everywhere. I smile, as I see the frown upon his face. He's just like me, not a morning person. I butter the bread and I make my coffee, then place the orange juice on the table.

I grab my cup and walk to the bottom of the stairs.

"Elliott time to get up now, monster."

"But moooom. I'm tired today, I want to stay in bed."

"Not today sunshine, get up now. Toasts done and your drinks on the table."

I hear him groan as I hear his heavy footsteps running across the landing, I make my way back into the kitchen and place my mug into the sink.

"Right, I'm going for a quick shower, please make sure you and Elliott have breakfast, Thomas."

"I will mum."

"Thank you Darling. Love you," I kiss the top of his head as I pass by.

Just as I reach the hall, Elliott charges down the stairs and lands at the bottom. I laugh because that child doesn't know anything below fast.

I grab my skinny jeans and put them on, I can hear Thomas in the shower as I finish getting myself ready to drop the boys off at school and then pick up Livvy. I rush through our routine as Elliott drags his feet and does everything but what I ask him too.

We just make it to school as the bell rings and I exhale a breath of relief. I'm hoping the day gets better before my interview. I can feel my nerves start to build the more I think about it, so I try to think of something else to help keep my nerves under control.

I pull into Livvy's drive and beep the horn as I wait for her to come out, I see her already making her way down the path with a spring in her step, and I dread to think what she's going to talk me into buying, she's the total opposite of me.

I hate the whole shopping experience, but Livvy loves trawling the shops for the best sales and discounts. I watch as she checks her mail before jumping into the car, bright as a button.

"Morning Bestie," Livvy sings.

"Morning, Sweets."

"What's up?"

"Nothing," I smile, trying to sound as excited as Livvy.

"Come on, it will be a laugh, it's been ages since we had a girly shopping day, in fact I can't remember the last time!"

"It will be a dream," I reply sarcastic.

Livvy raises her eyebrows like I've pissed on her chips.

"Someone's got out the bed on the wrong side this morning," she sings in her high-pitched singing voice.

"God, Livvy. How can you be as fresh as a daisy after all the wine we drank last night?"

"That my dear would be telling," she wiggles her eyebrows and grins, showing her full teeth grin.

I giggle. She always manages to make me laugh even with a niggling headache from the alcohol.

We pull into the parking space at the shopping centre and Livvy has not stopped talking from the moment she got into the car. It's a good job that I'm used to her waffling on, because I don't think she's stopped to draw breath.

Most people struggle to cope with Livvy's personality. She is confident, knows what she wants and has no problem voicing her opinions.

She was bullied all through her school years for being too helpful and caring but after all that, she hasn't turned nasty and bitter, she is still kind, caring and compassionate.

We understand each other, I'm the quiet one and she's the flamboyant one; we work off each other and we are loyal to one another. There is nothing I wouldn't do for this woman, and I know I can count on her too.

As we get out of the car, we decide to get a cup of coffee. As we enter the café the aroma of the coffee hits my nose. I smile because I'm so close to getting my caffeine fix, and I know I'm going to need it to survive the next few hours.

I leave the café with Livvy still talking about a client at work who keeps calling to ask her out on a date, while I'm wandering behind Liv trying to wake up and feel somewhat normal. Livvy pulls me into an expensive top-end market boutique.

"Livvy, I can't afford to shop in here," I exclaim under my breath, as I look around at all the top end clothes.

"Shhh, stop panicking. They have an amazing sale on. We can just have a look, but you want to look your best for your interview and clothes from here, say style, sexy and employ me." She wiggles her eyebrows.

I know it's a bad idea but trying to argue with my bestie never ends well. She only wants the best for me but it's just a shame that Liv's best is usually three or four hundred pounds more than I can afford.

As Livvy walks along the rails, she pulls dress after dress from the hangers, then shoves them at me and points me in the direction of the changing rooms telling me to try them on in the order, she has given them to me, while she waits in the dressing area to see what they look like on me.

I pull back the curtain and hang the clothes on the hook on the wall, and slowly undress as I look at all the dresses hanging there.

56

I'm not sure about this at all, I hate being on show, I much prefer being in the background.

I take the first dress and slide it on carefully. I'm frightened that I'll pull the silk material, but once the midnight blue dress is on, I fall in love. It hugs my curves perfectly and falls to just above my knee with a sweetheart neckline that makes my breast seem bigger, not that they need much help.

As I go in search of Liv to show her the dress, I feel the material flowing around my thighs as I walk. When I reach her sitting in the waiting room, she does a little squeal and her happy dance as she takes in what I'm wearing.

"That's it! That is the one Hannah. It was made for your body."

"Really? The first one?"

"Yes. I saw that dress and knew it was made for you. The others were just in case." She smiles.

I walk to the wall of mirrors and look over my shoulder to see what it looks like from behind and I have to say it does look good. It doesn't make my bum look big; it fits me like a glove. I look at myself from all angles in the mirror and for the first time ever, I actually feel good, confident even and definitely sexy.

"Okay, go and get your clothes on and while you're doing that, I'll go and pay for your dress."

"No, Livvy. I'm paying for it," I try to argue but it's no use as she rips the label from the dress and heads out onto the shop floor.

I sigh, I should have known she would do this because she always likes to treat me, but she shouldn't keep wasting her money on me.

Once I'm dressed, I head out the way I came in with the dresses draped across my arm, I see Livvy talking to the cashier and see they are both laughing.

Liv can always light up the room wherever she is, she has this aura that draws people to her.

When we were younger, I used to be jealous but now I'm glad; she draws the attention away from me.

As I approach them, Livvy beams and takes the dress from my arms. The cashier starts taking off the sale labels and bagging them up.

"Oh, I only want the dark blue one on the top," I start to panic.

But Livvy puts her hand on my shoulder and smiles.

"No, it's okay bestie, they are paid for."

"Livvy this is too much. You can't waste your money like that."

"I'm not, Hannah, Lenny's company has an account here and he said to put them on there. When you get the job later, you are going to need clothes to wear to the office every day."

I feel terrible, I feel like I'm always taking and never giving back. I smile tightly and nod my head. I make a mental note to speak to Lenny when I see him next and thank him, but I do feel slightly awkward as I know Lenny wants us to be a little more.

As we are leaving the shopping centre, Livvy decides we need to grab some lunch. I glance at the time and see it's nearly twelve already. We pop into a posh sandwich shop, and I order a salad and coffee, Livvy has the all-day breakfast and a cup of tea.

"So, are you looking forward to your first interview?"

"Define looking forward too." I laugh.

"Ah, off with ya. You know you'll smash it. Your hot, sexy as hell and polite, what more could they need to answer phones and take messages,"

"I don't know what the job will entail. I think it will be more to it than that, but I guess I will see later."

"We should get going soon. I'll do your hair and make-up too. What time do you need to be there?"

"Half five, and the closer it gets the more my nerves are getting the better of me."

"Hannah just be you! They will love you, just the way you are."

I smile because no matter how much I doubt myself, Liv's always behind me cheering me on, she's never once doubted my ability or made me feel less than perfect.

I pull the car to stop outside the building I have the address I've been given for the interview, and I swallow hard. This doesn't look like a building contractors' yard.

As I peered up at the glass building, I couldn't believe what I was seeing, and I wondered if I had the wrong address.

I pulled my phone from my bag and pulled up the business card that had been attached to the email and double checked the postcode that I had put in my satnav. They both tied up, so I was at the right place.

Confused, I climb from the car and walk through the entrance door.

As I approached the reception, I took in the clean appearance of the place.

"Hi, how can I help you?" The man from behind the desk asks.

I turn back to him and smile.

"Hi, I have an interview with Shepard's Construction. Can you tell me if I have the right place?"

"I can do more than that, I can show you to their offices," he walks from behind the desk, placing his hand on my lower back, guiding me towards the row of elevators on the left-hand side.

"Let me introduce myself. I'm Ben, I work the main desk in reception," he shakes my hand.

As we step into the lift, I let my hand drop as I introduce myself to him.

"I'm Hannah George,"

"Pleased to meet you Hannah. Shepard's Construction is based on the second floor and has the most gorgeous owner. I was hoping that one day he would swing the other way but unfortunately, I've been here three years and it's not happened yet," He winks.

I smile, Ben reminds me so much of Livvy, I think if I got the job, we could be good friends.

As I am directed down the corridor, I noticed some of the stunning pictures of houses and renovations, before and after pictures. I would not have believed they were the same buildings if I hadn't seen them side by side, they are stunning.

As we approach the last door, Ben knocks on the dark glass.

"Come in," I hear a small, delicate voice say from the other side.

Ben opens the door as we walk into the room, I glance around and see a glass wall of windows at the back of the room, that overlooked a cute park with a small lake. It's breath-taking on this glorious sunny evening.

Once I pull my eyes from the window, I see an older lady sitting to the right of the long rectangular table, silently watching me.

"Good evening, Mrs. Barkley, Ms. George has arrived for her interview,"

"Thank you, Ben. Ms. George would you like a drink?"

"I'm perfectly fine, thank you, Mrs. Barkley,"

"Very well dear, please take a seat." She smiled at me.

"Do you need anything else, Mrs. Barkley?"

"Ben, please call me Joyce. Maybe a jug of water and some glasses would be a good idea,"

"I'll be right back, Joyce," Ben disappeared from the room, and minutes later, he started to wheel in a trolley, with water, glasses and biscuits on the top. Ben blushed when he saw us watching him.

"I like to be prepared," he shrugs as I smile.

"This is why you're the heart of the reception; this place needs more people like you." Mrs. Barkley smiles.

"Thank you." Ben leaves us in the quietness of the room.

I hear the clock ticking in the silence of the office and raise my eyes to check the time. I was early to the interview, so I know I have a few minutes before the owner turns up.

After what Ben said about the owner, I'm a little nervous to meet him. I slowly move my eyes across the table until they meet Mrs. Barkley's, she smiles timidly as she places her pen down by her notepad.

"We are just waiting for Mr. Shepard. He said he might be slightly late, due to car trouble."

"That's okay, Mrs. Barkley. Have you worked here long?" I ask as I try to fill the silence.

"I don't work here, dear." She smiled. "I'm helping Mr. Shepard because I'm Mr. Shepard's father's P.A. and I offered to help as I've attended plenty of interviews over the years."

I smile as I hear footsteps rushing down the corridor. I turn my head in the direction of the noise and I wait for him to push open the door.

As I hold my breath the door flies open and who I assume is Mr. Shepard, enters but he trips and stumbles into the room, scattering everything he was carrying.

I gasp as I rush to help him pick up all the files, he had in his arms that are now on the floor. Flustered I see him trying to right himself.

"I'm so sorry I'm late ladies, I had car trouble then every damn light was on red when I reached it," he quickly explained.

I place the files on the end of the table and return to my seat, I watch him busily trying to sort out his personal items as he has his back to me. He asked Mrs. Barkley if she was okay and if she needed anything before we started. Then he turned his eyes to meet mine and he froze. I could see him trying to sort through his thoughts before he smiled and held out his hand to shake mine.

"Good evening, Ms. George. I hope you're okay. Can I get you anything before we start?" He asks frowning.

"I'm fine, Mr. Shepard. Mrs. Barkley has been very gracious, thank you."

With a nod of his head, he takes a seat in the chair at the head of the table and continues to look at me with fascination. It feels a little unnerving, but I try not to overthink it. I look at Mrs. Barkley and smile.

Mr. Shepard grabs a glass before filling it with water and downs it in one go, while keeping his eyes on me.

62

When he places the glass on the table, it tips over but luckily there was no water left so it didn't make a mess, I see Mrs. Barkley giving him a strange look, which he replies with a shake of his head.

"Okay, let's get started, shall we? Tell us a little about yourself, Ms. George," Mrs. Barkley starts.

This one I can answer, I take a big calming breath.

"Firstly, I'm a mum to two young boys, well not so young now. My eldest is eleven and my youngest is eight. I've recently finished an online course in Office Management as I wanted to improve my job prospects. I've been working the last two years in a café not far from here to help pay the bills and support the boys, but I need to find a better job and with better hours," I smile.

I look at them both to try to gage their reaction, but I can't pick up anything from their faces.

"What support system do you have around you? You know in case you are successful, and the boys are ill."

"I have my neighbour who watches the boys when I work and they aren't at school, I also have my best friend and her brother. They are really great with the boys and helps me as much as they can."

"Dad's not about then?" Mr. Shepard asks suddenly.

I hesitate as I look into his eyes and raise my eyebrow. I could have sworn I've seen him somewhere before as his eyes look so familiar.

"No, Dad isn't around." I shake my head.

He nods his head as he drops his eyes again to the notepad in front of him.

"What qualities do you have that you could bring to the job?" Mrs. Barkley asks.

I pause as I try to think of how best to answer this.

63

"I have great people skills and I'm polite." And that is all I could come up with as qualities they may be looking for. I know I'm failing at this; I feel my cheeks burn up in embarrassment.

"That's excellent," Mr. Shepard replied with a tight smile.

I drop my eyes, I know I'm fucking this up. They carry on for the next fifteen minutes firing questions at me and I trying to sound confident and assertive but failing miserably. As the interview finishes Mrs. Barkley stands and offers me her hand.

"We will be in touch, Ms. George. It was a pleasure to meet you." She sits back down.

"You too Mrs. Barkley, take care of yourself."

I lift my eyes to Mr. Shepard and he's watching me intently.

"Good evening Mr. Shepard," I turn and open the door as I rush down the corridor. I can feel the tears burning in my eyes as I push the elevator button. I can't wait to get out of here.

"Ms. George," I hear from behind me.

I turn on the spot as I see him rushing down the corridor towards me. As he reaches me, he pauses and takes a breath.

"The job." He bites on his bottom lip. "The job, it's yours if you want it."

"Really?"

"Yes,"

I stare up into his eyes, shocked. I see him struggling with something.

"Oh, Thank you, Mr. Shepard! I won't let you down I promise," I lurch forward and wrap my arms around him without thinking, I cringe as I realise what I have done, and I feel him stiffen in my arms.

I slowly step backwards as I thank God, I hear the door to the elevator open. I quickly apologise, before I step back into the lift, feeling my face blush.

As I press the button to the reception, I look up and see Mr. Shepard's stiff body retreating towards the conference room and I smack my hand to my forehead as I realise I've made a complete fool out of myself in front of my new boss.

Chapter Six

David

I stand at the kitchen island with my meal for one and pour myself a glass of whiskey. I don't usually drink in the house but after the last few hours, I don't think a bottle of water would calm the rampant energy running through my body. If the car breaking down wasn't enough stress, imagine my shock when I literary stagger into my first interview for the Office manager, to see the one woman who has haunted my dreams for the last month, sitting there in front of me.

I nearly swallowed my tongue in shock as I recalled what I did to her most delicate parts and how she rode my cock before coming all over it. I thought at one point I was hallucinating, that I had dreamed this all up or I had nodded off in the car waiting to be rescued and it was all a dream.

She was exactly how I remembered her. Her long mahogany hair trailed down her back and drifted around her shoulders, with her chocolate brown eyes looking up at me and voice like an answer to my prayers. I had to be dreaming, my throat was so dry it felt like the desert.

I grabbed a glass and poured the water until it nearly over flowed, but I managed to catch it before it did and then downed it in one gulp; all the while, my eyes were drinking in the beauty in front of me.

I left most of the questions to Joyce as she was the best at what she did for my father. But all through her first two answers there was one burning question, and I couldn't stop the words spilling from my mouth.

"Dad's not about then?"

I heard the sharp intake of breath from Joyce, and I knew I'd overstepped the mark, but I did need to know, it had been driving me mad for weeks, even though Shawn tried to put me right on the following Monday morning. I still needed to hear it from her lips, I wanted to know she wasn't giving her pleasure to anyone else, not that it really mattered as I wasn't in the position to give her what she needed but I just had this urgency in me to know.

"No, Dad's not around," she replied as she held her eyes to mine.

I drop my eyes to my notepad as many thoughts start flying through my head. My heart felt like it's going to beat out of my chest, and I feel the sweat coating my skin. We haven't even got halfway through, and I already know she's got the job.

As I sit here, the one night of passion I shared with her, runs through my mind on repeat like a movie on loop but as I watch Ms. George, it seems she can't remember me the same way I remember her.

I know I need my head tested, therefore setting myself up for a fall, but I need her close. I tell myself it's because I want to make sure she's taken care of financially and she can support her boys without worrying, but that would all be a lie. A big fat lie. I have this need to be close to her, there's something in me that's attracted to this beautiful woman.

Once she leaves the room, I see Joyce staring at me through the corner of my eye.

"Before you say anything, I know I overstepped the mark," I stand up and pace the floor.

My thoughts are running wild.

"Just slightly David. There are some questions you just shouldn't ask."

I nod, I know she's right. I just need my head to catch up.

"I think we should continue looking, it's obvious that something in your head is attached to this girl, and it won't end well."

I pause as the words work through my brain. Before I know what's happening my feet move towards the door and I open it. I halt at the doorway, if I continue and tell her she has the job, there's no going back. I didn't even really have to think because I knew, she's the one I wanted. She's the one my soul craves.

"I'll be right back," I tell Joyce over my shoulder.

I rush down the corridor like a hurricane. As I reach her, I pause and take a breath.

"The job." I bite on my bottom lip. "The job, it's yours if you want it."

"Really?"

"Yes,"

I stare down into her eyes; I see the shock written all over her face. As I stand two feet away from Ms. George, I feel the internal struggle inside. I hate being this close and not being able to touch her in the way in which I've dreamed of.

"Oh, thank you, Mr. Shepard! I won't let you down I promise," She lunges forward and wraps her arms around me without warning. I stiffen as I feel her body next to mine. After a second, I feel a shiver run through her body, and I feel her slowly step backwards as the door to the elevator opens as she quickly apologies and steps into the lift before she blushes.

I don't wait to see the doors close. I have turned and started back towards the conference room because I'm struggling to do the right thing. I can feel the internal battle raging inside. I want to jump in and fuck her against the wall of the elevator. So, I stiffly retreat towards Joyce and smack my head on the wall next to the door as I realise, I've made a complete idiot of myself in front of my new employee.

Once I walk back into the conference room, Joyce sits there with a raised eyebrow. She's never seen me behave so irrational before. I'm usually calm headed and never jump into things.

"Before you say anything, I think she'll be a good fit for the company," I hold my hands up in defeat before Joyce has a chance to say anything.

"Hey, it's your business David, it's your choice. I've known you since you were fourteen and I trust your judgement, but make sure you're thinking with the right head," she smiles.

That's one thing I love about Joyce, she's always the voice of reason but doesn't judge. I imagine after being my dad's P.A. for so many years she's seen some situations and ignored some bad decisions there too.

I've always had a lot of time for her, likewise she has for me. She's always felt like a grandmother. She would be the one to deal with any trouble I had in school as my father was always too busy and Clara didn't like what I stood for as she couldn't provide what my father needed, another son. So, Joyce became one of the most important people in my life and kept me on the straight and narrow.

"I will, but I think Ms. George needs a break. She's obviously dealt with a lot and now she needs a job with prospects."

"I agree. Just don't get too involved. You have a big heart and I know you don't have it easy but make sure you sort yourself out before you invite someone else in."

I agreed. I did need to sort my life out but how I was going to do that was what I was struggling with.

And that's where I'm at. I'm sitting here sipping my whiskey, with a meal for one, trying to sort through my thoughts and find where I genuinely want to be and there's only one thing that keeps coming to my mind and it's not the woman that lives in this house with me.

I spend all weekend locked in my room, trying to figure out how I can keep her from realising who I am. It's obvious she can't remember me, and I think that it's best it stays that way.

Maybe if we keep things formal in work, she won't realise who I really am but what about when clients or contractors come into meetings, and they call me David. Surely, she's going to eventually realise who I am. She is an intelligent woman. Unless she was too drunk that night to remember anything.

I've already warned Shawn to keep his mouth shut. I just hope he does as I ask but knowing him, he won't. I go over every scenario in my head and I know nothing good will come from them all but telling her the truth.

I've never lied in my life, but I'm so scared she'll run for the hills when she knows who I am and remembers our night together. I need to come clean; I know but maybe I could see how our first day goes and then if everything's okay, I can talk to her at the end before she finishes.

It's Monday morning and the sun is shining, the birds are singing, and I've just arrived at the office early. Just as I step out of the elevator, I notice a different smell in the air and a different feel to the office. I hesitate as I take in the light orchestral music playing softly in the background and I turn to look at the numbers above the elevator to make sure I'm on the right floor. I frown at the number highlighted because it's the right one, but something feels different.

I shake my head and head down towards my office. The music has a calming effect on me. I don't know why I hadn't thought of adding a light piece of music before? As I pass the office, I will be giving to Ms. George, as the Office manager; I see Ms. George already here sitting behind the desk, reading something intently on the desk in front of her.

I hover at the door as I take in how beautiful she is. She's dressed in a pale pink fitted dress, the colour really suits her, and the sweetheart neck shape makes her cleavage look delectable. I knock gently on the door frame as not to scare her; and she slowly lifts her eyes as a smile fills her beautiful face.

"Hi, Mr. Shepard. I got here early, and Mr. Matthews has shown me to the office. I hope that was okay?"

I freeze with panic. She must know we've met before now if she's met Shawn too. I wait to see if she says anything else, but she stays silent and frowns when I don't reply.

"Of course, it's okay. I don't usually arrive until after ten, so I'm glad Mr. Matthews was here to help."

"I have left your mail on your desk as it arrived the same time as I did, and Mr. Matthews asked if you could check your emails as he has sent you a plan to a new house that you've acquired." She smiles timidly.

"Yes, I'll do that straight away," I answer awkwardly.

"Is there anything else I can do for you Mr. Shepard?"

Suck my cock wasn't a suitable answer as I felt the slight movement in my trousers. I shake my head trying to clear all the dirty images from my mind.

71

"If you could check the diary for this week and see if there's any meetings booked in with contractors or suppliers, please and then email all the dates and times, so I have them all in one place."

"Certainly, Sir." She replied as she turned on the computer on her desk.

If my cock wasn't hard enough, hearing her call me Sir definitely did it. I am no way a dominant, but I can see the fascination when you have a sweet little thing like Ms. George calls you Sir.

I turn to leave the office and make my way into mine. I placed my laptop on the table and hang my jacket up on the coat stand. As I sit in my chair, I swivel it left to right as I try to pull my thoughts together to get some work done, but my mind is elsewhere.

I tap my fingers on the wood as I contemplate on what I should do first. The first thing that comes to mind is placing Ms. George across my desk and having my way with her, but I don't think that would go down well with it being her first day and all. I hear a gentle tap on the door and lift my eyes.

"I was wondering if you would like a drink Mr. Shepard or something to eat?" She smiled.

Oh god kill me now, the way she said 'something to eat' has my cock bursting from my pants. I need to get a grip or maybe she needs to get a grip on my hard on. I mentally shake my head; I feel like a fucking teenager.

"It's okay Ms. George, I will pop out and fetch us something. We need to celebrate your first day and it's my treat. What would you like?"

"It's Hannah,"

I hear her say and I frown, not understanding what she meant.

"My name is Hannah, not Ms. George. Well technically it is Ms. George, but I much prefer just Hannah, as the George part is my ex-husbands not mine." she clarifies.

I feel a complete arse, I see the sadness in her eyes and feel angry that I had made her sad in any way.

"Okay, Hannah it is. If you call me David," I freeze, as I realise what I had just said. I intently watch her to see if she recognises me.

I see her eyes widen as she rushes from the room. FUCK!!!!!!! I knew this would happen.

I chase after her as I see her dash for the lady's toilet. I don't think twice as I barge through the door. I hear the latch slide across as I approach the only locked cubicle.

"Hannah, are you okay?" What a stupid thing to say, you idiot!

I hear her breathing heavily behind the stall door, I know she's upset. I tap gently.

"Please come out, so we can talk." I whisper as I lean my head against the cold wooden door.

I hear the lock slide across and now she has opened the door. I step back, leaning against the sinks to give her some room and the time she needs to face me.

After a few minutes she appears from inside the stall, her mascara running down her cheeks. I was at a loss for words, I didn't know how to make this right, but I needed to find the way because there was no way I was letting her leave.

We stand there staring at each other, neither wanting to be the first to speak. I could feel my heart beating out of my chest and knew I would do anything to keep her close.

"I didn't know who you were when I was in the interview, I promise, or I would never have agreed to take the job. I thought I recognised your eyes, but I thought I'd probably served you in the café." She paused with a look of defeat on her face. "I'll get my things and leave, I'm sorry I wasted your time."

She went to walk past me and back out into the corridor but before she reached the door, I grabbed her arm, stopping her from leaving. I feel the electric energy pass between us and quickly drop her arm.

"I should have said when I walked into the interview, but I was in shock." I admitted.

"I couldn't believe the woman who had haunted my dreams for the past month was sitting in my conference room." I take a deep breath as she turns to face me. "I know what happened shouldn't have happened, but it did. Was it the best night of my life? Yes. Would I want it to happen again? God, yes. But it can't, you have responsibilities and so do I. But I'm sure we can be responsible adults about this and work together." I can't believe the words as they come from my mouth, but they sounded good, right? There was so much more I wanted to say and do, but I needed to be an adult and accept defeat.

With the nod of her head, she wipes her fingers under her eyes. I want to pull her into my arms and comfort her, but I know that's not an option. As she leaves the toilets, I lean over the sinks, and I splash my face with freezing water. I honestly don't know what's going through my head right now but at least it's all out in the open and we can move forward and learn to work side by side or so I hope.

Chapter Seven

Hannah

I rush to the bank of the elevators as I glance down at my watch, damn I'm ten minutes late. I've never been late for anything and after our show down yesterday, I didn't want David thinking I was taking liberties.

After our talk in the toilets, I went back to my office and hid out there for the rest of the day. I spent my time getting used to the computer system and how they do the invoices, which Shawn helped me understand better while he popped in to speak with David.

I can't believe I never put his face to the man that Livvy was hanging off on our girl's night out last month, when he showed me to my office yesterday. I thought he looked familiar but again I thought I must have served him in the cafe. It never crossed my mind that he was the best friend of the man who set my body on fire in a dark corridor in a nightclub many nights ago. I could kick myself for being so drunk that night.

When Shawn first offered to help me understand how they do the invoices, I refused and said I'd find a way to understand it, that I didn't want to put him out, but he said that he really didn't mind. I didn't want to seem ungrateful, so I thanked him, and he pulled up a chair beside me.

After several attempts at showing me the ins and outs, it finally clicked and I got one right. Shawn jumped up and did a happy dance, clapping and cheering loudly. I was laughing so hard; it was just what I needed after this morning.

"Stop, stop! I'm going to wet myself," I roll with laughter.

"Hmm.... I haven't even tried my moves on you yet and you're already wet," he winked as someone from the door cleared their throat.

Shawn spun on the spot and nearly choked when he saw the look on David's face.

"My office now!" He bellowed.

Shawn turned back to me as an angry David stormed into his own office. My eyes bulged as I began to panic, I didn't want him to think I wasn't pulling my weight or willing to put the hours in.

I dropped my head into my hands as my elbows rested on the desk. I couldn't believe I'd made David so angry on my first day, especially after our confrontation. I could feel my eyes fill as I begged the tears not to fall.

"Don't worry Hannah, his bark is worse than his bite. I'll smooth it over, it's not your fault he's wandering around like a bear with a sore head," he smiled but I couldn't bring myself to smile back.

I looked down, trying to tidy up all the paperwork that was scattered all over the desk from Shawn's lesson on the invoices. Once they are all in a pile, I try to busy myself. I can feel Shawn's eyes on me, but I refuse to look at him because I know I'll break down.

I see him turn and leave my office out of the corner of my eye and feel relieved. I spent the rest of the afternoon locked in my office, answering phone calls, making appointments and sending the contractors their monthly statements.

When I glanced up it was after half past five, and I had totally lost track of time. I sat for a minute contemplating if I should go and say goodbye to David before I left for the day. I didn't know if he would want to speak to me, even though he did say that we need to behave like adults and that's what an adult would do.

So, I grab my stuff together and slowly walk towards his office. I pause as I reach the door, I'm trying to talk myself out of it.

I don't want to make the situation worse but before I could turn and leave, David's door flies open. I feel his hard body hit mine as I stagger backwards but before I hit the floor, I feel his arms grab me and pull me to him.

As I stand in his arms for a second, his touch makes my body sag in relief from all the tension of the day. I forgot for a moment that he was my boss and leaned forward to take in his scent. I suddenly realise how much I have missed the feeling of being in a mans arms and what I would give to feel that every day.

I closed my eyes, then stepped back before I did something silly like kiss him. When I open my eyes, David was looking at me like he's having the same battle.

"I was just going to say goodbye, I've finished for the day." I whisper breathlessly.

"Hannah, I'm sorry about earlier. I wasn't angry with you." He reached out and ran his finger along my jaw, leaving a tingling sensation trailing behind it. "I don't know how to explain how I felt seeing Shawn flirting with you like that. I felt like tearing the place down, I was so jealous, not that I have any right to be, but I am sorry if I upset you."

I look into David's eyes and see the sincerity in them, though I was shocked at his honesty, I didn't know how to reply. I wanted to push him back into his office and fuck him on his desk but I knew that wasn't an option while he was still married. So, I step back.

"I'll see you tomorrow, if I still have a job," I smile.

"Of course, you still have a job. I've been extremely impressed with what I've seen today. Well done, Hannah."

"Thank you."

I turn and head back towards the elevator and I feel David's eyes on me the whole time, but I didn't look back. I knew if I did I would be tempted to go back and kiss him. So, I silently waited for the elevator to arrive, glad to have my first disastrous day over and hope that tomorrow would be better now everything was out in the open.

So here we are day two, late as I glance back down at my watch. I'm twelve minutes delayed now, what's taking so long to get to the bottom floor. I tap my foot as a nervous energy runs through my body. I really hope that today's better than yesterday. I mean, it couldn't get much worse. As the elevator reaches the bottom, Ben comes hurrying out and nearly collides with me looking at his phone and not where he was going.

"Oh Hannah, I'm so sorry. I didn't see you there." He beamed at me.

"No worries Ben, I should have been paying attention too."

"How's working for Mr Sexy, I mean Mr. Shepard?"

He must see me cringe because his face drops.

"That good, huh?"

"No, it's been great, I mean I just need to get used to the computer system and routine," I smile timidly.

"Well, if you want to swap one day, I'll work under him any time." He winks.

I laugh aloud and enter the elevator. I watch Ben turn and make his way across the marbled floor to his reception desk as the doors close.

Yeah, I'd like to be under Mr. Sexy too, but I know it's never going to happen, well not in this lifetime anyway. I smile sadly to myself as I leave the lift; I pause as I hear the soft tinkling of an orchestra playing.

I try to think back to when I left last night to see if I can remember turning it off, and I could have sworn I did. Maybe I had forgotten but I do vaguely remember switching it off.

I continue towards my office trying to work out who might have turned it on but coming up blank. David won't be in for another forty minutes; I wonder if Shawn's popped in before going out on site but as I reach my office door I freeze.

There is the most gorgeous red roses bouquet sitting in the middle of my desk and a big red balloon with 'Congratulations on your first day' written on it.

I feel his presence before I smell him coming up behind me. I don't want to turn around because he'll see the tears streaming down my face and I don't want to destroy this moment.

"Did you do this?" I whisper loud enough for him to hear but not too loud to hear the wobble in my voice.

"I wanted to make up for us missing lunch yesterday." He paused.

We were silent for a long time, and I didn't think he was going to say anything else but then he placed his hand on my shoulder.

"It wasn't just about us missing lunch, it's about everything that happened yesterday. I made your first day so hard, when I really wanted it to be as special as you are. I'm sorry."

I feel him step back as his hand drops from my shoulder. I feel bereft from the feeling of his touch. I quickly wipe the tears away and turn to face him but all I see is his back retreating into his office. I walk into my office and drop my bag into the seat in front of my desk, then walk around to my chair to see David had a cup of coffee, milk, sugar and a plate of pancakes with bacon, sitting on my desk with a little note.

Yesterday has gone, tomorrow is yet to come.
Let's hope today is everything you hoped for and desired.
D xx

I slump into my chair, completely blown away, I am struggling so hard to keep my feelings professional. I want to go to his office and jump him, but I know that would make everything so much worse. I decided to write him a quick email to say thank you.

From: h.george-shepardscontructionlimited@gmail.com
To: shepardconstructionlimited@gmail.com
Subject: Thank you!

David, I just wanted to thank you for my surprise this morning. It meant the world to me, Thank you!

Is there anything you need me to do today?
H x

I press send and start my pancakes. Just as I'm finishing my coffee, I hear my emails go off.

From: shepardconstructionlimited@gmail.com
To: h.george-shepardconstructionlimited@gmail.com
Re: Thank you.

Hannah you are most welcome, I know it doesn't make up for yesterday, but I hope it goes some way to showing how sorry I am.

If you could go through my emails and star any important correspondence, so I can reply to them after lunch would be great. Thank you for not quitting on me.

D x

I frown, as if I could quit on him, yesterday might have been the biggest fuck up to a start of a new job ever. I mean how many people start a new job to find out their new boss was a one-night stand that they couldn't remember because they were too drunk. I honestly don't think anything else could be any worse but I'm willing to do my best and give my all, even if it's only to the job and not the man.

I send a quick reply letting him know I'll start it now and load his emails.

After two hours, his emails had been sorted. I'd starred all the important stuff, removed all the junk mail. Well, what I hope was junk mail, unless he's really into finding a Russian wife to come over and do dirty things to him. Then organised all his folders, so everything can be accessed more easily.

I stand from my seat and stretch. I feel stiff after sitting still for so long and not getting much sleep last night hasn't helped the situation either but every time, I closed my eyes, David's crystal blue eyes were staring back at me, and I could still feel his arms wrapped around me.

I look around my office trying to decide what to do next and glance over at the filing cabinet. I wonder what kind of state they will be in and whether I should try to organise them so that I can easily access them when David or Shawn is looking for something.

I glance at the clock above the door and notice it's half past eleven, so I know I have plenty of time to get them sorted. I set about taking the files out, one by one and putting them in alphabetical order and then I put the finished projects at the back and the newer files at the front with all the suppliers and contractors in their own draw on the filing cabinet.

When Shawn puts his head around the door, I glance at the time and realise it's nearly home time,

"I like a lady on her knees." He winks.

I smile.

"It's a good job I'm not a lady then," I wink back.

"Me and you are going to be best of friends."

I laugh aloud; Shawn is always joking around. I already really liked Shawn, but I definitely have no romantic feelings for him whatsoever.

"I'm getting off, now. Do you need any help with anything before I leave?" Shawn asks.

"I'm good thanks Shawn. I'll just finish off and I'll be on my way soon too,"

"Okay, I shall see you in the morning."

He turns as he leaves, letting the door shut behind him. After a few minutes I hear the door open again, thinking Shawn had forgotten to ask me something. So, I continue to lean behind the cabinet to reach a file that has fallen behind with my arse in the air, I hear a sharp intake of breath and realise it's not Shawn at my door but David. I slowly stand back up as my cheeks flood with colour, I blush the colour of my flowers. As I raise my eyes to his and I see his breathing is laboured.

"I was popping in to see if you needed help carrying your flowers to your car, but I see you're not ready yet,"

"I have just finished organising your files but noticed one had fallen behind the cabinet," I smile.

"You should have called me. I would have got it for you, you could have hurt yourself," He fussed but he wouldn't meet my eyes.

"I was fine, don't worry David. I'll just shut down my computer and then I will be on my way."

I turn and walk to my desk as I lean over to switch it off, I feel David approach from behind. I stiffen as I'm not sure what to do. I feel his hips line up against my backside and I close my eyes. I would love to turn around and wrap him in my arms and kiss his glorious face but I'm trying to keep myself in check, especially after this morning.

"I'm just reaching for your flowers," He whispers as I feel his breath down my neck, and I shiver.

"Thank you."

Is the only thing I can hoarsely whisper as I'm lost for words. He steps back as I turn around. I slowly follow David to the elevator as my thoughts are running wild. I long to feel his arms around me again or his mouth on mine.

We both step into the lift and I watch as he presses the button to reception. I lift my eyes and keep them focused on the information sticker on the door, as I feel his eyes on me. As we stand side by side, shoulder to shoulder, I feel his hand softly graze mine and I can feel the energy fizzing around us, but I concentrate on keeping my breathing steady.

The door opens, and David steps back to let me step out first, as I wave goodbye to Ben, I glance back and catch his eyes on my arse, so I walk away with a little more swagger. I love having the feeling of his eyes on my body as I walk out the main reception.

Once we reach my car, David places my flowers on the floor in the passenger's side and gently closes the door. He pauses like he wants to say something but doesn't know if he should.

"See you in the morning?" he says as he leans on the roof of my car.

"Yeah, and thanks for breakfast, it was a lovely surprise," I smile as I blush when I catch his eyes.

"There's no thanks needed. It was an apology for yesterday. I think I was so worried about you realising who I was and that you would quit; it put me in a bad mood, sorry."

"There's nothing to be sorry for David, we are work colleagues and that's all," I gave him a tight smile as I got into the car. I hated that the slightest touch or his eyes on mine, set my body on fire. If only my heart would listen to my head, and I wouldn't feel as much as I do.

I'm falling in love with my boss, but he's already married.

Chapter Eight

David

I thought once we got over the first few days that everything would calm down and it would be like the one-night stand never happened. I was hopeful we could move forward and just be friends but being friends with a woman you're head over heels in love, isn't an easy feat.

Being close enough to fantasise, to smell and feel the heat of, but not being able to touch is driving me crazy. As I sit at the head of the conference room table for a meeting, I have next on cost cutting supplies, all I can think about is her.

I gaze out of the window and spin my pen on the table, as our one night plays out like a movie in my head. I turn my gaze to the pen and watch as it spins and all I can think is it's mimicking my thoughts. I can hear the voices around me, but nothing makes sense.

I glanced back up towards the gentlemen sitting round the table as my eyes connected with Shawn's. I see the frown on his face and as I turn to the rest of the table, everyone is looking at me as though I've grown a second head. They've all been asking me questions and I have sat here lost in another world, a world where I was free to be who I wanted and have the woman I loved beside me.

"Sorry Gentlemen, where were we?" I try to sound confident and in control.

"We were just saying that the suppliers we use are one of the cheapest in the area and think changing them would be a stupid move in the current climate. Where were you?" Shawn throws back.

I sigh, I know I wasn't paying attention, but he didn't need to throw me under the bus with the accountants and HR, like that.

"Sounds good to me," I reply with a short tone.

I stand and shake everyone's hand, then head to my office without so much as a backward glance. I don't need Shawn's smart-arse comments and I certainly don't need him questioning me.

Just as I'm shutting my office door, I feel Shawn right behind me pushing his way into the room.

"David, what the hell is going on?" he demands.

"I don't know what you mean, Shawn,"

"You've never been that distracted ever in a meeting. Has something happened? Is Gaynor busting your balls?"

"No of course not. I've just a lot on my mind." I pause, wondering if I should tell him what really has me in a spin? I decide not to go down that route, he'll never let me forget.

"I just need to concentrate on work, I have heaps of new contracts to review and a plan to finalise. So, if there's nothing else?" I raise my eyebrow.

"Oh, okay if, you're sure. Remember, drinks after work tonight."

Oh great, I had totally forgotten about drinks with Hannah and the crew after work. I swear to God, the universe is setting me up to fall.

"Great," I say flatly. "See you later." I drop down into my chair.

When Shawn leaves the room, I release a breath of relief.

My head is all over the place and my nerves are completely shot. After our shaky start at the beginning of the week; Hannah and I have found our rhythm.

I have to say she is one of the most efficient Office Manager I've ever had, she knows what I need before I do and she's organised my office and files, so I don't have to spend half my day looking for something. It's all on hand and easy to access.

It's so great we've gotten into a routine.

Hannah arrives at nine and by the time I'm here she's got my coffee on my desk, a pastry and all correspondence sitting there waiting for me. I have an email sitting in my inbox with all my appointments on and all the emails requiring a reply starred and waiting there. It's such a relief and I look forward to coming into work, knowing all the trivial things are sorted.

There's only one issue. I want her with everything inside of me. I'm drawn to her like a moth to a flame. Hannah walks into the room and no matter what I'm doing my eyes follow her, whether I'm on a phone call or I'm in a meeting; my eyes eat up the vision of her.

As soon as I walk into the office, I smell her delicious perfume. She just has an aura around her that pulls at me and makes me want things I know I can't have. Just as I turn on my computer to start going through my emails, Hannah comes walking in with a cup of coffee in her hands. I pause as I watch her move around my desk to place the coffee down on the coaster and lean across me to collect some of the finished contracts to file but as I feel the side of her breast glide across my arm, my cock silently hardens in my trousers, and I want to whimper at the constant ache.

Any time she is near, my cock has a mind of its own and springs to life. I try to hold my breath as I try not to take in her smell. I close my eyes briefly as the vision of Hannah spread across my desk flashes into my mind. I should be locked up at the number of times a day I have this vision and the number of times I've wanked to it. I feel her move away when she draws me from my thought's.

"Is there anything that you need me to do?"

Oh God, YES, I want to shout. Fuck me, seven shades of Sunday but I just shake my head as I don't trust my words.

As she reaches the door, I call her name.

"Hannah," she pauses and glances back.

"If you have finished everything, why not take the afternoon off? You deserve it, you've worked really hard this week and it will give you time to get ready for drinks tonight,"

She smiles but declines.

"It's okay David, I don't want to take advantage. I'll get these filed and type up the minutes from your meeting this morning that Shawn has dropped off."

I smile but want to cry as I watch her retreating from my office. I wasn't giving her the afternoon off to be nice, I was giving her the afternoon off so I could have a few hours to control my hunger for her and get a grip on my manly urges.

I decide I need a few hours out of the office once I've sorted the emails, so I gather all the things I need. I look at the time and see it's half past three, I'll check with Shawn what time we are supposed to be meeting at The Moon Under the Water, the pub nearest the yard. I shoot him a quick text and head for Hannah's office. I pop my head around the door, and she looks up.

"I'll be out of the office for the rest of the day, if I have anything urgent, just drop me an email and I'll pick it up later."

"Okay David, I'll see you later." she smiles.

I walk to the elevator and press the button as I enter, I glance back towards her office. I don't know what it is about her that has me so screwed, I mean I know she's gorgeous, she has a funny personality, but I feel drawn to her all the time.

Maybe it's because when I look into her eyes, I see myself reflecting back. There's a vulnerability I see in her that I feel in myself, a loneliness that resonates with me. It's like my subconscious sees myself in her and wants to merge with hers, to become one.

As I enter the house, I hear Gaynor talking on the phone. I walk past her room and straight into mine. I strip out of my suit and chuck on some shorts and a t-shirt. I walk to my desk in the corner and start pricing up the materials we'll need for the new project we've taken on.

I get lost in my joy of renovating and planning the architecture of the new build that Shawn has managed to win from right under a competitor.

I love looking at all the workable options, the clean lines and exquisite soft furnishings. I must remember to talk to Shawn and the project manager tomorrow to get the ball rolling. As I make notes on the size of the land and the requirements from the owners. I hear my phone vibrate and lift my eyes from the screen of my laptop to my phone and notice Shawn has messaged me back.

I pick up my phone and see that he'd messaged a couple of hours ago. I look up at the time on the alarm clock next to my bed and see it's five fifty-five. As I turn my phone screen on, I see we are meeting at six thirty, so I book an uber and then jump into the shower. I let the hot water roll down my neck, across my shoulders and down my back. I love the feel of the water loosening all my muscles, but I need to get a shift on, if I'm going to be on time.

I rush from the bathroom with a towel around my waist as I pick my black fitted jeans, white cotton t-shirt and black leather jacket with my Rockport boots, once I'm dressed, I run my fingers through my slightly damp hair as I head out the bedroom door and straight into Gaynor.

"Are you off out?" She enquires.

"Yeah, I'm meeting Shawn."

"Okay. It must be nice to just go out and enjoy yourself."

"You could come too, but every time I've offered, you tell me no. I never stopped you going or doing anything Gaynor."

"Yep, because you love spending time with your disabled wife."

"Don't! You put this divide between us, not me. I tried everything to involve you in my life, even before the accident but you were never interested. I was just a means to an end. A social standing." I shout.

I take a deep breath, while I try to control my breathing. I don't need this shit. I need a heavy drink.

I charge past Gaynor and head straight for the front door. I see the uber pulling up along the curb and I jump straight in.

I direct him to the pub as I try to calm my racing heart. Once we arrive at the door, I chuck some money on the seat in front and jump from the car, heading straight for the bar.

I ordered a double whiskey and shockwave. I down the shot and swig the whiskey, then I rest my head down on the cold wood of the bar as I let the alcohol work its magic. I then remember why I'm here and lift my head to look for the others. The first person my eyes collide with is the one that my eyes always seem to find, Hannah.

She's dressed more casually than last time she was out. I didn't think I could see her looking any more beautiful than the night at the nightclub, but I was so wrong, tonight she is stunning. Dressed in a plain off the shoulder black top, blue skinny jeans and black ankle boots with her hair in a messy bun. I'm frozen in the vision before me that I don't realize that Shawn has joined me at the bar until he puts a pint of lager in front of me.

"I know you don't want to talk about it, but you'd be brain dead to let her get away," he holds his hands up in defeat as I glance towards him. I shake my head, then glance back towards Hannah and notice her friend was with her.

"You know that's not an option, so I'm not even going there." I pick my beer up and make my way over to the guys. I sit down and position myself so I can watch Hannah, without drawing attention to myself. I greet the boys and they order another round of drinks and I pay.

Hannah and her friend take the seats opposite me. Tim, the site supervisor asks her how her first week was and then they all start firing questions, before long they are quizzing her on the partner situation.

I see her glance up at me from under her long lashes and blush as she tells them she's single and not looking for a new love interest.

I smile to myself as a few of them wouldn't think twice about trying it on with her but I'm glad she's shot them down before they've got any ideas. I sit back and watch her interact with all the staff, she's very attentive to whoever she talks too and gives them all her full attention.

I finish my fourth drink and head over to the pool table; I rack up the balls and call Hannah over to see if she wants a game, she approaches the table with a gleam in her eyes.

"Are you sure you want to lose in front of all your employees, Mr. Bossman?" She winks.

"Game on, Ms. George,"

"Who wants to break?"

"Ladies should always go first," I smile.

I know I'm playing with fire, but I need an excuse to be close to her. I watch as she picks up the cue and walks to the top of the table. She leans forward to line up the cue with the white ball as her eyes connect to mine and the view from where I am standing robs me of my breath. I nearly come in my pants as I see her pert breasts, bulge over the top of her black lacey bra.

As she pulls back the cue, she pushes it forward and then connects with the cue ball, I watch as it hits the balls spread across the table, and she pots two red balls before she lifts her eyes to mine and grins.

"I think someone's good at playing with balls," I wink.

"I do believe I know my way around a long stick and it's balls."

I turn away from the pool table for a second to have a drink and rearrange my junk. This woman has me in all types of trouble. After two games and three drinks, I call it. Hannah is just too good and I'm not too proud to admit that she won both games and kicked my backside.

We move over to the bar where the others are standing and chatting. I see Shawn has Livvy wrapped around him, and I sense someone might be getting laid again tonight as I try to ignore the need to see where Hannah is.

I down the last of my drink and glance at my watch, I see it's half ten and the pub will be shutting soon, so I make my way to the toilets and then head back towards the bar. I see in the distance Hannah's talking to Joe, I know she's safe with him, he's been married thirty years, so I decide to slip away quietly.

Just as I reach the sidewalk, I pull my phone out to call for an uber, when I hear the door open behind me. I turn on the spot to see Hannah, standing there frozen as she eyes me.

"I'm just getting some fresh air," she says.

"I'm just getting a uber,"

"No goodnight then?"

"I thought you were busy with Joe, I didn't want to be rude,"

Hannah nods her head, but frowns at me.

I take a step nearer at the same time as Hannah steps towards me, I know we are walking a thin line, I feel the energy between us, but I can't help remembering what it feels like to touch her delicate skin.

"Where's Livvy?"

"I think she's left with Shawn. I haven't seen them for a while."

"Okay. I'll order two Ubers." She smiles timidly.

Once I've finished on the phone, I turn back to see her leaning against the wall. I walk closer but try to keep a safe distance, I know one touch from her, and I will forget everything else but her glorious body.

"Thank you," she says out of nowhere.

"For?" I ask.

"The Uber." She whispers as she turns her body to face mine. "I really enjoyed tonight." Hannah gazes into my eyes.

I feel my body burning with nervous energy.

"Me too but next time I'll have to remember not to play pool against you," I smirk. Hannah laughs aloud, and the sound is like music to my ears.

She looks so beautiful when she laughs, and I decide that she needs to laugh more.

Before I know what is happening, I feel myself moving towards her. I lift my hands to her face and guide her lips to mine. I feel her mouth touch mine and I lose all of my senses.

I push Hannah up against the brick wall and kiss her like she's the last person on this planet. I lick the seam of her lips asking for entry. I know I'm about to jump off the edge of the cliff and then I hear her muffled groans. I feel her lift her hands until they are in my hair as she runs her nails along my scalp. I growl, I would have never thought of that small action as erotic but fuck it turned me on.

Our tongues dance to the rhythm of our own music as I nudged my erection into her stomach. Suddenly, I hear the horn from a car, and we jump apart. We stand staring at each other, panting like we've run a marathon.

"Mate, did either of you need a uber?"

I turned my head to see one cab parked and another arriving around the corner.

"Yeah," I turn back to Hannah. "You can get the first. Mines just arrived." She nods her head and makes her way over the car and climbs in. I lean in through the window to speak to the driver.

"There's fifty in it to make sure she gets to her door safely," I show him the fifty-pound note.

"Yeah, no problem, mate." I pass the money over and looked at the back window to make sure Hannah was okay, but she had turned her back to the window. I just wanted to see her face to make sure she was alright, I nearly tapped on the glass, but I knew if I saw her, I would have done something stupid, like fuck her again. So, I let the uber pull away from the curb, as a sigh fell from my lips.

I'm just hoping as I see the taxi drive off that, I haven't fucked everything up, once and for all.

Chapter Nine

Hannah

I roll over as I feel the bed dip, it can't be morning already, surely. I test my eyes and open them to see if the room is full of light. I look towards the window and the sun is blazing through the gap at the edge of the wall. I close my eyes again as I replay the kiss with David last night. I couldn't believe it when I felt his lips on mine. I lost all sense of time. I was jubilant, my heart leapt with a warm fuzzy feeling.

I had been flirting with him for an hour and half while playing pool and apart from the occasional touch as he walked past me, he hadn't give me anything. I could feel him holding back but I suppose his situation is a lot different to mine.

I love being in his presence, I love his personality, he always makes me laugh, he helps me feel alive. I just wished things were different. I wish I had met him first. I thought I loved Ian, but it was nothing to how I feel when I am with David.

With David, he makes me feel like I have been asleep all my life, and now he's awakened something deep inside of me. He gives me confidence to step outside the box I've always kept myself in. I have never been overly confident, I have always been the one in the background, the one that was at the party but didn't really partake as I was always worried what everyone would think of me. I would stand at the side with a drink in my hand while Livvy took the limelight, and I was always happy that way but being in David's presence gives me something different. He makes me feel different. When I talk, he listens, with genuine interest, it's like he wants to hear my thoughts and ideas. He doesn't make me feel stupid.

I feel the bed move again and I get the distinct feeling someone is watching me, but with my head feeling slightly fuzzy I just want to live in my memories for a little while longer. However, I know that's not an option, but I can live and hope.

I eventually peel my eyes open, and find Elliott is sitting on the edge of my bed waiting for me to wake up.

"Good morning, baby," I yawn.

"Morning Mum. Are you getting up yet?"

"What time is it El?"

"Half nine mum. Aunt Livvy will be here soon."

"Okay. I'm coming, I'm coming. Ask Thomas to put the kettle on, while I go to the toilet."

"Will do mum." he rushes from the room, like his bums on fire.

I smile as I'm really looking forward to spending some good quality time with boys and have a chill weekend but first things first; toilet, coffee and painkillers. In that order.

I climb from the bed and head across the landing. As I reach the mirror, I cringe; I'm still wearing last night's makeup and the mascara is running down my face. I grab my face balm and while I'm having a wee, I apply to my face. After I've finished, I stand at the sink and let the water heat up before rubbing it off my face. Once I've rinsed my skin and washed my hands, I head for the stairs, as I hear the front doorbell ring and I hear Elliott charging for the door in excitement.

As I reach the bottom, Elliott is dragging Lenny through the door by the hand. I must look surprised as he blushes.

"Livvy said to come round and join you both in taking the boys out as you both might feel a little tender today, after the drinks last night. I hope that's okay?"

How can I say no? I'm sure Livvy is trying to push us together, even though I've told her countless times I'm not interested.

"Yeah, that's fine by me, Lenny. The boys love spending time with you too."

I smile tightly.

"I'm just making a coffee; do you want one?"

"Yeah, that would be lovely, thank you."

I continue through to the kitchen with Lenny hot on my heels. It's far too early to be dealing with him and having no caffeine yet doesn't help. I pull the mugs down from the cupboard then realise that the night-shirt I'm wearing has ridden up and barely covers my arse. I blush as I nearly drop the mugs onto the kitchen counter, then before I know what's happening, I feel Lenny's body cover mine as he tries to rescue the cups. I stiffen, as I feel his arms come around me and brushes the outside of my breast.

"Wow, careful." he whispers in my ear, as I feel his steady breath flow down my neck. "If you couldn't reach, you only had to ask, and I would have got them for you."

I tried to step out of his arms as he must have realised, I felt uncomfortable because he stepped back.

"They slipped from my hands." I tell him. "Why don't you finish them off, while I go and get dressed. Boy's sort yourselves out please." I shout as I head out of the room.

I couldn't get out of the kitchen fast enough. I need to start to be careful around him, I don't want him to see any interest from my side.

I have just finished getting ready when I hear Livvy's voice at the bottom of the stairs talking. I take a breath as I start my way downstairs. I made a conscious choice to wear jeans and a jumper so that I'm covered and don't give Lenny the wrong idea. I reach the kitchen, and I hear Livvy giving Lenny all the gory details of her and Shawn, from last night but stops once she sees me enter the kitchen.

"Carry on, I'm sure he was a stud in bed," I smirk.

"If it's going to interfere with your work, I will stop all contact with him now but he's so hot and funny and sexy," she stops when she sees my face.

"Livvy you can fuck who you like, Shawn is a friend and my boss's best friend, what you do with him has nothing to do with me."

"Thank God because he's asked me on a date next weekend. Ekkkk." She beams as she claps her hands in excitement. "And I didn't want to have to say I cannot go,"

"I'm glad you've found someone, honestly. Shawn's a great chap and a good friend, you both deserve to be happy. Now give me coffee and painkillers before we take the boys out."

After we finish our drinks, get the boys into Lenny's car, we stop off to get brunch before we head to the theme park. We wait in a queue for what feels like a lifetime and when we finally get in, the boys rush off with Lenny towards the rides, while Livvy and I lag behind.

"Sooo... What happened between you and David last night? When we left you were playing pool and you had him eating out of your hand. He couldn't take his eye off of you." she rambled on.

I blush as I remember playing pool and trying to flirt with him to no effect.

99

"Nothing. We played pool, I won both games, he was graceful in defeat and then we stood at the bar with the others chatting, he spoke to Tim, I spoke to Joe and then he left."

"There's more to it than that missis, I can see it on your face."

"Nothing happened."

"Yeah, the lady does protest too much," she winks.

I know I will have to come clean about the kiss at the end of the night, but I really don't want to make a big deal of it because I know that when I return to work on Monday, last night will be forgotten and I will have to pretend like nothing happened again.

I really want a relationship with David more than a work one, but I accept his marriage and respect his vows, so I decided from the beginning that nothing could ever come from my feelings.

I watch as Lenny, Thomas and Elliott join the queue for a big ride, while Livvy grabs my hand and shouts to the boys we were going to get drinks. I knew it was just an excuse to get me away from them to try to get the juicy gossip. We found the concession stand and waited to be served.

"So, are you going to tell me what really happened?" she asks out of nowhere.

I fidget as I try to think of something to change the subject to, not that it will do any good because she's like a dog with a bone.

"What do you want me to tell you?"

"That he fucked you so hard, until you couldn't remember your own name and when you came to stand up, your legs felt like jelly from the orgasm,"

"I wish," I laughed. "Nothing like that happened."

100

"But something happened, didn't it? I can see it written all over your face."

I sigh. I know I'm going to have to tell her, or she will never let it go.

I blush, "Okay, I admit something happened but not what you had going on in your head by a long shot,"

"Well??"

"After I watched David leave the pub, I went outside for some fresh air and he was looking down at his phone at the curb side, but when he heard the door close behind me, he turned but I do not think he thought it would be me." I take a deep breath.

"Go on,"

"When he saw it was me standing there, I think it threw him for a minute, he froze. We were both in shock at seeing each other. Then like an idiot, I asked him why he never said goodbye. He said something about me being too busy chatting with Joe, even though I was just nodding along to Joe's conversation. That man can talk for England," I smile.

"Sooooo.."

"I stepped forward, he stepped forward."

"And?"

"He asked where you and Shawn were. I told him that I hadn't seen either of you for a while, so I gathered you'd left together."

"For the love of God woman, tell me what the fuck happened," Livvy exclaimed.

"He called for two separate Ubers to make sure I got home."

"Yeah, then what?"

"I moved to lean against the wall, while he was on the phone. After he disconnected, he moved to stand by me but left a little distance between us. I thanked him for ordering the taxi, I tried to think of something to say, because the silence between us was deafening."

"Are you telling me that nothing really happened?"

"Liv, if you gave me chance to finish, instead of keep jumping in every time I take a breath, I would tell you that, we chatted about the games of pool, he couldn't believe he lost to me, then out of nowhere David turned, lifted his hands to my face and pulled my lips to his. He kissed me like his life depended on it, that he explored more of my mouth than my dentist has in a good many years. I felt his arousal poking me in my stomach as I ran my nails through his hair," I took another deep breath, just talking about it had me all hot and bothered.

"AND!"

"The ubers arrived, we jumped apart. David told me to take the first one and paid the driver fifty pound to make sure I got home safe."

I sigh. I wished so much; I didn't want it to have ended that way, but I knew he had loyalties to someone else.

"Oh, Livvy, I couldn't look at him through the car window because I knew that if I made eye contact, I would have jumped from the uber and forced him to fuck me."

"Hannah, I know I shouldn't say this but you're my best friend, so you know I'll be one hundred per cent straight with you. I watched him last night and he couldn't take his eyes off you. There is definitely something between you both,"

"Why is it the only time I really connect with a man does it turn out to be with my new boss? And my married new boss at that!"

"It will all work out, I'm sure of it, Han,"

"Well, it couldn't get much worse," I smile gloomily. "I decided last night when I reached my bed, that I'm going to concentrate on my job and the boys. If I'm meant to be with someone then I'm sure, I'll meet them when fate decides."

"I think fate has already decided Hannah, it just needs everything else to fall into place,"

I smile tiredly. I don't want to set myself up for heartache, so I let Livvy's comments wash over me, I need to put myself and the boys first.

Once we reach the front of the line, we purchase drinks for us all and set off through the crowds looking for Lenny and the boys. As we approached the ride, we left them waiting, I see them just getting off. We give them their drinks as the boys decide what they want to go on next, we pass several rides before we reach the log flume. As soon as I see it in the distance, I knew which one they will want to go on. They love the whole getting soaked crap, I just wished I was so enthused about it as they were.

Livvy manages to convince the boys to go on the flume towards the end as she doesn't want to walk around all day with wet knickers, which I am extremely happy about. I look at the time and see it's one o'clock, so we decide to get a burger from the restaurant. While the boys are eating, they study the map of the park with Lenny, circling all the rides they want to go on. When I see how many are circled, I'm not sure we'll have enough time to fit them all in.

"Boys we only have three hours left so you may need to whittle those rides down from twenty to maybe ten or less," I smile.

"But Mum, we've never been to a theme park before and we want to go on all the rides," Thomas whines.

"I understand that Thomas, but we will come back next month, so it won't be your only time here."

"Okay." He blows out a frustrated breath.

"We could make it a monthly family day out thingy," Lenny jumps in.

The boy's face lights up at his suggestion, they really do love spending time with Lenny. Everything would be so much easier if I saw him as anything but an older brother. I have never had those thoughts about him. I think it will be hard for the boys If I decide to bring another man into their life but that's something I need to worry about, if or when I decide to date.

We place all the rubbish in the bin and make a move to the ride nearest to the restaurant. As we start to approach the ride my eyes widen when I see it doing a loop over our heads.

"I am not going on that thing!"

"Don't worry Mum, Uncle Lenny will hold your hand,"

"Nope. Not happening. I'll stay here on solid ground, thank you very much, I'll hold the drinks while you all go on,"

I glance at Lenny as I see his face drop, I am determined to not give him the wrong idea, so they all pass me their things while I watch them all run off to join the queue.

While I wait for them to finish on the ride, I see some benches and make the choice to sit under the oak tree watching the world pass me by. As I watch all the couples walking around with their children, I have a feeling of emptiness. I thought that would be me and Ian, but it wasn't meant to be. I wasn't meant to have the happily ever after.

I see Liv, Lenny, Thomas and Elliott walking back towards me and I suddenly realise how lucky I really am. I feel a little guilty for wishing for more when I have so much in my life, I should be grateful for what I have.

104

We spent the rest of the afternoon being dragged on the rides and ending on the log flume. I haven't laughed that much in many years. I forgot what it was like to lose all the pressures of being an adult and really let my hair down.

When I stepped out of the log, I looked like I had been standing in the shower, I was drenched. I don't suppose it helped that Lenny and Thomas had been chucking water at me throughout the whole ride. I couldn't wait to get home and in a hot bath, soaking my poor tired feet and an enjoyable book before bed and that's how I spent my night after we were dropped back by Lenny before they carried on to their houses. It was a perfect ending to a perfect day. It was just a shame I didn't pass the first chapter before I gave into sleep.

Chapter Ten

David

I stir my coffee and bring the cup to my lips. As I stand in the quiet of the kitchen, I stare out of the window into the darkness of the night. I can't believe I kissed her again. What was I thinking? I have barely slept because I kept replaying the feel of her lips on mine. I would like to say that if the uber hadn't turned up that I would have done the right thing, but I knew that wouldn't have been the case. I knew once my mouth touched hers that there was no hope of walking away and saying no to her glorious lips.

I could still feel the touch of her skin, her fingernails running through my hair and scraping my scalp. I feel my cock twitch from the memories of her tongue touching mine. Do I feel guilty? God, yes, but I'm struggling to keep a lid on my feelings. Every time I see Hannah, I have an urge to do naughty things to her delicious body. How I manage to control myself is still a mystery to me. I hear Gaynor's wheelchair come into the kitchen, that's the last thing I need. I turn to see her staring at me.

"You're back then?"

"Yeah, I wasn't out late,"

"I heard,"

"Do you want a coffee?"

"Not at this time in the morning."

I glance at the clock and see it's five in the morning.

"You're probably right."

I put my empty mug in the sink and go to move past Gaynor, as she grabs my arm to stop me moving around her.

"I was thinking about what you said."

"What did I say?" I dolefully ask.

"About me putting this divide between us."

I take a deep breath. I know that what comes from her mouth next is not something I want to hear. No doubt it will be my fault as everything else is.

"Gaynor, can we not do this now! I am tired, I'm going to be on site at seven and I want to try to get some sleep,"

"Do you know what, David...." She pauses. "Fucking forget it. Enjoy your fucking day!"

She turns her chair around, then wheels herself back down the hallway to her room. I feel the guilt settling in my gut. I shake my head to clear my thoughts as I make my way to my bedroom. I know I should go and check on her, but I just do not have the energy. I lie down on top of my bed as thoughts of Hannah flood my mind. My once floppy cock is now hard as rock. I try to think of something to rid me of my need to come to the thoughts of her but no matter how much I try, all I can see is her dark chocolate brown eyes.

I pull my boxers down to just below my cock and hold the shaft in my hand as I feel the warmth of my flesh, I slowly move my hand up and down my hardened dick. I stroke it from the base to tip, as I feel my desire start to grow. Closing my eyes, I imagine that Hannah has her hands on my manhood, and she is softly running her fingers up and down, from root to tip, collecting all the precum on her tongue as she slowly swipes it across my tip.

The firmness of her grip has me hungry for my release. Just when I think it cannot get any better, my fantasy takes it up another level. I imagine I can feel Hannah's mouth engulf my dick and it touches the back of her throat and I know I am so close to exploding.

I imagine her pulling my dick back out of her mouth as her tongue licks and her lips suck along the head. I move my hands so fast that I feel myself getting ready to shoot all over my belly. I take a deep breath as I finally allow myself to come, I see stars as I start to fall back down to earth. I quickly grab a dirty t-shirt from the floor beside my bed and clean myself up before I nod off to sleep with thoughts of her flooding my mind.

Before I know what's going on, my alarm is going off and it feels like I have just closed my eyes. I am so tempted to turn over and go back to sleep, but I know it won't do me any good. I will just be constantly dreaming or thinking of her, I would much prefer to keep busy. So, I pull my tired mind and body from the bed and head for the shower. I stand under the hot water longer than normal, but I need to try to wake myself up before I head onto the site Shawn is overseeing.

I jump from the shower and wander into my room naked. I don't bother grabbing a towel as nobody will see me anyway. I head straight to my wardrobe and grab my old worn jeans, black fitted t-shirt, and my old work boots. I take them all and place them in the bathroom as I start getting ready. I rush into the kitchen, pick up my phone, fill my travel mug and then grab my jacket as I make my way to my car.

I breathed a sigh of relief that I had not bumped into Gaynor again. I have tried so many times to connect with her, but she retreats from me. I just do not have the energy to deal with her now. As I pull through the gates of the construction site, I see I am the first one here, but it is Saturday, they usually have a later start on the weekend.

I look up at the beautiful house that is starting to take shape. This is one of my favourite parts, when you stare out at an empty space and over days, weeks, or months you see how the crew turn that empty spot into a masterpiece. It takes my breath away from me, even when we take a shell of a building and turn it into something fully functioning. I grab my hard hat and I start to take a walk around. I admire the amount of work the lads have put in Shawn has constructed a dedicated team around him. This is the one thing I miss about working on the sites, getting my hands dirty. I love running the company and make sure it is going in the right direction but getting my hands dirty is what I really like.

I stand on the scaffolding on the top level, checking out the joinery on the roof, when I hear a truck pulling into the site, I turn and see Shawn getting out with his hard hat on.

"Hey Bossman, what are you doing here this early?"

"I fancied getting my hands dirty." I shouted down.

"Well, seeing as you're here, I think you should buy the drinks this morning then. We don't know when we'll get another one," he laughs.

I roll my eyes as I start making my way back down the ladders to Shawn.

"So, what happened to you last night?" I enquire.

"I got a better offer than hanging out with you losers, so I took it," he smirks.

"Well, it's a good job I hung around or Hannah would have been left to fend for herself asshole,"

"I'm sure she managed. Livvy was as horny as I was, so we couldn't wait any longer."

"I don't want to know, thank you very much," I turn away and start walking around the back of the building. I am so glad

109

Shawn took my advice and kept the old oak tree in the back garden. That will look gorgeous in the summer in the evening with some twinkling lights in it. I feel Shawn walking up behind me.

"So, how was the rest of your evening last night?"

"I stood talking to the lads, had a piss, then left." That's all he was getting from me.

"Nothing happened with Hannah?" he asked with a raised eyebrow.

"No."

"No. Is that all I'm going to get?"

"Yes."

"Nice to see you haven't lost the ability to have an adult conversation."

"I know, right?" I smirk. "Right, I'm off to get the drinks for the crew; text me their order." I back away from Shawn and the whole Hannah conversation.

"This conversation is far from over, David."

"What conversation is that, Shawn?" I throw back as I reach the front of the house and make my way over to my car.

Once I have got everyone's drinks, I place them in the boot of my car and make my way back to the site. As I pull the car in, I see a few of the older crew sitting on some wooden pallets that are stacked around the site for them to use as seats, rather than them sitting on the floor.

When Joe sees me undoing my seat belt, he ambles over to help carry the drinks over to the little canteen. I thank Joe for his help as I place the drinks on the table. I pick mine up and I grab Shawn's as I go to look for him. I greet a few of the lads as I head inside, into what will be the living room but couldn't see him, maybe he's measuring up in the kitchen or he's back on the roof.

I head towards the kitchen, and I hear a group of the crew laughing and joking, but I couldn't quite hear what they were saying. As I round the corner, they have their backs to me, but the closer I get the clearer their conversation became, and I could hear Tim and his big fucking mouth spouting how he was thinking of asking Hannah out on a date and how he thought she'd be an easy lay.

I hold my breath as I try to control my temper. Then I hear the other two laugh and joke about the size of her tits, and how he would love to fuck her from behind, and how warm her cunt would feel as she comes.

"Come again, Tim. Tell me how you plan to ask her out when you will be eating through a straw."

"Oh, come on Dave, don't tell me you haven't notice what a piece of meat she is,"

I place the drinks down, and take a step towards him, until I'm right in his face. Chest to chest, nose to nose, breath mixed breath.

"Be careful with your next words, Dick."

"Why? Do you want her first? I'm sure if we get her drunk enough, she'll let us all take a turn. You know what those quiet ones are like."

I see red. I am so angry; I lift my right fist and connect with his face. I've never fought over a girl before, but Hannah isn't just any girl.

"You bastard." Tim shouts.

I grab him by the scruff of his top and pull him until his eyes are level with mine.

"If I ever hear her name fall from your mouth again, I will make sure I hit more than your eye. Do you understand me??" I pant.

111

I let him go and he fell to the floor, flat on his back.

"Oh, and Tim, you have ten minutes to get your things and get off this site before I change my mind and kick your ass anyway." I say as I walk away.

I don't hear Tim stand up, but I feel the side of his shoulder connect with the left side of my torso, I grunt as I collide with the wall. I push him back with all my energy and see him land against the wall.

I quickly regain my footing and punch Tim with a right hook, right on his chin. I hear my finger crack as I connect the punch square on, and the pain shoots up my arm. Tim manages to stand to full height and lands a punch to my left eye.

I want to scream like a girl but concentrate on connecting another blow just as Shawn comes charging through the hall and pulls me off him, while he holds me back.

"What the fuck is going on?" he bellows at the top of his voice.

I pant as I try to control my breathing.

"You." he points at Tim. "Get to my office!"

And then he turned to me.

"You stay where you are. Everyone else get back to work and fuck off out of my sight."

I lean against the wall as I watch the crew scurry like mice in a kitchen that had been disturbed. I see Shawn counting slowly in his head.

"Do you want to tell me what the fuck just happened here?"

"Not really." I stand with my arms crossed like a petulant child. "All you need to know is that that prick is going to need his P45 and the number for the job centre for Monday. He doesn't work for my company anymore."

"I can't just sack him, David. Well not unless I know what the fuck happened."

I take a deep breath and step forward to pick up my coffee. I take a swig and look at Shawn.

"You aren't, I am. He talks smack about Hannah again, next time he will be needing a hospital."

"I'll sort it, go and get your eye looked at. I'll speak to HR today, see where we go from here."

I don't reply. I make my way through the building and out onto the site. I glance around looking for Tim, but I can't see him. So, I continue onto my car, once I'm in my seat I look in the rearview mirror and see the bruise starting to form.

Just what I need. How am I going to explain this on Monday morning? I rest my forehead down onto the steering wheel and try to calm the unsettled feeling in my gut. After a few minutes I hear a tap on the window, I move my head to the side and see Shawn standing there.

I start the car and open the window.

"Jim just told me what really happened." he pauses like he has a million things he would like to say.

I nod. I have nothing I want to add. I've never been the fighting type but when I heard the way he was talking about Hannah I nearly lost my mind.

"I know, I shouldn't say this but as your best friend I want what's best for you." I watch as he draws a deep breath. "How many Hannah's do you think there are in this world, David? I know you are struggling with the whole situation but don't waste your life on someone who never really wanted you anyway. Maybe fate has stepped in and realised that you've punished yourself for way too long over something that was never your fault."

113

Shawn steps back from the car with a glint in his eye. I know what he's said is true but until Gaynor decides to end things I'm stuck where I am. I hear his words rattling around my head, 'How many Hannah's do I think there are in the world?' None that's why I'm so drawn to her.

I put my foot down on the accelerator and wheel spin in the gravel. I turn up my music and make my way to Joyce's. I need to feel some comfort and at the moment that's the only place I need to be.

Chapter Eleven

Hannah

Phew, what a second week it's been. David turned up at work Monday morning sporting a black eye and an attitude to match. God knows what happened as he wouldn't tell me. When I left him Friday evening, he was fine, but something happened between then and Monday.

I was so shocked, and my heart sank when I saw the bruise around his eye. I asked several times what happened, and I fussed over him, but he remained tight lipped. I had endless paperwork on Monday and Tuesday, contracts that needed signing, checking for mistakes and typing up minutes from the meetings from the previous week.

There was a low hum of gossip about an incident, and it was said it happened on one of the sites at the weekend, but I hadn't heard anything specific, nothing but rumours. I tried to see if Ben knew anything, but he said that he hadn't heard a thing. I even tried to bribe him with coffee and cakes on his break Tuesday in my office, but I got nothing. He ate the goods and left, leaving me wanting more.

I tried to question Shawn too, but he said he didn't know anything either, which I found strange as he knew everything that went on with David. I found it hard to believe that he knew nothing as he was David's best friend and they do basically everything together. I knew he knew what happened because he avoided all eye contact with me at the mention of David's face.

When I arrived at the office on that Monday morning, I had hoped that David would want a repeat of the kiss on Friday, but he never mentioned our kiss and acted like it never happened. It truly hurt my feelings, I was hurt that he felt nothing, and I felt everything.

I feel like I'm constantly being pulled one way and then another. All weekend I was so desperate to see him, to speak to him, I wanted to call David so badly but refrained. I am trying so hard to do the right thing but it's tearing me apart.

I spent the rest of Monday fretting and going over our night out with the crew, the way he looked at me, the lingering glances, hidden smiles, the subtle touches and the way he made me feel.

I know I must either face the situation and say something to him or move on. I don't want to be the weak girl who hangs around waiting for something that is never going to happen. This stupid crush is silly, and I need to be strong. My heart can't keep taking the backwards and forwards game that we keep playing.

On Tuesday I decided that maybe trying to hold onto David was just pathetic, that maybe meeting someone else, outside of work, might be a clever idea. I'm not desperate to meet someone new but having someone there at the end of the day and to share my hopes and dreams with would be nice.

I contemplate joining a dating site, but I worry all the stories you hear about all the nutters that are waiting to stalk you, are true. I don't want to put the boys at risk. So, after work on Wednesday I invite Livvy over for some wine and a girly catch up. While I open the wine and find the glass, I send the boys to bed. After the first bottle I started to relax for the first time since last Friday evening. I really needed this time with my best friend, she always makes everything better.

When I fill her in on the first half of my week, she can't believe that David never acknowledged the kiss or apologised for overstepping the line again. I asked her if she had spoken to Shawn since Friday.

"We spoke briefly on the phone Sunday, but he seemed distracted, and we didn't say much, why?"

"I wondered if he mentioned what had happened to David?"

"No, he didn't but he doesn't really talk at all about David. If I bring him up, he'll change the subject."

"Oh, okay."

"Hannah, I'm sure it's nothing to worry about missis," she says as she opens the second bottle.

After she filled my glass, I started telling her how I've been thinking of dating again, but I wasn't sure dating apps were the way I wanted to go. I told her that I wanted to try and put some distance between myself and David.

She agreed that maybe dating someone else might help, she decides to set me up with someone from her work, for Friday. To say I was nervous was an understatement. I hadn't been on a date since I was sixteen and that was many moons ago.

After work on Thursday, I met up with Liv in town as we agreed the night before a new outfit was needed. I had decided to buy a new dress, underwear and shoes. She had me traipsing around the shops for over an hour, when all I really wanted to do was to be at home with a glass of wine and watching a movie with the boys.

After buying several dresses, two pairs of high heels and seven panty and bra sets, I leave Livvy to carry on with her purchases while I head home to sort the boys.

I seriously couldn't wait for Friday to end, the atmosphere in the office was so heavy. David was in a foul mood and snapped all day. Livvy couldn't help but open her big mouth and tell Shawn about my date, who then in turn told David. I swear to God they both love causing me trouble. So, David has been walking around like a tornado, causing disruption wherever he's been today.

Things came to ahead during his afternoon meeting with his lawyer. David lost his shit and balled at him, several times. I just couldn't hear what was being said. After ten minutes of constantly shouting, Shawn rushed in and told him to calm the fuck down and they would sort it as the door slammed shut behind him.

I don't know what was going on with him but I'm learning to stay out of his way. I decided to work through my lunch so I could finish half an hour earlier, as I want to make sure the boys are sorted before my date tonight. As I walk to David's office, I'm not sure I am doing right by saying goodbye, but I hate leaving without speaking, so I knock on his door.

"For fuck's sake Shawn, I said I didn't want disturbing," he growls angrily.

I pause and take a deep breath, debating whether I should just turn and walkway.

"Sorry, I didn't know. I just wanted to say goodnight, I'm getting off early."

I see him look up as I start to speak.

"Sorry I thought it was Shawn again. Okay. Enjoy your date." he grunts.

I gasp at the tone of his voice; he has no right to be pissed at me.

118

"I'm sure I will. Thank you." I replied before I turned and left.

When I reach home, I pull into the drive and climb from my car. I look at Martha's and notice she's standing at the kitchen window looking out. I walked across the drive and opened the side door to retrieve the boys.

"Hey, Martha, how are you feeling today?" I asked.

"Much better today, dear. How was work?"

"Tiring," I smile. "Are you ready boys," I shout through to the living room.

"Have you been good?" I asked Elliott.

"Yes, mum." I hear Elliott moan.

I kiss Martha on her cheek and thank her for watching them. I follow the boys around the side and through the back door, busying myself with getting dinner ready and trying to keep my thoughts away from my frustrating boss.

As the time nears to me getting ready, I start to think I've made a big mistake, I'm trying to contemplate whether I should text Matty with an excuse, but I think back to my stupid crush on David and I know I need to try to move passed how I feel about him.

I move up the stairs to get ready, while the boys play on their games console, and it feels like I'm on my final walk to the gallows. Once I'm stripped out of my work clothes. I jump in the shower, I stand under the hot water and let it loosen all the knots in my shoulders.

Then I step out of the shower, wrap the towel around myself and move into my room. As I towel dry my skin, I put on my white lacey bra and panty set, while I flick through all my dresses deciding on what to wear, but nothing catches my

119

attention. If I'm honest I only had one man in mind when I brought them and he's not the one taking me on the date.

I pull out a fitted white blouse and a pale blue pencil skirt. I decide to leave my hair flowing with soft curls descending my back and keep my makeup light, I grab my heels and head downstairs waiting for Livvy to come and watch the boys.

I pull up to the restaurant and look up at the quaint looking Indian. It only opened eight weeks previously, so I hadn't been here before and was looking forward to the food. I looked down at my blouse and frowned; I hadn't maybe thought this through properly. I pull into one of the parking spaces around the back and leave the warmth of the car, heading for the door to the restaurant.

As I walk in, I see the bar along the back wall and decide to take a seat on the stool while I wait for Matty to arrive. The bartender asks what I would like to drink, so I order a vodka and coke. I know I shouldn't drink as I'm driving but I need something to calm my nerves. I watch as he picks a can of coke from the fridge and pours it into a tall glass with a shot of vodka.

He places it in front of me, I pick the glass up to have a drink and welcome the cool liquid. I hear the bell ring above the door, so I glance in that direction. I close my eyes as I see a man walk in, I have never met this Matty or seen a picture, but I have a feeling the man I'm having this date with has just walked in, and I sigh.

Why didn't I request a picture of him before saying yes? I feel him approach as I inhale a breath. Now I wouldn't say he was ugly, but he was not tall, dark and handsome, like David. In fact, he was the complete opposite. Short-Ish, blonde and stocky.

Maybe that could work in my favour. At least every time I looked at him, I wouldn't see David. I shake my head trying to clear my thoughts, I seriously need to get my boss out of my head.

"Hannah?"

I want to say no but there's no escaping this now. I turn on my seat and plaster a smile on my face.

"Yes," I nod. "Matty?"

"That's me. I'm pleased to meet you."

"Me too. Do you want to get a drink?"

Fuck! What have I agreed too? I think to myself as I eye the man in front of me.

"I'll have a glass of water please," he smiles at the bartender as he takes the seat beside me.

We watch the bartender walk down to the other end of the bar. My mind runs wild trying to think of something to say to him. The silence stretches on, and I see him ogling me like I'm a piece of meat. It's starting to feel uncomfortable; I'm going to have to come up with something quick.

"So, tell me about yourself, Matty." I ask.

"Well, I live at home with my mum, my dad passed away when I was fifteen. We have three cats and two dogs...."

"Oh lovely. I bet it's good to have your mum look after you?"

"Well, it has its advantages," he snorts, laughing, I raise my eyebrows at the horrid sound. "She washes my clothes, cleans and cooks, so I really don't see the point in finding my own place,"

"I bet," Great a mummy's boy. "But you'll want to move out eventually, right? You know, to settle down, find a good woman and have kids."

"Eww, no way. I don't ever want kids, they are gross. I mean why would anyone want a kid's snotty nose to wipe and

121

arse to clean. It's not for me." I smile while biting my tongue, I can see how this night will end.

As the waiter moves us to a table, he pauses what he was rambling on about. I think this has been the first time he's drawn breath, but as soon as we are seated, he picks up exactly where he left off. Telling me about his job and Livvy.

"I work with Livvy in her brother's accountancy agency, I've worked there for the last four years...."

While the waiter takes our food order, I drink some of my vodka & coke and order another one.

"The water's free, right?" Matty enquires. The waiter nods his head as moves away from the table and I cringe. Who asks those types of questions?

"So, where was I? Oh, yes. I've worked with Livvy for four months, since she joined her brother and I have to say she's hot as fuck," I raise my eyebrows. What a douche! He's on a date, while telling her that someone else is hot as fuck. Wow! I think he's stooped to a new low.

On a plus side at least I know he has someone to fall back on when I don't return for a second date.

Just when I think he might be ready to change the subject, he comes back to himself. What have I done? I asked one simple question and he's still talking. I can now see why he's still single. Nobody and I mean, nobody will ever want to be with this idiot twenty-four, seven.

I see the waiter bringing our drinks over and I politely ask where the toilets are as I need five minutes to clear my thoughts before I smack him in the face. He points to the side of the bar with sympathy. I excuse myself, telling Matty I will be back shortly and grab my clutch. As soon as I walk into the toilets, I grab my phone and call Livvy, she answers after one ring.

"What the fuck, Liv??"

I hear her start to giggle, which adds to my annoyance.

"Tell me you haven't set me up with a dick,"

Still, all I can hear is her laughing on the other end.

"Liv, you owe me big time, bitch."

"What? Matty's perfect. He has no other attachments, like a wife and he's highly intelligent." she manages to say between the bouts of laughing.

"I swear, Liv, this man isn't looking for a partner, he's looking for a blow-up Glenda. Someone with a hole and doesn't want a conversation." I sigh.

"Just get to know him, he really is a nice simple man, once you get past the self-imposed attitude."

"Yeah, not going to happen. When a man is on a date with you and tells you, your best friend is gorgeous; it's pretty much over before it starts."

"He didn't."

"Oh, he did. We had twenty minutes of him talking about how gorgeous your hair was and how you make him laugh; so yes, you're welcome."

I hear Livvy snort a breath at the thought of Matty liking her.

"Nope, not happening."

"Yeah, well it isn't happening here, either."

"You do realise you've been talking to me for the last twenty minutes?"

"Oops. Do not make me go back out there! I wonder if there's an exit door or window I can climb out of?"

"And risk breaking your neck?"

"Hospital sounds an effective way out of this date." I laugh.

"Surely he isn't that bad?"

123

"Well let's say, if I was offered twenty-four hours sitting in front of a wall watching paint dry or going back to the table to finish this date, I'm picking the paint drying."

"Okay. Do you need an emergency call?"

"Several." I burst out laughing.

"Give me five."

I huff and say goodbye, before making my way back out to the table.

"Sorry, where were we?"

"I'm sorry to do this Hannah, but this isn't working for me?"

I scoff and my eyes bulge, he isn't saying what I think he's saying.

"I don't understand?"

"When I agreed to this date, I thought we might have something in common or at least you'd be interesting but you're not."

I completely lose control and burst out laughing.

"Matty, here's a little friendly advice. When you agree to a date, please give your date some attention and please don't be so self-absorbed. It's not hot and it certainly doesn't set you off in the right light." Just as I finish speaking, my phone rings.

"Hey Livvy, Thanks but there's no need for the emergency call I requested, missis, Matty is about as much fun as a wet lettuce." I smile as I hear Livvy wetting herself laughing on the other end.

I can honestly say I've never seen a man's face that shade of red before in my entire life. I reached into my clutch and chucked some money on the table before I turned and marched out of the restaurant, back to the car. Maybe dating might not be the way forward, after that disaster I'm becoming a nun.

Chapter Twelve

David

I glance up at the window and see the sun setting, so I know it must be getting late. I have been sitting in the same position for the past hour, staring into space with nothing else on my mind but Hannah.

My mind is running wild with images of Hannah on her date with a man that looks like a surfer. I have no clue what this geezer looks like but if Livvy has anything to do with it, I cannot see him being a decent bloke.

It killed me when I got the text first thing this morning from Shawn saying he had spoken to Livvy, she told him that she had set Hannah up on a date with one of her work colleagues. My blood boiled when I thought of some idiot touching what was mine. But she wasn't mine, was she? She might have been in my heart, in my soul but in real life she was free to choose anyone she saw fit to fill that spot, because I have no way of making her mine.

I rub my tired eyes as I try to focus on the screen again, I need to get this finished before I can leave. The problem is I am not sure I want to go back home.

This week has been a total shit storm, from last Friday's kiss to the law case against me, today.

My head is throbbing, the stress I have felt this week has been immense. Monday morning, after I dragged myself from my bed, I came face to face with Gaynor in the kitchen. I had not seen her since she stormed from the kitchen the morning before and the look on her face at the sight of my black eye, was not one of concern, more of a smirk, like I got what I deserved.

"So, what happened to your face?" she sneered.

"Nothing, I walked into the bathroom door in the night." I quipped.

I did not have the energy to deal with her shit. I flicked on the kettle and waited for it to boil, so I could make myself a coffee before I showered. I could sense her staring at my back, I knew she wanted to say something.

"Say what you need to say, Gaynor. I'm in no mood for games."

I heard her draw in a breath as I added the milk to my coffee and brought the cup to my mouth.

"What's going on, David?"

"Nothing is going on Gaynor, why would there be?"

She pauses as if there's lot's she wants to say but doesn't know how to voice it.

"I know what we have isn't what either of us expected," She starts. "But are you seeing someone else?"

I nearly sprayed my drink all over the kitchen counter. I turn and look her in the eye.

"No, I am not! Why are you?"

I see a look of something move across her face, but it has gone before I can register what it was. Her eyes drop to the floor.

"Of course, not." she pauses not sounding too sure, she sighs. "But when someone's husband returns home with a black eye, usually there's something not quite right."

"In a normal marriage, yes, but ours isn't normal, is it?"

"I walked down the aisle, didn't I?"

127

"Yeah, to all the cash that was promised to you. I have always been a means to an end for you all and I'm tired, Gaynor. Tired of always putting everyone else before myself."

I storm out of the kitchen and straight into the shower. I had to leave before I said something I shouldn't, and I did not want to hear anything more come from her mouth.

Once I was dressed, I returned to the kitchen and felt relieved that Gaynor had gone back to her room. I did not think I had enough energy to deal with her again this morning. I made myself another coffee in my travel mug and made my way outside to the car.

While I was driving to work, every time I looked in my back mirror my black eye shone like a beacon. I frowned because I knew I was in for a day of questioning; everyone will want to make it their business, but I do not want the argument getting back to Hannah. I did not want her to know what that vile individual was saying about her behind her back.

Tim had worked for me pretty much since the start, but not once had I heard him talk about a female like that before, especially not about another female employee. To say I was shocked was an understatement. I mean, I had heard stories about him being an animal between the sheets and that he had particular needs. Do not get me wrong, we all have desires but to talk about women like meat is not something I could let go. Especially not about Hannah. She was my weakness and I have never had one before. I have never had someone who has gotten under my skin as much as she did. Even when I was a teenager, I never let anyone get too close but for some unknown reason, she calls to me.

When I reach the works carpark, I just want to try to sneak in and hide out in my office for the day, I do not want to attract attention to my face and the questions that will start flying in after.

I think I have safely made it to the elevators without being detected, so I sigh with relief, I push the call button and keep my head down.

I hear the door ping, so I know they are about to open, I poise myself, ready to step in, when I hear Ben.

"Well, hello there sexy,"

My head sinks further as my shoulders slump, not what I needed today. He is like the town crier. There is no need for a newspaper with Ben in the building.

"Hey Ben," I mutter with my head still low.

"Are you okay, Mr. Shepard?"

I forget for a brief moment and lift my head.

"I'm fine, thank you."

"OMG!!! What happened to your beautiful face?"

Shit! I try to drop my head again, but Ben places his hands on either side of my face, shaking it from side to side, taking in all the bruising.

"Do we need to call the police? Were you robbed? Raped? Oh, God, they did not do that. Tell me who they are, and I'll find them."

"Don't panic, no robbing or raping took place, Ben. Just a good old man walked into the door in the dark, kinda situation." I smiled.

"Are you sure sir? There is nothing wrong in admitting you'd been mugged or internally interfered with!"

I try to hold in my laughter.

"I can assure you, nothing happened but can we keep this between us as I don't want people thinking I'm a wimp." I wink.

I thought he was going to faint. Ben blushed and promised to keep this conversation between us, as I wished him a good day and walked into the lift.

It is a standing joke that Ben has a big crush on me and If I batted for the other team, I would be interested, he is a very good-looking man, but I don't, so I just let him flatter me.

As I step off the elevator, I take a quick glance down towards Hannah's office, debating how I can get past her door without her seeing me. I move slowly down the corridor, taking my time as I do not want to make any noise that will bring Hannah out to see what is happening.

If anyone were watching me, they would think I have lost my marbles, prowling down here like a pink panther, just before I reach her office door.

"What the fuck are you doing, man?"

I hear Shawn behind me.

"Shhhh..." I put my finger to my mouth and nod my head in the direction of my room, hoping Shawn understands my silent message to talk in my office.

I turn and start creeping again, trying to be quiet past her office.

"You do remember, Hannah's late today?" Shawn laughs behind me.

I freeze, then frown, before I stand up straight and turn back to my friend as he bursts out laughing.

"Twat." I mutter as I continue to my office.

Once I reach my desk, I put my jacket on the back of my chair and switch on my computer. I look at the spot that usually has my coffee waiting for me, but it is empty. I should have remembered to pick my travel mug up out of the car, I bet the little bit I had left would have still been hot. I hear my office door shut and I look up to see Shawn moving to the chair in front of me.

"So, are you going to tell me what you were doing in the corridor?" he laughs.

"Shut it, dick."

"What? Am I not allowed to find enjoyment out of your dramatic ways? It's the only reason you are my best friend."

"Yeah, because you had hundreds lining up for the job," I smirk.

"Thousands, more like. Anyway, what was that really about?"

I sigh, I know he is not going to let it drop.

"I didn't want Hannah to see my black eye."

"Well unless it's going to disappear in the next..." he glances at his watch. "Fifteen minutes, I think you'll have no choice."

"Look, before she gets here, please whatever you do, do not tell her about Saturday morning."

"Why? She will love it. You on your white horse, defending her honour."

"Yeah, from a dick that was spewing how warm her cunt would feel as she came." I pin Shawn with a look of anger. "I do not want Hannah hearing anything about this, Shawn. It would destroy her, knowing that they were talking about her like that."

"Okay, okay. She will not hear anything from me. I'm going to get going, I'm needed back on the site as I am going to try to replace Tim today,"

I nod as I know this has not made things easy for Shawn, but I'm not having someone like Tim working for me. I watch as Shawn stands up and leaves the office, I swing my chair around as I look out of the window, watching the wind blowing in the trees. I heard the door open, and thought it was Shawn coming back because he had forgotten something but as I swung around, I saw the shock and horror on Hannah's face as she took in my glorious eye.

She rushes around the desk and takes my face in her hands.

"Oh, David, what happened? Are you okay? Do you need me to take you to the hospital? Have you called the police?"

As I sit there staring up into her eyes, I wanted to grab her, pull her into my lap and finish what we started on Friday, but I knew I could not cross that line again. I needed to be strong, but the way she was looking into my eyes made my cock harden and my resolve weaken. I move out of her hands and pull back from her touch because I could not think straight with her hands on me.

"Hannah, I'm fine, honestly. I just bumped into the bathroom door, Friday after I got home."

"Oh, are you sure? Because that looks bad,"

"Yes, I'm sure." I smile.

She walks back around to the front of my desk and frowns but does not say anything else.

"I came to see if you wanted me to fetch you a drink?"

"That would be lovely, thank you."

Hannah turns and leaves but as she gets to the door she hesitates for a moment before she continues to fetch my drink. And that is how I spend most of my week.

Locked away in my office, trying not to draw attention to my black eye, that is until today.

Friday used to be my second favourite F-word but today it feels like it is never ending. It is the day from hell. I arrived at work with a stick up my arse, for no real reason only that I did not sleep well.

I received a call from my lawyer at the crack of dawn, saying he had received papers from the courts, telling him I was being sued for unfair dismissal and he needed to come into the office for a meeting, but that he was not available until after lunch. So, when I arrived at the office, I was ready to bounce off the walls, I literally took it out on everyone.

Just as I start to look at some plans for the new renovation, we have taken on, I glance down at my phone and notice I have a text from Shawn. I open the text and my eyes nearly bulge from their sockets.

'Hey Shep, I will be in the office after lunch, I am just measuring up the old barn for the conversion.

Look I was not going to say anything, but Hannah has a date tonight, according to Liv, she was going to join a dating site but changed her mind.

I know with your situation it is hard but think about what I said, before it is too late.

See you soon S.

I re-read the text several times, but I do not have time to deal with the emotions running through me at the moment. I need to sort Tim out before I can think of anything else.

I hear a knock on my office door and shout for them to come in, it is probably Hannah fussing again but it is Mr. Kelly, my Lawyer.

"Please take a seat, James. Can I get you a drink?"

"Coffee would be great, thank you."

"I'll be right back." I head to the break room to make his drink.

Once I am back in my office, I make sure the door is shut behind me, the last thing I need is Hannah hearing everything I have been trying to protect her from.

"So, where do we start?" I ask as I take my seat.

"Well, I need a blow-by-blow account of what happened, David. He's claiming you sacked him because your P.A. chose him over you."

"He's what!" I bellow.

"He's said that you have a thing for your P.A., and you asked her out. She turned you down but when he asked, she agreed and you lost it, resulting in you sacking him."

"That's bollocks," I shout with steam coming out of my ears.

"Well, can your assistant testify? She might put a stop to his claims. Unless you had problems with his work?"

I knew in that moment I was fucked, I had no problem with his work, as his work was always finished to the highest level. I wanted to hunt him down and fucking hit him again for the shit he is causing.

"I am not bringing Hannah into this." I shout. Just as my office door flies open and Shawn comes storming in and slams it behind him.

"Fucking hell, David, I could hear you when I walked off the elevator. What the fuck is going on?" he glances across the room and sees James sitting in front of my desk.

"Take a seat Shawn," I sigh as I run my fingers through my hair.

"Hi James, what's up?" Shawn greets him.

"Hi Shawn, a shit storm," he smiles.

So, we fill Shawn in on what was going on and then spend the next few hours going over every little detail of last Saturday at the site. James took endless notes and we looked at it from all angles, before he agreed to work on it over the next few days, then get back to me with the best way forward.

I had asked that we try to keep Hannah out of it as much as I could as I did not want her upset by the whole situation.

After Shawn shows James out, I rest my head in my hands as I try to massage my temples to relieve my head from the pain that was now throbbing in it. A little while later Shawn returns with a coffee and pat's me on the shoulder.

"We'll get it sorted, mate; he's just trying it on."

"Yeah, I'm sure he is." I sigh. "Right, I've got work to do, I'll catch you later."

"Okay. Maybe we could get drinks after work?" he asks hopeful.

"Nah, I have too much work to do, I don't want disturbing and I'm not feeling it tonight, but tomorrow might be another day." I smile.

I watch out of the corner of my eye as he leaves my office, closing the door behind him quietly. I sat back in my chair, dropping my head back and closed my eyes. I feel like everything is coming down around me and I have no control over my life.

I roll my neck, trying to loosen the knots in my shoulders and back from the tension of the meeting, I then sit up to try to concentrate on the computer screen and the work I must finish.

In the silence of the room, I'm struggling to focus on anything that's on the screen as I hear a knock on the door.

"For fuck's sake Shawn, I said I didn't want disturbing," I growl angrily.

There's a pause, and I think he's left without entering, so I take a deep breath, and turn my eyes back to the screen.

"Sorry, I didn't know. I just wanted to say goodnight, I'm getting off early."

135

I look up and see Hannah standing just outside the door and I remember the text from Shawn earlier and my mood darkens more.

"Sorry, I thought it was Shawn again. Okay. Enjoy your date." I grunt, as I cut her off and basically cut the conversation short.

She gasps at the tone of my voice; and I feel like shit. I had no right to be pissed at Hannah. She was unattached and could do what the fuck she wanted.

"I'm sure I will. Thank you." She replied before she turned and sprinted for the elevator.

I sit there for a few moments, just staring into space as I try to reason with myself and the way I feel about her upcoming date, but I know I've just treated her like shit and that in turn means I am a dick.

I jump up from my seat and dash in the direction of the elevators, trying to reach her before she leaves, but when I get close, I see the doors just shutting.

Fuck.... I scream in my head.

I stand, staring at the closed doors on the elevator and know I need to let her go and enjoy the rest of her evening.

So, I do the right thing, I turn around and make my way back to my desk. I try to work through the pile of paperwork and the plans for the barn conversion, but my mind keeps drifting back to Hannah.

When I see the sun setting, I know I'm not going to get much more done, so I open the bottom drawer on my filing cabinet and pull a bottle of Jack Daniels out, before returning to my seat. I pull my glass tumbler from the drawer on my desk and pour a large glass. I tip the drink back and swallow with a gulp.

I cough and choke from the burn of alcohol. I bang my chest trying to catch my breath, I remember why I hate this stuff, but I need something to try to calm my thoughts.

After a few hours, and so many drinks, I start to feel a little buzzed, my mind replays the time in the club with Hannah in my arms and her in the throes of her orgasm. My cock throbs, as much as my head and heart but I know I'm not going to get any relief anytime soon. I glance at the time and see it's only eleven o'clock, I wonder where Hannah is and if she's helped her date find relief.

I know she's not really that type of girl. I know she's not a loose woman, but jealousy is taking over my thoughts with the more alcohol I drink. I look down at my mobile phone on my desk, I hesitate for a second, but I need to hear her voice.

I press in my code to open my phone screen, then click open my contacts, I scroll down until Hannah's name appears. I contemplate putting my phone down but the need to hear her voice is far greater. I put the phone to my ear, as I listen to the ringing tone.

"Hello..."

I hear a sleepy Hannah on the other end of the phone, but I lose all ability to speak.

"David, is that you?"

"Yeah." Is my only reply. I held my breath and waited for her to slam the phone down.

"What's happened? Are you okay?" I hear her stutter. I love to hear her concern in her voice, it left me feeling all warm inside.

"Nothing." I freeze, not knowing what I was doing.

"There has to be some reason why you called at..." she pauses, must be to look at the time. "Eleven o'clock."

"I wanted to ask if you managed to file all of the minutes from the meeting last week?" I slur.

"So, you called me on a Friday evening at eleven o'clock, just to see if I had filed the minutes from the meetings last week."

"Well, yeah."

"Really? So, you wanted nothing else?" she whispered. "Where are you anyway?"

"I'm still in the office," I quietly reply. Just listening to her talk is enough to harden my cock in my trousers. "How was your date?" I ask, trying not to sound too bitter.

"So, that's why you called?" I hear the smirk in her voice. "Do you really want to know?"

"No. Not if you loved it." I tell her.

"Well, there's not much to say. I met him at that new Indian restaurant, he spent the whole time talking about himself and he told me he thought Liv was beautiful, so I think it officially sucked balls."

"I'm sorry, Hannah."

"But are you? Or are you just saying that to make yourself feel better?"

"I am sorry but not that it sucked balls, more that you wasted your time on someone who was a stupid dickhead and let you walk away, because if I had that chance there would be no way I'd let you go."

I knew I needed to get off the phone before I said something I couldn't take back. There was a long pause, both of us lost in our thoughts. There was so much I wanted to say, I sigh. So, much I wanted to listen to Hannah say, but we couldn't cross that line.

"I'm going to go and let you get some sleep. Thank you for all your hard work and sorry for being a twat this week and I'll see you Monday,"

I end the call before I drop myself in it further and place the phone on my desk, as I pick up my tumbler with the last of my drink and down it in one.

Chapter Thirteen

Hannah

I look through the window and see the skies are blue. I love this time in the morning. Everything is so still and calming. I walk out onto the back step as I sit down, enjoying the peace, while I wait for the birds to wake. I was planning to have a lie in today, but the sun was too bright, and I did not want to waste a glorious day lying in bed.

The past four weeks have flown by. I cannot believe I have been working at Shepard's Construction for a whole six weeks and what six weeks it has been. After those first few days I didn't think I would see the first month out, but once we got past the one-night stand, I fell in love with my job. Things with David are bearable, we have managed to find our stride, and we pretty much work amicably.

Those first few weeks were torture, but I have decided to put my attraction to him behind me and just concentrate on myself and the boys. I cannot say that I am doing an excellent job at keeping my attraction secret but at least I am trying. David on the other hand is really struggling.

Every time I look at him, I can see the heat in his eyes, but I just ignore it now. The couple of days following the drunk dialling incident, after my disastrous date, I really struggled to keep my feelings in check, but until he took the leap of faith and ended his marriage, I am keeping my distance at all costs.

I learned the truth about the whole black eye incident via a third party after overhearing that someone was trying to sue David after he had sacked him. Once I learned what had happened, I was shocked that not only had he had stood up for me, but he risked losing thousands of pounds, I could not allow that to happen. So, I charged into his meeting he was having with his lawyer and told him I would not allow him to be sued if all they needed was a statement from me, concerning my supposed date with Tim. David refused my help saying it was his problem to sort, that it was nothing to do with me, but I stood my ground and I spoke to his Lawyer.

"What do I need to do?"

"You're not doing anything Hannah,"

"Oh, please!" I quipped. "This would have never happened if I hadn't been so friendly with him David,"

"Hannah, you are friendly with everyone, but that doesn't give him or anyone, the right to talk about you like that,"

I ignore David's glare and turn to his lawyer once more.

"What do you need?"

"A statement saying you've not been on a date with Tim or ever agreed to one, nor would you be interested in a date with him. Include that you've only met him once on the night out and have no intentions of being with him."

"Done. Will this sort it out?"

"It will help. As for sorting it out, that is a little difficult because he was sacked on the spot and did not throw the first punch," he glances over towards David.

"Just do what you have to do to sort this James, I want it finished with. If I must pay him off, so be it."

I shake my head and head for the door, just as I am closing the door behind me, I hear James say to David.

"Keep that one David, she is strong willed and not easily scared. I would say that one's a keeper,"

141

I can only imagine he meant it in a work capacity, but God did I wish it were directed at a relationship one. The rest of the day was spent doing my statement, making sure it put Tim in a bad light and continuing with my paperwork while thinking about David and what he did.

Since that day, I have asked David a few times if he has heard anything else, but he is still being tight lipped. I sometimes wonder if he is still angry that I got involved but I could not let him take the blame for this when it was over me, it happened.

As the weeks pass, the more I love my job. Shawn is a scream and Ben just knows how to cheer me up. Every Tuesday break and lunch have become our catch-up day. We have cakes for break and Chinese for lunch, which Ben has delivered to his desk.

My responsibilities have increased over time, and I am now involved in meetings and taking notes, which I find easier as before all meetings were recorded and then I would type them up, but if someone at the far end of the room spoke, it was hard to hear what they had said.

David had started going on site a little more too. You can tell he loves to be hands on and enjoys the demanding work. Shawn and Livvy are officially dating now, which is nice. Liv needs someone who challenges her, and Shawn definitely does that. I'm so glad they have found each other and seem settled.

I take a sip of my coffee as I hear the boys come downstairs; I know my peace has ended but I need to take the boys shoe shopping. While we are there, I might manage to grab them some clothes too, so the sooner we get going, the sooner we will be back. I hate shopping at the best of times, but shopping with crowds and the boys is hell.

The thought of taking the two of them to the shopping centre sends a shiver down my spine and hives breakout on my skin. But when you've two boys that look like they have been in a grow bag, I have no choice. So, I finish my coffee and walk into the kitchen.

As I reach the kitchen table the boys are already eating bowls of cereal, so I kiss them both on the head as I make my way upstairs and get dressed.

After we are all ready, we jump in the car and make our way to the shopping centre. The boys are not happy that we had to go shopping, so they were sulking big time and dragging their feet. I'm sick of the number of times I've had to tell them to hurry up but they are pissed that they couldn't go and hang out with friends so I end up talking to myself. I was tempted to tell them we would go home and let them go play with their friends, but as their shoes were hanging off their feet and their trousers had divorced their ankles, I didn't have much choice.

As I hurry through the crowded street to the shops, I glance back over my shoulder to make sure they were both following behind and had not disappeared. I approach the shoe shop and pause by the door, waiting for the boys to catch up. Once inside we peruse the many assorted styles and they both pick two pairs each, one pair for school and trainers to wear any other time.

Just as I am standing in the queue to buy them, I feel like I am being watched. I look up and my eyes connect with David's as he stands just inside the shop door watching me. I see his eyes drop to the boys and smile. I have never introduced them to David as I wanted to keep my private life away from my work one. But now Liv is dating Shawn, they are bound to meet eventually as Shawn is usually where David is. I see him lift his eyes back to mine, like he is trying to decide if he should come over to speak. I hold my breath as I wait to see what he decides. Finally, I see him moving his feet in my direction.

"Hey," He greets me. "And who are these handsome dudes?"

"Hey David, this is Thomas and my little man Elliott." I smile.

"Mum, I'm not little anymore," Elliott pipes up.

"I know, I know," I hold my hands up in defence. "But you'll always be my little man," I kiss his forehead.

"Hey boys, how are you? What are you up to today?"

I see Thomas frowning at David out of the corner of his eye, he really struggles letting new people into our lives.

"We are shopping, but I hate shopping," Elliott replies sadly.

"Yeah, I'm not a fan of shopping either, mate." David bends his knees, so he is on the same level as Elliott and smiles. "What are you buying? Anything exciting?"

"Shoes," Elliott answers shyly.

"Well, we all need new shoes,"

I hear the cashier call for me to go over and pay. I smile and look back towards the boys, while I see David chatting to them, I start to move forward to the empty cashier and pass her the shoes. As I am paying, I keep peering over my shoulder to watch David talking to the boys and see them all giggle to something they find funny.

My heart warms to see David with the boys. It makes me long for something that I could never have. Once I have finished paying, I move back towards them and hear Elliott telling David about him not being allowed to a play date with Adam because he had to come shoe shopping.

"Well, I know it's not exactly how you wanted to spend the day but just think if mum didn't buy you any and it rained, your feet would get wet, buddy." I see him smile at Elliott.

"Don't get fooled by the big brown puppy eyes he's making." I grin. "He knows how to use them and how to get what he wants," I laugh aloud.

David stands and turns back to me and beams, trying not to laugh.

"So, what are your plans for this afternoon?" He asks as he looks from one to the other, waiting on a reply.

"We hadn't really thought, had we boys?" I smile, I see Thomas glancing between myself and David like he is trying to work out world hunger.

"Well, I was planning to grab some lunch, then maybe visit the fair that arrived in the Park last weekend. If you have nothing planned, do you want to come?" He raises his eyebrow in question to me before dropping his eyes to the boys.

I could see the boy's face light up with excitement. They had asked last weekend to go to the fair at the park, but I didn't want to go alone with them as Livvy and Lenny had both been busy the last few weeks and we had not had our monthly outing.

I looked between them all and waited while the boys cheered and begged for me to agree to allowing us to go with David. Though in the back of my mind I knew it was a bad idea, I could not say no to the boys.

"Okay, but if I get sick from the Waltzer's, you are all going to have to look after me," I smile at the boys.

"Oh, don't worry, I will hold your hand, while they spin you around," David winked.

I shook my head as we made our way out of the shopping centre. David went left at the entrance, and we went right as we

145

both moved towards our cars, after we agreed to meet at the park within twenty minutes.

I could feel a moment of excitement build as the thought of spending the afternoon with my three favourite people filled my mind but as I got closer to the park my nerves were on edge, I tried to stop my racing thoughts as I realise it will have been the first time since the night of our passionate kiss that I had spent any time with him outside of work.

I have always been careful who I bring into the boy's life, that's why dating has always been at the back of my mind. I know the work of my battery-operated boyfriend is not the most fulfilling way to release my frustrations, but I was content with not having to worry about another person in the equation.

As I drove to the park, I could hear the boys excitedly chatting about the fair and how a couple of their friends had been and loved it. I smiled as I listened.

"Mum, I like David." Elliott says out of nowhere as we parked the car.

"Do you sweetheart?" I raise my eyebrow in surprise.

"Yeah." and that was all he said, I smiled at the simplistic way that Elliott saw things.

I glanced towards Thomas, and I could see his face scrunch up at Elliott's words. It is a little harder for Thomas as he still misses his dad terribly. I think it has really affected him not being in contact with Ian.

Even though I have tried several times to make contact with Ian, I am starting to think after two years of silence that we may never hear from him again.

I sigh. I wish I could wave a magic wand and make everything better for them both, but it really was beyond my powers. We walk towards the entrance of the park and I see

David already waiting for us. As he sees me approach, his face lights up and I feel the butterflies in my stomach.

"Hey," David smiles.

"Hey yourself."

"Shall we get food first, boys?" David asks Thomas and Elliott when he looks at them.

"Yeah!" Elliott excitedly cheers, as Thomas looks past David towards the fair.

"You hungry Thomas?" David asks.

"I suppose," he mumbles.

"Come on then, let's go and see what we can get from the burger van." I say coolly trying not to sound too excited at the thought of spending some time with him.

We walk through the gates of the park, and I take a second to stop and look around. I can see all the families milling around, with an air of excitement in the atmosphere. I glanced to the left, and I noticed a man with his two boys lining up to take them on the bumper cars, and I frowned. That should have been Ian and the boys, but he decided we were not good enough for him.

I shake the saddening thoughts from my mind, I really need to stop thinking about the stuff the boys are missing and concentrate on making their futures better. I hear Thomas shout out to me, and I realise they have walked on without me, while I have been standing here daydreaming.

I rush to follow them across the fair until we reach the burger van. I sit the boys down on the wooden picnic bench, while I go to fetch food. David offered to help me carry the food, but I had a sense it was more to find out if I was okay.

"Hey, are you okay?" he whispers as we stand in the queue.

"Yeah, I'm fine. Why?" I question with a frown.

"You just seem a little distant and away with the fairies."

147

"I can assure you I am fine, David. I was just over thinking things."

"If you would prefer me to disappear, I can. I'll just tell the boys that I've had a phone call, and something's come up." He frowns. "You didn't want me to offer to take you all to the fair, did you? Fuck, I'm such a dick."

"David it's fine. They would meet you eventually anyway."

He raised his eyebrows surprised with my words.

"Well Liv's with Shawn now and you are Shawn's best friend, so I'm sure they would have met you at some point."

"But you wanted to keep your work life separate," he shakes his head.

"Don't worry about it. I can have more than Liv and Lenny as a friend, you know."

I see the lines on his forehead crinkle as he frowns at the word friend. I know there is this chemistry between us, but I need to keep the lines clear, or I would end up so lost in him, I would not be able to keep hold of my morals.

"Yeah, friends." he mumbles.

As we reach the front of the queue, I place our orders and the server asks David what he wants, thinking we are separate.

"We're together," he corrects her as he gives her his order and then pays for all the food.

"No, I'm paying." I sigh heavily.

"No, you are not, it was my idea to come and there is no way you are paying, Hannah."

"But David...."

"There are no buts, I've paid."

I swallow a string of profanities as I want to curse him out. I hate owing people something, even though I know he will not see it as owing him, but I still feel I do.

"I sense another but coming," he winks.

I rolled my eyes as the lady started putting our order on the ledge at the side of the burger van and I lean forward.

"There would be another 'but,' but we are in public, so I'll be good for once," I smile as I turn away to walk back to the bench. I look over my shoulder to see his eyes on my arse and start to feel the butterflies again, but I quickly trample them down.

Once we had finished eating, David and Thomas were like long lost friends. They were talking about building and how David got into it. Elliott was asking lots of questions about the machines they use, and David offered to take them one weekend to the site. So they could see how everything worked and he would show them how to build a wall because there was a skill to brick laying, who knew? I smiled as I watched them all getting on.

Once we had put all the rubbish in the bin, we walked through the fair until we found the Waltzer's. I hated this ride with a passion. The last time I went on one, I was fifteen and Livvy fancied the man that used to mind the ride, so she talked me into going on it to try to catch his attention but my God, all it did do was make me sick to my stomach.

I swore I would never go on them again, but seeing the excitement in Elliott's face, I knew I could not say no. So I bit my lip and climbed in the car with David to my left and Thomas and Elliott to my right as they dropped the bar down to make sure we were secure. I took a few calming breaths as David moved in a little closer.

"Do you need to hold my hand?" he whispered softly into my ear.

His breath blew down my neck, causing my skin to prickle as he waited for my response.

I opened my eyes, not that I had realised I had closed them in the first place, to find David's deep ocean blue eyes locked with mine.

"I think I'll be okay," I reply breathlessly.

I can feel my pulse racing as the ride starts to spin, and my eyes are glued to his. I feel the butterflies start to bubble in my tummy.

Everything around us becomes a kaleidoscope of colours spinning around us, our surroundings are just whooshing past, like we are trapped in our own little world. I could not tear my eyes away from his darkened pupils.

I heard the boy's cheering in laughter but there was only one place I could look. His eyes held me captive, as everything around us froze, I got lost in the depths of his gaze.

When the ride slows down, I try to look away, but I am stuck in the moment, I do not want it to end. It's like I am flying. I feel like he's the moon and I am the earth, and I want more than to be just rotating around each other.

I feel the bar lift as the boys jump from the ride pumped and full of excitement, but I am yet to peel my eyes away from his. Then he leans forward.

"When I look into your eyes, I can get lost in them for hours, you make me feel free." he whispers, millimetres from my lips as I hold my breath.

My breathing falters and I pray that he will take me in his arms. I feel the warmth spreading through my body as my desire starts to peak and I know I am in serious trouble with this man, I would do anything to make him mine.

I blink several times trying to bring myself back to the moment. Then, I hear the ride assistant telling us the ride has finished, and I finally drop my eyes down to my feet as I want them to move. When we climbed from the car, and I felt him guide me off with his hand on my lower back, to catch up with Thomas and Elliott. I feel like I am walking on air around the fair. For the next few hours, everything is like a dream.

We have a go on the Ferris wheel, the view over the park and town was breath-taking. Thomas has a go on the fair games and wins me a cute big rabbit to sit on the bottom of my bed. While Elliot has a couple of goes on the hook a duck and wins a bouncy ball. David helps both of them to have a go at the darts game and wins a 'number one girl' teddy, with a pink bow in its hair. When David presents it to me, I could not have swooned anymore.

I watched him with the boys through the afternoon and he was amazing with them. It had been the first time in a long time, I had seen Thomas drop his guard and laugh all afternoon.

Chapter Fourteen

David

Have you ever known real love?

The kind that makes you feel, love?

No, this ain't let's make a deal love,

Make an angel give up his wings,

It makes you guilty ' cause you want more....

I sing quietly to myself, as I pour myself a glass of whiskey. I have had the most glorious afternoon with Hannah, Thomas and Elliott and I never want this feeling to ever end.

"What has you so happy"

I hear from behind me. I look over my shoulder to see Gaynor glaring at me from the hallway.

"Nothing, why?"

"I've never heard you sing before, so there's something definitely going on."

"Can I not just be in a good mood, Gaynor; I don't need an excuse to sing." I frown.

"I never said you needed one." The anger crept into her voice. "I just said, there must be one."

I sigh, after the afternoon I've had, the last thing I want is her to destroy my good mood. I can never remember feeling this relaxed or happy ever, I knew that it was too good to be true for her not to say something to bring me down. I close my eyes and count to five.

I am not going to lose this good mood; I chant to myself. I bring my whiskey back to my lips and take a sip. I feel the sting of the alcohol burn as it slides down my throat. I look back at Gaynor and down the rest.

"Do you ever think there's more to life than what we have now?" I ask absentmindedly.

I hear her sigh.

"I know there's more David, sometimes you just have to take the chance,"

I look back at her and see the sadness in her eyes.

If I must deal with her cryptic chatter, I need to have a certain amount of alcohol running through my veins.

"I need a shower,"

I place my tumbler in the sink and turn to walk out of the kitchen.

"Your Dad was here earlier; he was looking for you."

"I'm sure he'll find me," I say trying to shake the dark mood from my mind. After the good day I've had, I don't want to think about that asshole. I reach my bedroom door and pause; I feel unsettled by the way I dismissed Gaynor. I hate behaving like a knob. It wasn't who my mum taught me to be. I turn to go back before I could move, I see Gaynor wheeling herself back towards her room.

"Gaynor,"

She pauses but doesn't look back.

"I'm sorry. I shouldn't have been an arse. I'm tired."

"Forget it."

I watch her push her bedroom door open and wait until she's completely in her room before I continue into mine. Once I'm in my room, I sit on the edge of the bed. I smile as I think about this afternoon. I loved spending time with Hannah, Thomas and Elliott. It gave me an insight into the life I really wanted, the feeling of belonging to someone.

When we were on the ride, I could feel my heart beating out of my chest with the look that was in her eyes, I could see the desire dancing in her chocolate brown irises.

I wanted so badly to climb into her eyes. I was so desperate to lean over and kiss her beautiful face.

I knew it wasn't a possibility with Thomas and Elliott there, but my need nearly pushed me over the edge. The more time I spend with Hannah, I know the closer I'm getting to say fuck it. I feel ready to jump; to fall from the skies and take the leap of faith.

When she smiles, she sets my heart soaring. When she laughs, my heart skips a beat. I've never felt love before, only from my mum but what I feel when I'm close to Hannah, frightens me to death.

I rub my hand across my tired and weary face, when I think back to sitting across the bench from her and watching how they all talked and interacted, it made me long for something I might never have. But then I start to feel guilty when I think of Gaynor in her wheelchair, she never wanted children or a family. I remember one day asking her why she agreed to the wedding, her reply made my heart sink.

"I needed security,"

Not because I loved you, or because of what I offered or what my dad offered. That was the night our shameful marriage started to fall apart. I really believed on the morning of my wedding that if I went through with it, we would eventually fall in love and have the happily ever after, like my mum dreamed of but it wasn't to be.

In hindsight I wished I hadn't gone through with the wedding. I should have walked away from my father and his demands. I should have grown some balls and told him to do one.

154

I never had the perfect married mom and dad role models growing up, so I didn't know what marriage was supposed to look like but surely there had to be more to it than what we have.

I fall backwards onto the bed as I feel the emptiness in my heart and this place feels more like a prison than a home. I glance around the room and there are no real personal items, like photos, memories or mementos of anything that means anything to me. I have never felt so lost or lonely.

I jump from the bed and walk over to my desk, while I open my top drawer and pull out a bottle of jack and a tumbler. I drop the glass back in and pull the lid from the bottle and bring it to my lips and take a long swig. I feel the burn and place it back down, then head for the bathroom, where I switch on the shower.

While I waited for it to warm up, I heard my phone ping, so I know I've received a text. I walk to my bedside table and pick it up. My heart rate starts to increase as I see Hannah's name on the screen. I take a steady breath before opening up my phone.

"Hey. I just wanted to thank you for today. Thomas and Elliott haven't shut up about it yet. I really appreciate you making such a fuss of the boys. Thank you again H x"

I smiled as my heart skipped a beat.

"No thanks are needed. I loved spending time with you and the boys. You should be immensely proud of how well you have brought them up, they are a credit to you. I mean that. D x"

I mute my phone. I don't want to get hung up waiting for a reply that might not come, and I've had a drink, so I won't to be tempted to give Hannah another drunk dial call.

I drop my phone on the bed as I strip out of my clothes and step into the shower with thoughts of Hannah at the front of my mind.

What I would give to have her pressed against the cold shower wall, with my hands exploring all her gorgeous curves. I feel myself hardening at the thought of her soft, supple skin, pressed against me while standing under the hot flow of water.

I imagine my hands traveling up her thigh until I reach her soft folds, as I glide my fingertips over her skin. I imagine myself pushing my finger between her lips until I find her clit. I hear her sharp intake of breath, so I know I've hit the jackpot.

I apply just the right amount of pressure to cause her breathing to increase, then I slide my finger further down until I reach her core. I push two fingers past her entrance as I continue to circle her clit with my thumb.

I could practically hear her cry in pleasure as I continued to tease her clit and her G-spot simultaneously. I feel her starting to clench around my fingers, so I know she won't last long as I steadily grip my cock ready to blow my load.

I swiftly move my hand up and down the shaft as I continue to drive myself insane with my fantasy.

Since the day I met Hannah, she has always played the main star in any fantasy I have had. I grip my cock with determination to reach my orgasm as quickly as possible. I can feel my balls starting to pull closer to my body, so I know I'm close and as I imagine entering Hannah's core. I hiss as I shoot all over the tiles in the shower.

I stand a few minutes with my head bowed and my hand bracing the wall as I try to catch my breath. I take a deep breath as I start to wash myself. I turn off the water and step out as I grab a towel. I towel dry my hair, before putting another one around my waist.

I make my way to my bed, as I drop down too tired to dry myself, I feel my phone digging into my side and realize that I had left it on the bed. I pick it up and see Hannah's name again, so I glance at the time and see it's past ten pm, so I quickly open the message.

"Thank you, David, that means a lot. Sleep well. H x"

I wish I didn't have to say goodnight over text, I'd much rather say it in person, preferably lying in the same bed with my head between her legs but I'm just torturing myself thinking about it.

"Night Hannah, Sweet dreams Dx"

I switched off my phone before I made the mistake of calling to hear her voice. I flung my arm over my head as I slowly drifted off to a restless night of hot steamy dreams of sex with my office manager.

⸻

I groan as the light from the crack in the curtain tries to penetrate my eyelids. I roll over as a dull, aching, thud fills my head. I lie motionless for a second as I try to remember what day it is. As I try to get my brain to function, the events of the afternoon before flash through my head, I smile as I think about how much I enjoyed myself. I had never really put much thought into wanting my own children but being with Thomas and Elliott made me realize I was probably missing something great.

I can't believe how Hannah's ex just walked out on her and the boys. He must have been mad to walk away from his perfect family.

I wriggle about as the urge to piss becomes too much; I know I need to leave my warm covers but not wanting to face the day. Eventually I give up trying to hold it in anymore, I jump from my bed and walk naked across to the bathroom.

As I finished, I didn't expect to hear raised voices coming from the front entrance, so I walked to my door and opened it slightly to hear Gaynor's voice.

"Shhh will you. You are going to wake David up."

"Well don't be so stupid then," I hear her mother reply.

"It's not your decision. I don't love him, and he certainly doesn't love me. I married him for Dad, and Dad only." I hear her hiss. "I've done a lot of thinking while being trapped in this thing and I want someone who loves me, and who wants to be with me."

"And you think Luke will want you now? After all this time," her mom sighs heavily.

What? Luke... I haven't heard from Luke since just after the accident, four years earlier. Though now that I think of it, how can someone who was around all the time, just disappear overnight.

Luke was a good friend. I wasn't as involved with Luke as I was with Shawn but when we were in college, he was always everywhere we were, and we continued our friendship a long time after.

We spent so much time together, and I always considered him a close friend. He even tried to talk me out of marrying Gaynor, saying that I deserved more than a make shift marriage, that she was a money digging whore. I told him I knew what I was doing and that I had hoped that we would grow to love each other over time.

I try to calm my rolling thoughts as I try to listen to the rest of the conversation.

"We've kept in touch; he blames himself for what happened."

Why would Luke blame himself?

158

"Gaynor, you need to stop living in the clouds. You need to stay with David." I hear the anger in her mum's voice as Gaynor slams the door.

I stagger back to the bed and drop my head into my hands. I missed some of the conversation between my racing thoughts and the shock I felt, I wanted to rush out and confront her, but about what?

I only heard her mention Luke's name, and they kept in touch. I struggled to piece together all that I heard. My mind was spinning with all my thoughts.

I need to get out of here and try to clear my head. I glance at the time on my alarm clock on the bedside table and I am surprised to see it's half past eleven. I never sleep in this late. I've always been an early riser.

I skip my morning shower as I had one before bed, after I've brushed my teeth, and got dressed, I head out the front door. I didn't want to risk bumping into Gaynor.

I start the car, reverse off the drive and point the car in Joyce's direction. I think I need some calm time and Joyce has always provided a safe haven for me to relax in. Once I pull on to the drive, I see Joyce in the front garden pottering around, I smile when I see her lift her hand and I head for the gate. Just as I reach the front steps, Joyce pulls me into a warm hug as the front door swings open. As she pulls back, she eyes me.

"What has you here this morning, David?"

"Can't I visit my two-favourite people." I raise my eyebrow.

"Yes, if that was the only reason, what is bothering you?"

I loved how she could read me before I even had to open my mouth.

159

"Leave the poor guy alone." I hear Albert say behind Joyce. "Let him get through the door before the interrogation starts."

"I'm not interrogating him, Bert, but I can see that something is bothering him."

"Well, let's go and put the kettle on before we have him spilling his guts."

I smile, these two people right here are exactly what I needed. We make our way into the kitchen and sit at the old country style dinner table, as Bert puts the kettle on.

"Something smells delicious in here."

"My famous Beef roast, are you staying for dinner?"

"I don't want to put you out, Joy,"

"Ah, you never put me out, you know that."

While I'm sitting there, I suddenly feel all my stresses drain away, and my shoulders feel light.

"I would love to as long as you don't mind, Joyce."

I feel Bert's hand on my shoulder as he reaches over to put my coffee down in front of me.

"Son, you never put us out. We love when you come over, even though it has been a few weeks." he raises his eyebrows.

"I know, I'm sorry. Things at work have been hectic."

"Wouldn't be due to a certain brunette, would it?" I see Joy's eyes light up in humour.

I drop my head to the wooden table harrowingly just missing my mug and groan.

"I will never live that interview down, will I?"

I hear them both chuckle. To tell you the truth, I knew coming here would cause me to face some of my life issues but maybe that's what I need, someone to point me in the right direction. I lift my head and start telling them everything from the start, I decided to keep the part where I fucked her up against the wall in the club to myself, as even though Joy and Bert are open minded, I didn't want them to think any less of Hannah.

I tell them about my afternoon with the boys and how I had never felt so relaxed. I finish telling them how I feel like I am missing out on a big part of my life and even though children really hadn't been a thought up until now, I would love to have some in my future but staying in a loveless marriage with someone who never wanted children isn't what I want anymore, I see the gleam in Joy's eyes.

"That's fifty you owe me, Mr. Barkley." she grins, as I frown.

"For the love of God, David, why do you like to prove Joy correct. She came back from that interview and said something had happened previously and I was convinced nothing had or else you wouldn't have employed her." He frowns as he pulls his wallet from his pocket and chucks two twenties and a ten towards Joy.

"What can I say? I know my boy better than you," she laughs. "But now that is over, what are you going to do David? I mean you know my thoughts on Gaynor and the whole wedding thing, and I saw the way your eyes lit up at the site of Hannah."

"I don't know, I just feel there's something missing. You both know since mum died, I have always just wanted to belong somewhere, and I thought if I agreed to marrying Gaynor, I would kill two birds with one stone. Help Dad with the business in some way as I know he was disappointed in me not joining the company like he wanted, and I would finally have someone to belong to but that never happened. The more I've tried over the years, the more she's pushed me away. I just want to feel some real love and for someone to love me, for me." I blow out a frustrated breath.

I feel Joy take my hand in hers, as I look up and see the sadness in her eyes.

"Do you know what I think?" she pauses as I shrug my shoulders.

"I think you have finally seen the future you never imagined having. I think you have seen what you could have with Hannah, and she has slowly woken you up to the fact, you deserve so much more than you allow yourself to have."

"And." Bert starts as I turn my head in his direction.

"And" I repeat.

"I think if you look into this Luke issue that you overheard this morning, you will find the courage to do what is best for YOU at last." I smile timidly.

"But how will it look, me walking away from the woman I married, who is in a wheelchair, through running errands for me."

"David, my sweet boy. That accident was never your fault. Sometimes things happen, but it doesn't mean we have to stop living or stay in a situation that we are not happy about. You can be happy too." Joy stood and dropped a kiss on my forehead as she walked to the oven to start dishing up the roast beef dinner.

I stay quiet for a while as I let her words swim around in my head. Then I remember I forgot to switch my phone back on, so I turn it on and I waited for it to power up, I think back to my time with Hannah and the way she looked on the Waltzer's. She looked perfectly adorable, she made my heart feel light and my spirit free. As my mind rambles on, Bert pulls me from my thoughts.

"So, when do I get to meet this beautiful woman who has you all twisted up?"

"I'm not sure. I need to work on leaving Gaynor, if that's what I decide to do. Hannah deserves one hundred per cent and I would never allow her to be the other woman."

"I think your heart has already worked it out, and maybe your head just needs to catch up," he smiles at me.

"Oh, Bert, leave the poor man alone, he has a lot to consider,"

The flashing light on my phone catches my attention from the table as Joy places my dinner in front of me. I snatch my phone up and open the text, as I see it's been sent from Hannah and my heart rate picks up.

"In case you decide not to mention today on Monday, I just wanted to say thank you for making the boys feel special, it's been a long time since a man has gone out of his way to make them happy. I'm really glad it was you xx"

My heart skips a beat, and I cannot keep the smile off my face. I looked at the time the text was sent, and Hannah had sent it just after I turned my phone off.

"Me too, Hannah, Me too. I had the best time with you all. Hopefully in the future we can do it again. D xx"

"That must be a good text, to create a smile as big as that." Bert pulls me from my screen.

"You could say that." I don't explain.

"David, you know I never interfere with your life or the way you run it but if one text from Hannah can make your face shine like that, you need to follow your heart. We have known you since you were fourteen and I have never seen a look like that cross your face, even on your wedding day." Joy swallowed.

I know they were both right but just walking away won't be easy; I need to really think everything through and hope my brain catches up with my heart.

Chapter Fifteen

Hannah

I drop down in my chair and take a deep breath. I could quite happily drop my head back and fall asleep. After a while I hear the cleaners finishing off, I look at the time, and sigh.

I'm not usually here this late on a Friday, but I had some files that I wanted to type up, so Livvy asked if she could take the boys to the movies with Shawn and as I knew it was too much to ask Martha to watch them late tonight as she hadn't been too well all week, I agreed.

I rub my tired eyes and loosen the bobble from my hair. These past few weeks have been like torture. Since the afternoon with David and the boys at the fair, things have felt so different between us. You could cut the tension with a knife.

David pays me more compliments. I like that he pays more attention to how I look, and I am forever catching him watching me during meetings and conference calls, but we are yet to have a real conversation about the way things are going, apart from me telling him I needed more this morning.

I reached for the folder I was going to type up next and remember I had taken it into David's office earlier for him to double check the plans and statements before I mail them out. I take a deep breath and walk to his office. We hadn't really spoken today, at least not since I had my little chat, where I spoke, he just nodded. I need to lay out everything I wanted, instead of this back-and-forth game we had going on. I was trying to be an adult because it was driving me crazy, but he just replied he didn't have time as he had a telephone call in the next five minutes.

I stormed from his office and slammed my door but as the day went on, I knew we needed to have the talk, or I would need to leave the company because it was breaking my heart being so close but not being able to touch.

So, the file I needed was a good enough excuse to be in his office.

I stood by the door, leaning on the wooden frame with my arms folded, waiting for him to look at me. I needed to see his crystal blue eyes, I needed to know we were on the same page, but he kept them firmly on his computer screen.

"Yes, Hannah?" he must have sensed me at the door.

"I... I..." I stutter as I step into his office. "Have you thought anymore about what I said earlier?"

"I don't know what you want me to say Hannah?"

"I want you to say, you feel it too David. To say that I'm not losing my mind." I pause. "You play these games. You get my attention and then step back. Why?"

"I'm trying to do the right thing, Han. You walked into my life with that tight arse and fuck me legs. Lips to die for and tits that should be illegal. You distract me, you tease me, you make me want something I can't give." He sighs.

"I only want to love you. I only want…." I stop.

"You only want what?" He lifts his eyes to mine.

I shake my head; I can't speak the words.

"Tell me!"

"Tell you what David! That since you came into my life you've destroyed me for every man before and after?? Is that it?" I stare at him in anger. "Or that since I met you, you're all I see, all I think about, all I want in my life?" I pant, feeling like my lungs can't get enough oxygen.

166

I step back because being this close to him is sending my pulse wild. I watch him grinding his teeth, as I see the frustration in his eyes.

"You think it's easy being this close to someone I want to build my life around?" He stands up. "You think I don't lie awake at night wishing it was you who was lying in bed next me, not some empty space?" I gasp. "Do you think I chose this life? Do you think I chose her?" He took three quick steps until he was standing in front of me.

"I did what I had too out of duty. I know it was wrong, but I just wanted my dad to love me, to make me feel part of the family, to feel like I belonged." His voice strained. "I have never felt like I do with you, I have never had a connection to anyone but you, my life is such a mess. I can't ask you to be the mistress." He looked down, defeated. "But I'm struggling to walk away or so I thought."

David takes a step back, I feel completely distraught, but I can't let him go either, so I take a step forward.

"I can't walk away either." I whisper.

I slowly run my fingers down his cheek until I reach his jaw. I gently lift his chin until his eyes meet mine. With a ghost of a smile, I look deep into his eyes.

"Do you want me to walk away?" I whisper.

I need him to say it, I need David to make that decision, then when I leave the best job I've ever had, I'll know it wasn't because I couldn't do it.

"DO I WANT YOU TO WALK AWAY?" he explodes, making me jump.

"No, I don't want you to walk away, Hannah but what else can I do?"

"Let me love you?" I softly say.

167

"You have no idea the internal fight I'm having to do the right thing,"

David drops his eyes to my lips, and I think he's going to send me home. I hear his breathing change.

"Strip."

I look up, my eyes connect with his, I'm sure I heard him wrong.

"What are you waiting for, Hannah?" He smirks.

I step back. I keep him pinned with my eyes on his.

I lift my hands to the top button of my blouse. I flick the first button open, then pause with a raised eyebrow. I drop my head onto the side, eyeing him.

Is this a test or another game?

I slowly drop my fingers to the next button and repeat it until all the buttons are open and my blouse hangs open loosely in front of this gorgeous man.

I let my arms drop to my side as the material slowly floats down and lands on the floor.

I stand before David in my bra and suit trousers, I can see he's dying to drop his eyes to my cleavage, but he continues to hold my gaze as I move my fingers to the button on the waistband.

I pull the zip down and undo the button, feeling my face blush with the anticipation of what's to come.

I wiggle my bum and feel the material slide down my hips, thighs and land at my feet. I step to the right and out of my trousers, I'm so proud of myself that I did it so gracefully.

I stand before him in just my deep red bra and thong set and my most favourite pair of heels. I see his Adams apple dip as he swallows.

Starting from my face, he cautiously let's his eyes travel over every inch of my body. I drop my eyes to his mouth and see him biting on his bottom lip.

"My mind is telling me to stop. To tell you to walk away, that this isn't right but for you, I'm willing to lose it all."

I freeze, I'm under his spell. He steps forward until our chest touches. David carefully removes each bra strap off my shoulders, walking around me he glides his fingertip across my skin until he reaches my back. His touch is sending a shiver down my spine. He flicks the clasp on my bra, and it quickly drops to the floor. I feel his lips delicately kiss along my shoulders, then his nose runs up my neck until I hear him smell me just behind my ear. He moves until I feel his teeth on my earlobe, and I gasp.

"There's so much I want to do to you." I hear him say in a soft hum.

"I'm not going to stop you, David." I turn my head until our lips are within centimetres of each other.

He steps back and he moves in front of me again. I watch as he slowly undoes his shirt and drops it on top of my bra. David flicks the button on his trousers, undoes the zip and steps out of them. He reaches for my hand and pulls me into his embrace as he slowly devours my mouth. I feel his hands in my hair, then I feel the slight pull and my insides turn to jelly.

I feel him pull back from me, leaving a feeling of loss.

"How can something feel so right, be so wrong?"

"Just shut up and kiss me, David."

Slamming his mouth back to mine, I feel my need for him increasing, and the ache in the pit of my stomach is growing. I feel his hardening erection instantly as it digs into me, I want to do so many naughty things to him.

I run my fingers through his sexy chestnut hair, dragging my nails back down his neck.

Hissing, David lifts me into his arms as he moves across his office effortlessly, until he reaches his desk. As he places me on the edge, I let my arms drop to the cool wood, trying to support myself as he consumes my mouth.

I feel his hands travelling up my torso as they make their way to my breasts. My nipples pebble as David delicately caresses them. He drops his head as his tongue circles each one, then continues to travel down until he reaches my navel. I take a sharp breath of air, as he continues south, I feel him pause just before my panties.

"Once I take these off, there's no going back. Do you understand?"

I bring my eyes down to meet his, as I stare into his icy blue eyes, I know that I could never love anyone the way I love him. I nod.

With a blink of an eye my panties were gone, David ripped them straight off my body.

"Hey," I shout. "I loved those panties; they were my favourite colour." I smirked.

"I'll buy you new ones, in fact I'll buy you a hundred," he winks.

I watched him return his gaze down to my mound, he licked his lips and my insides tremble with desire. I drop my eyes to his fingers as they trace the inside of my thigh, travelling towards my centre. I can feel my arousal building. I don't think I'll last long once he reaches there. I groan and close my eyes. I feel him glide along my skin and it's making my need for release unbearable, and my head spins.

David pauses for a moment, I wait. Is he having second thoughts?

I slowly open my eyes and meet his blue ones. He drops his eyes as he slides his thumb across my wet pussy, gently pushing his way in and circling my clit. I take a deep breath as I feel the tingling begin to rise.

David slowly drops his thumb lower until he reaches my soaked core. I slide forward until I feel his thumb enter me, and we both take a sharp intake of breath, together. We are so in tune with just one look he can set my whole body on fire.

"You have no idea what you do to me," he whispers.

I lift my head until our forehead meets, we watch each other as David delicately slides his fingers in and out of my core.

"I need you. I need to feel you wrapped around my shaft,"

"Please David, I need more, I need to feel your cock." I whisper.

I can see his face strain with frustration as he slowly withdraws his fingers. David drops his hand until they reach his boxers, without hesitation he pulls out his cock and lines it up with my slit. After a slight pause he forced his way into my pussy with one vigorous push, he filled me completely with a hiss as he clenched his teeth.

"Oh, Hannah, you feel so good," David groans.

I couldn't seem to form any thoughts because I was overwhelmed by the feeling of David. Pulling back, I could feel him gliding all the way to the tip and then plunging back inside me, groaning, I was lost in all sensations of him.

My head drops back, making my back arch, pushing my breasts into David's chest. I love the feeling of his skin on my skin. Our hearts beating close to each other, our connection growing.

David increases his speed and I feel my orgasm building. I love how strong he feels and how hard he is between my legs. Delicately David drops his hands between us and softly touches my clit, circling it in a figure of eight. Oh, God, I'm so close.

"Han, you need to come, Baby." David grunts.

I see David clench his teeth as he waits for me to succumb to the sensations that are taking over my body. I gasp for breath as I feel my orgasm crash inside me, my nerve endings tingle as my pussy pulsates around his cock, before allowing himself to take his pleasure.

I scream my release as David's lips meet mine, taking all my cries as he emptied himself inside me.

I feel him slowing down as our foreheads meet again, both of us breathing heavily as our eyes open and smile at each other.

"I knew I was in trouble the first time I met you," David pants.

I smile, "I knew you were the one the moment you fucked me up against the wall,"

We both laughed as David pulled out, I hissed with soreness.

"Was I too rough?" He asked with what sounded like regret.

"No, you were perfect," I gently kiss his lips.

We both stood and searched for our clothes, David found my bra and I found his tie. We moved coordinated around the office as if this wasn't the first time, we'd both stepped over the line.

Once I was fully dressed, I turned to leave the office as the reality of what had just happened hit me. I sense my tears starting to build as I reached for the handle on the door.

"Where are you going?" David grabs my hand.

172

"Back to my office to finish up." I sigh. I can't make eye contact as I know I'm about to get rejected again.

"We need to talk."

Was the only words David said as he dragged me back to his chair. Once he sat down, he pulled me into his lap, and lifted my eyes to his.

"I'm not walking away this time," he raised his eyebrow waiting for the words to sink in. As the words spun around my mind, I frowned. How could he say that? Was he leaving his wife? Was I going to be the other woman? I didn't think I could do that. I feel his finger smoothing out the creases on my forehead. "I mean what I said, Hannah, I am not walking away."

"So, I am going to be your bit on the side?" I mumble as I try to control my temper, I have never felt so crap or used.

"Do you really think I would treat you that way?"

I pause, as I look into his eyes.

"No." I whisper, as I try to steady my heartbeat and try to work out how this was going to work and how we could be together.

"I need you to trust me." his hands cup my face as he brings his lips to mine. "The next few weeks or months, maybe; will be rough, but I need you to trust me."

"Trust you?" I ask in confusion, "The last person I trusted destroyed my life and trampled all over my heart," I nibbled on my bottom lip.

"I'm not him," he places his lips on mine in a tender kiss. As he pulls back, he looks into my eyes. "I just need a little time to work things out. I will be leaving Gaynor but there were something's I need to sort before that can happen. When I walk away, I don't want to drag you down too."

"Are you sure you want to do this," I ask in a timid voice.

173

"Yes."

I look at his face and for the first time ever he looks radiant. There was a light in his eyes that I hadn't seen since our first night together.

As I sit there in his lap, all of my thoughts are running wild at the possibilities for the future we could have, but what if he can't do it in the end? What if he finds that he still loves his wife and then I'm back to square one?

"Don't overthink things," he whispers.

"David, why now? And how?" was all I could say because I couldn't calm my thoughts enough to think straight.

"Our marriage isn't a conventional marriage, we married to appease our fathers, her dad wanted to buy into my dad's family business and my dad needed a cash injection to stop the company going under." he frowned as he spoke. "Six years ago, when I met Gaynor at a family function, my dad introduced us. I should have known he wasn't being fatherly, but I was so desperate to please him that I let things go. She was never my type, but she was enough to keep my father off my back and back in his good books but then one day he called me to meet him at his office, I should have known he was up to something." he pauses. I stroke his face to comfort him.

"He asked how things were going with Gaynor, I said okay, but she wasn't really my type and he told me, to make her my type as he needed me to marry her. I was shocked and declined instantly but he laid the guilt trip of my mum and how she would want me to be married and how I kind of owed him one because I didn't want to be part of the family business. So, I agreed. I hoped that Gaynor would put a stop to it, but she must have been promised something from her dad to get her to agree too." He took another breath as he drew circles with his finger on my palm.

"I had no one, other than Joyce, Albert, her husband and Shawn. I just wanted to feel like I belonged somewhere and that someone wanted me. Over the coming months, I convinced myself that I could love Gaynor and after the vows we would fall in love and everything would work out, but it never happened and then when we had been married just over twelve months, Gaynor was involved in a big car accident while fetching my suit from the dry cleaners and she was paralysed from the waist down. The guilt gnawed at me, she became distant, but I stayed. I tried to make things work, well at first but over the years I stopped trying and every time she spoke to me it just made me angry. She never has anything nice to say and that was before the accident and over time it's got worse." He lifts his eyes to mine as I take in all that he's said, and I feel so much compassion for him.

We both sit silent for a moment as we both try to process our thoughts.

"Oh, wow." Is all that I can say.

"Do you now understand why I've been trying to do the right thing? And not just by her but you too."

I nod.

"I never wanted to push you away, Hannah, but I couldn't have you seen as the other woman or the woman who split my marriage." He smiled timidly.

"I know, I'm sorry I've pushed so hard today."

"I'm not." He beams. "When you spoke to me this morning, my head caught up with my heart and I knew the internal battle I have going on isn't needed."

"It isn't." I frown.

"No." he looks away for a second and then brings his eyes back to mine, taking my face into his hands so he could make sure I didn't look away. "I fell in love with you the night we met and my love for you each day has grown. The day I spent with you and the boys, confirmed my heart ache for you and I wanted to build a life with you all, but I just needed my head to catch up." He smiled. "But I just need one thing from you."

"Anything," I whispered.

"Trust me," he kissed me so passionately that he stole my breath and made me lightheaded.

I knew with all my heart that I would trust this man until my last breath.

Chapter Sixteen

David

I see the car lights flash, as I switch the alarm off and make my way across the carpark. I walk Hannah to her car and push her up against the cool metal door, while I pull her lips to mine. I can't keep the smile off my face, as I look into her eyes.

"Thank you for tonight," I whisper against her lips.

"It's me that should be thanking you." she smiles.

"I know I'm asking a lot of you but all I ask is you don't give up on me, Hannah. I also know things are pretty fucked up now, but I will make it right, I just need a little time to put together a plan."

"I know," she spoke quietly. "I will wait until the end of time if I have to."

My heart leapt at her words, the love I feel for this woman is immense.

"See you Monday, Beautiful." I sighed heavily, all I wanted to do was to go home with Hannah and snuggle on the sofa before bed but that wasn't meant to be yet.

"See you Monday," she repeated sadly.

I stepped back so I could give her the room to open her car door. As she sat in her seat, I leaned in and fastened her seatbelt before placing a soft kiss on her forehead. I stood back up and closed her door as I watched her drive off, my heart felt heavy.

I didn't have it in me to go home and face another cold and lonely night in my prison. I push my hands through my hair as I make my way to my car, this is fucked up and I must make it right, someway, or somehow.

How am I going to sort this mess out? I climb in and sit quietly in my seat and try to work out what's next. I look up and watch the moon sitting brightly in the dark night sky and wished my mum was here to help me sort out this shit show that's called my life.

I sit there and try to think of what she would say to me if she were here. I know she'd tell me to end my marriage properly before anything else happens between myself and Hannah. The conversation I overheard the other week pops into my mind, and I wonder why Gaynor was talking about Luke. I try to think back to when we were all close friends and I wondered if there was something I wasn't picking up on.

I wreck my head trying to remember if there was anything that would have raised my suspicions but there was nothing that came to mind. Luke and Gaynor got on but not that well that would make me think that there was something more was going on.

I think back to my stag night. He was a little cagey; he tried to convince me that marrying Gaynor was going to be the worst mistake of my life.

He dribbled on for an hour telling me that she wasn't the one and that I deserved someone that loved and treasured me, but I put it down to him being drunk, but maybe it wasn't. Maybe he was trying to warn me off to leave the space for him to step in. I start my car and make my way back to my prison.

ᥫᩣ

I sit on the cold wooden floor in the sitting room, looking through the dresser as I search for the mortgage papers and house deeds. I wanted to put things in place for when I leave.

178

It's been a week since the night with Hannah in my office and I'm so desperate to move out.

After I overheard the conversation between Gaynor and her mum a few weeks ago, I've been trying to do some digging but I haven't been able to find anything out, so I've decided to just end things. Neither of us are happy, we were never meant to be forever, she was never my destiny.

As I shift through the paperwork and move some boxes, I still can't find where the stuff I'm looking for is. I sigh, as I'm so sure we put the paperwork in here. I haven't touched them since we signed them. I move another box that I don't recognise, as I place it on the floor by the side of me, a few of the books fall out onto the floor and as the pages drop open, the writing catches my eye. I collected the top one off the floor and notice the writing, then frown, while I flip it over to look at the cover and the cute teddy bear sitting on the front.

As I look at the box, I realise they must be Gaynor's, she said she wrote sometimes when she was younger, so she must have put all her old diaries and bits of paper into a box but as I shuffle through, I notice they are old dairies.

I know I should put them back in the box and ignore them, but I wonder what's written in them. My mum used to keep dairies but I'm sure they were destroyed when I was uprooted and moved to Dad's.

I stand slowly and try to gain the feelings again in my legs from sitting on the floor for too long. I bend down and pick up the box, carrying it into my room, curiosity has taken hold and you know what they say, 'Curiosity killed the cat,' so I sit on the bed with the box at my feet.

I grab it and I tip the box onto the bed and picking up the first diary to catch my eye.

179

I look at the lovely teddy bear sitting on the front in the corner of each sheet, I open it and scan through the pages, noticing the date, May 18th, 2007.

I blink several times and wonder if I should continue, I know that I shouldn't be reading it but what will it hurt, it's not like I'm going to tell anyone.

So, I scan down the lines and see that they are Gaynor's as she signed the bottom of the page. They are entries to her grandma. I knew her Grandma had died when she was eleven, and she adored her.

From the date this one was two years before we met. I know it's wrong, but I continue to read the letter.

Dear, Grandma.

I saw the most beautiful boy today. He lives in the same town as me, and he looks slightly older, so we are probably in a different year. I saw him look at me but as I smiled, he looked away. I wish I'd had the guts to talk to him, but I didn't. I was too shy to approach him, I feel like it's a missed chance but maybe next time. I loved the colour of his eyes and the way the sun glinted in his dirty blonde hair. I'm not sure what my father would think of me salivating all over this boy, but he'll never know, well not yet anyway.

Best wishes, Gaynor

I pause, I don't know if I should carry on, it's a serious violation of her privacy, but I can't help myself, so I flick to the next page and scan the writing as the anticipation takes over.

September 21st, 2007

'Dear Grandma,

I was walking across the green at lunch and yet again I saw his beautiful face. He was with his two friends; he didn't even look my way this time. It hurt that I didn't even see his

180

beautiful eyes but maybe next time I will build enough courage to talk to him. He was fooling around with his friends; I wish I had friends that I could hang out with like that, but my father wouldn't like it unless I was studying for some exam.

Best wishes, Gaynor'

I picked up another diary and opened the page.

March 18th, 2008,
'Dear Grandma,

I finally did it! After all the months of watching him from a distance, I plucked up the courage to speak to him. It was heaven, we didn't say much, well in fact I asked him if he would mind passing me the milk, he smiled and nodded. My heart is full. I am so in love with him. His eyes sparkled as his hair fell over his forehead, I really wanted to reach out and touch it, but I didn't want him to think I was strange. Next time I want to have a longer conversation, but something is better than nothing, right?

Best wishes, Gaynor.

I flicked to another page and again I paused as I scanned the writing.

June 22nd, 2008,

I pause as I read the top line, because something about that date sends alarm bells to my mind. I continue to read.

'Dear Grandma,

Tonight, I was forced to attend a function with my parents, and I hated it. I don't know why I was made to go. I stood in a big hall, all smiles and laughter, when really, I wanted to be anywhere else but there. I was introduced to my father's friend's son.

Imagine my shock when I realized who he was, although he was handsome, he's not the one I want. I don't know what was worse about tonight, David is my loves best friend or that it was hinted that I would date him.

Best wishes, Gaynor

My eyes bulge when I finish reading the page. I need to stop reading them, but I just can't seem to be able to. I flicked to another one again and read the next entry.

December 20th, 2008,

'Dear Grandma,

I feel like Juliet, I feel like my life is being decided without my consent. I have finally spoken to my love and found out his name is Luke Matthews, he offered to buy me a coffee and a muffin while I waited for the bus, but I got so nervous and made an excuse, then I told him I had to rush to meet my friend so I couldn't stand to talk. I was on cloud nine until I got home, and I was called into my father's study to be told that he needs me to marry David. My heart is so broken. I agreed as the tears ran down my face because I knew if I didn't my father's business would lose millions in revenue, even though his business was struggling; joining forces with the Shepard's would bring a better clientele and more clients. I wish I could run away but I know that's not an option.

Best wishes, Gaynor'

I feel my heart sink, I always thought she was a spoiled brat and had no compassion for anyone but herself. I know I need to stop reading but I can't. I pick up another diary from the pile and the one I so happened to fall to was the worst day in my life.

June 1st, 2009

'Dear Grandma,

182

Well, it's here. I sit in front of the mirror in my wedding dress and veil. I try to steady my heavy heart. I know marrying David is wrong, but my father promised me it would be only short-term, until he had his feet properly under the table. I hate that I'm being made to marry someone I don't love. I've told Luke and he's not happy. He wants me to walk away from my family and my father's wishes, but I won't get my trust fund, and I've been waiting for it for so long. I wanted to start my own business, so I needed the money to start up. It's breaking my heart to go through with it, and Luke has said he won't wait for me. I'm torn. I want to run to Luke, but I need the money as well.

> *Best regards, Gaynor'*

I pause and attempt to understand the situation. They were in love. Why didn't they say anything? I close up the diary and place it back onto the bed, while puffing out an unsteady breath.

We had both married out of loyalties to our fathers, me because I was trying to fit into the family and wanted to feel like I belonged. Her because of a trust fund and her future.

I drop the diary to the floor, and sigh. Then I pick up another one and I flick through a few of her pages until I find the one, I'm looking for and my heartbeat speeds up, she talks about meeting Luke in hotels and their time spent together while I was at work. I stop at the last diary on the pile and held my breath as I reach down, I flick through the pages, until I find the one, I want.

July 28th, 2010,

> *'Dear Grandma,*

I plan to meet Luke this afternoon to tell him I want to leave all this behind and run away with him. I have tried to stay away and live a full life with David, but I don't love him any more than a friend and I don't want to deny my heart anymore.

I have cried myself to sleep every night since the wedding, but I need to do what's right. I know David isn't happy either, I know he would like to be anywhere else but here with me. I've asked Luke to meet me at the Roman Way Hotel, I just pray he turns up. I'm so excited, my heart feels full.

Best wishes, Gaynor.

I frown as I turn to look at the bottom of the box, and there's nothing else or any other diaries written but that was the day of the accident. I do not know how to explain how I feel; I don't think I could put a name to these feelings running through my veins.

She had been having an affair, she'd been sneaking off to see my very good friend.

She was going to run off with him and leave me.

This is all too much to take in, I can feel the anger building. I place all the diaries back into the box and place it on my bedroom floor, I pace as I try to control my feelings. I need to get out before I explode, I drop Shawn a text.

"I need to talk. Do you fancy meeting for a drink?"

I leave my bedroom and walk down the hall as I leave the house towards my car. I jumped in the seat as I started the engine and I switched on the heater; I was starting to feel a little chilly. I see my screen light up and see a message back from Shawn.

"Yeah, no probs. I'm just leaving Hannah's; I'll meet you at the moon under the water in twenty."

I frown, why would Shawn be at Hannah's? I was going to shoot off a text asking but I knew I could trust both him and Hannah, I think all these thoughts of Gaynor and Luke are sending my mind into a whirlwind.

I shake all the negative thoughts away and reverse out my drive and pull out into the traffic as I head in the direction of the

184

pub. I think a stiff drink is needed to try to calm all these thoughts.

I push through the door, looking around for Shawn as I make my way to the bar. I came up short so I must have gotten there first. I order two lagers as I wait for Shawn to show up. I take the seat at the bar and wait for the drinks to be brought over as I feel a hand on my shoulder, I glance back and see Shawn taking the seat beside me.

"What's up mate? You look like someone's run over your cat."

"I don't have a cat." I say as I bring my pint up to my mouth.

"I know, but if you did and it was run over, that face is exactly how I would suspect you to look,"

"I'm not in the mood Shawn."

"So, who's died?"

"No one."

"What's going on then?"

"She was having an affair,"

"Who? Hannah?"

"No." I frown as I remember his text. "Unless you have something to tell me?" I raise my brow.

"Why would I? And stop talking in riddles. What's up mate, talk to me."

So, I started from the beginning and told him how I've struggled to contain my feelings for Hannah, which he said you needed to be blind not to see it.

I told him how I spent the afternoon with Hannah, Thomas and Elliott and loved every second of it, then how last week Hannah lay everything out and I decided to follow my heart and ignore my head.

I explained how I had been trying to find the deeds and mortgage paperwork to the bungalow because I needed to look at what I was tied into. How I was just going to sign it over to Gaynor because I didn't want anything to do with it and how I found her diaries and read some of what she had put.

"Did you know that her and Luke were in love?"

"What??"

"As I was reading the diary at first, she talked about this boy she liked the look of, but no name was mentioned, and it was before I'd met her but as the entries went on, she said his name and how in love she was with him." I gulp my lager back before I continue. "It was Luke."

"As in Luke Matthews?"

I nod as I catch the attention of the bartender and point to my empty glass.

"Oh, Wow. I wasn't expecting that."

"Imagine my shock," I say bitterly.

"No wonder he just disappeared. That bastard."

"Hey, I'm not really bothered by the whole situation of them being in love, but they never said anything. He should have come to me as his friend and told me straight." I take a deep breath. "No wonder things have always been strained between us."

I nod to the Barman as he places the pint in front of me.

"Can we have two double whiskies as well please," Shawn asks.

"Yeah, sure. I'll be right back."

"So, what's the plan now?" Shawn asks as he turns away from the bartender.

"I suppose I should talk to Gaynor but what do I say? Hey, I found your diaries, oh and by the way I read them, I know it's a

186

invasion on your privacy, but I was just curious," I sigh in frustration. "Oh, and thanks for being honest about your feelings for Luke and shagging behind my back." I laugh aloud.

"Yeah, I can't see that going down with Duckface very well." he laughs too.

I down my drink in one and enjoy the feeling of the warm alcohol sliding down my throat.

"So, why were you at Hannah's?" I raise my eyes to his. "Don't tell me you're fucking her too behind my back," I smile.

"Nah, mate. I was dropping Liv off. They are having a girl's night in or some shit."

I laugh.

"I really can't believe I never saw it or had any idea it was happening."

"Maybe she hid it well."

"Well let's face it, we've never been that close anyway." I smile. "At least I know she's not a completely heartless bitch, hey."

"You're both not bad people David, just thrown together for other people's gains. Maybe being with Hannah, is what you have been waiting for."

"I think it really is Shawn." I think of her beautiful face and smile. "I can't function unless I see her beautiful face. I hate weekends because I don't see her. To me she is the one. I know it, I feel it in my soul."

"Well, you need to do something about it then because I can tell you she feels the same, every time I catch her watching you, she has love hearts in her eyes."

I smile. I really hope what he was saying was true because I really didn't want to live another day without her and the boys next to me.

187

"Talking about the future, I wanted to ask you something."

"Sound conspicuous,"

"The owner of the remodelling house that we've been working on,"

"Yeah, Mr. Wilson."

"Yeah, he phoned yesterday to say he'd have to pause on the work until next year as his funds had run out and he couldn't afford to carry on, so I asked him if he would be interested in selling it."

"Okay," he frowns.

"It's being valued on Tuesday, and If I can get it cheap enough, I'm going to buy it."

"It has four bedrooms, David."

"Yeah, I know."

"So, it's a bit big, isn't it?"

"Not when Hannah and the boys move in."

"Ah, I'm with you now."

"I want us both to have a fresh start and the house is beautiful. It also has a pool for the boys."

"They'll love it."

"Just keep it under wraps at the moment. I want to see how much they value it and what Mr. Wilson will accept."

"Do you need me to work my magic?" Shawn wiggles his eyebrows. "You know I have a way with the estate agents."

"Only because you've bedded most of them."

"True, but I'm a changed man," he winks.

"Hmmm, has Liv managed to tame the untameable?"

"Mate, Livvy can tame my dick any day of the week. That woman is a tiger in bed," He roars, and I roll around laughing.

I love this man more than life; he has stood by me through some truly awful times and been there when I needed him. He is

188

my soul brother. He gets me like no other. We finish our drinks and I get a taxi; I need to try and sort this mess out as soon as possible.

Chapter Seventeen

Hannah

It's been three whole weeks since my night in the office with David, and I'm starting to feel uneasy, he hasn't mentioned anything about what is happening in his life or if he's talked to his wife about him leaving. He has just turned up to work as normal and acted as if that night and our conversation never happened. I really wanted to march into his office and demand some answers, but he asked for me to trust him, and that's what I am trying to do.

Even if I feel like my mind is going to explode. Each day at the office has been harder than the one before, and with each day that comes there seems to be more conference meetings to torture me with. Every time I must sit beside him and listen to his silky voice demand the attention of everyone in the room and listening to him turns me on. I watch him laugh, joke and just generally be himself with everyone he meets but this waiting is driving me insane.

It is late Thursday afternoon, and for some mad reason I agreed to go for drinks after work with Ben and we are meeting up with Liv, for some food. At the time it seemed like a good idea, but now I'm not feeling it.

As I sit at my computer, I realise I never got to go through the mail this morning because when it came in, I was in a meeting with David, Shawn and a new window company that wanted to be considered for any future work. Therefore, it's been sitting on the edge of my desk since eleven o'clock. I move my coffee and pick up the mail. I skim through the pile, putting the junk in the wastepaper bin, it amazes me how much junk is sent daily.

I then flick through the rest and move them into piles putting David's, into one pile, while Shawn's in another pile.

As I reach the last letter in the pile, I notice it has my name on the envelope, which surprised me as I never have mail sent to my work office. I frown, I can't think of anyone who would send me a letter here and it has been hand delivered as it doesn't contain the address or postage stamp on the envelope.

I place it back on the edge of the desk and think to myself I'll open it a little later as I need to get these sorted and deliver them to David and Shawn, because I'm running out of time. I'm so busy for the next few hours that the letter slips my mind. By the time I finally sit back down in my chair, I have half an hour before I must meet Ben in reception.

As I start tidying my desk up, it catches my eye, so I pick it up and eye it wearily. I have no idea who would send me a letter, but there's only one way to find out. I run my finger under the lip of the envelope and hear the paper rip. I pause as I take a deep breath before pulling the letter from its casing.

I drop the letter to my desk and wonder if I really want to know what is in it? It can only come from a few people and I'm not sure if I want to allow them back into my thoughts. I sit staring emotionless for a few minutes just staring at the paper, lightly biting my bottom lip. As I stare at it, my thoughts run wild, I mean, I don't even know who it has come from, and my pulse is racing.

I close my eyes and decide to just rip the band aid off, so to speak, and pick the damn thing up. So, I do. I reach and pick up the paper with a heavy heart and open the page.

Dearest Hannah,

191

I know I should have made the effort a long time before now and I should have never let your father cast you out. My biggest regret is that I never stopped it before it went too far. Every day I have wished to see you again, and to know you are happy. You will never know how heartbroken I was over your fathers' actions, but life is not always as it seems and if I had my time again, I would have stood up for you and made him see how his behaviour was wrong. I hope that one day you will forgive your loving mother, and we can become known to each other again.

I know you probably don't want anything to do with me and your father passed last month so you will never get to hear how sorry he was from him, but I hope you will listen to my words of sadness and find it in your heart to forgive me.

I know you'll probably find it hard to believe, but your father really did regret his actions, but he was a bigger fool for not admitting it sooner. He will never get the chance to make it right, but I want to. I pray you allow me to re-join your life, I miss my baby girl.

I hope to hear from you, my beautiful daughter soon.

You are forever in my heart,

Mom xx

I take a deep breath of air as my lungs burn because I had held my breath all the while I was reading the letter, not that I had realised I'd done it. I feel the tears building in my eyes as I realise that my father had passed away, I wasn't sure how I felt about that or the fact that my mom wanted to get back in touch.

At nearly twenty-nine, she had been out of my life for twelve whole years, that's a long time for someone to toss you to the side and then expect you to just walk back in. I sigh, I don't know what to make of it all, as if I haven't got enough going on

192

with David, I've now got all the issues of deciding what to do with my family.

I drop my head into my hands as I try to calm my breathing and will, my tears not to drop. If this had dropped in my lap a few years ago, I would have jumped as the chance to have her back in my life, hell maybe even twelve months ago but now, I don't think I'm in the right frame of mind to make this decision.

I hear someone clear their throat at the door, I look up and see a worried Ben, looking back.

"Hey, are you okay?"

I smiled.

"Yeah, I'm fine. I just need to finish off and I'm all yours."

I rush to drop the letter into the top draw of my desk and turn off the computer, while standing and collecting my jacket and bag. As I meet Ben at the door, David is leaving his office too, we make eye contact, and he frowns.

"What's happened?" he strides towards me.

"Nothing, why?"

"Why are you upset then?"

I smile, I love how he can look into my eyes and instantly know something is bothering me.

"I'm fine, honestly. I'm just off out with Ben, enjoy your evening." I smile, even though I'm not feeling it.

⌒⌒⌒⌒⌒⌒⌒⌒⌒

Once we reach Bella Italia, I follow Ben inside. I love this little Italian restaurant, it's so quant and feels like you could be back in a little village in Italy.

I hadn't been here in a few years so when Liv suggested here, I jumped at the chance. Martha was having the boys over night as she had her son's boys staying too, so she thought they would keep each other company.

When we arrived at the restaurant, the hostess directed us to our table at the far-right corner, my favourite place to sit as it gave me a great view of the restaurant and I loved to watch the customers soaking up the Italian atmosphere.

The waiter approached and we told him we were waiting for a friend, so he left us with the wine menu, while he went to serve some others.

I heard the door open and saw Livvy striding in. It always amazed me how she looked perfect even after a nine-hour shift. After I've worked that long; I look like a bird made a nest in my hair with the number of times I've run my fingers through it and my makeup barely makes it to lunchtime.

As she approaches the hostess, she guides her over to our table, and Liv takes the seat opposite mine.

"How's it diddling muckers," she beams.

Ben rolls around laughing, he loves Livvy's personality, I roll my eyes because she loves the attention.

"Fine, until you asked," I winked.

"Well, it's a good job I don't ask often then," she smirked, before turning to Ben.

"How's it hanging Ben,"

"Oh, you know, more to the right than the left,"

"I would see a doctor about that dude, doesn't sound healthy." she grinned.

I actually thought Ben was going to have a heart attack as he continued to laugh, I see a few of the other customers shooting dirty looks our way as we giggled away,

"All right, all right, let's pipe down. We don't want to get thrown out before we eat, now do we?"

"I suppose you're correct," Ben chuckles.

The waiter chooses that moment to come over to take our drink orders and drop off the food menu. I am just looking down the menu as Liv and Ben argue over the bottle of wine we would have; they both saw themselves as wine connoisseurs, while me, I preferred a shot of Taboo with lemonade.

After several changes and a frustrated waiter, the house special rosé is the winner.

While waiting for the waiter to return with our drinks, we take a look at the menu, as I'm scanning down the appetisers, I hear the bell above the door chime again, so I glance up and my eyes bulge.

"Oh my God!! Is that who I think it is?" I say to no one in particular. Out of the corner of my eye I see the other two spin in their seats to see who I was talking about.

"Don't draw attention to us," I whisper to them both.

"Who? What?" Livvy whispers back.

"I can't believe it, David has just walked in. He's talking to the hostess." I watch as he walks back out the main door, then two minutes later I see the top of his head as he comes back in and I peer around the table to the left, where I see a gorgeous lady in a wheelchair, pushing herself towards the furthest table away.

"I can't believe it, he's here having dinner with his wife,"

"Are you sure, Han. It could be a business meeting he forgot to mention," Liv tries to pacify me.

"No, it's definitely his wife. His wife had an accident four or five years ago, which left her in a wheelchair, it's definitely her."

I feel my pulse rising as I watch him help her to the table, moving the chair so she can push her wheelchair in. As I watch them interact, I don't see the animosity that he talks about, from the outside it looks like a couple enjoying a beautiful meal.

The waiter arrives back, he opens the wine, and pours a little into the three glasses sitting on the table. I take my glass and chug the wine down, not tasting a single drop.

"Yep, that will do, can we have a couple of bottles, please?"

I see the waiter frown at my words but proceeds to fill our glasses as I continue to gulp the delicious wine. I feel the alcohol warm my blood as I continue to watch David's exchange with his wife. I know I need to look away, but I can't manage to drag my eyes from them both. I pull the menu up to cover my face as I feel a defeated sigh leaves my lips. I try to concentrate on the items listed on the menu, but I've read the same meal for the last few minutes.

"Do you want to leave?" Ben askes. I shake my head as I know if we got up and left, we would draw attention to us, and David would see me.

"I don't know about you two, but let's get pissed," Livvy suggests.

I smile at her.

"That's the best idea you've had for a good few months." I reply flatly.

"Well, I do have them, occasionally." she smiles as she refills our drinks.

I pick up my glass and take a sip of the wine, as my eyes glide across the restaurant again. I see her smile at the waiter as he places a bottle of wine on the table, and they order their food.

I flip my eyes back to my friends as I see them both watching me intently. I think they're waiting for me to break down, which I might, if not about David being with his wife, then

196

about the letter I received from my mum earlier. I smile as another waiter arrives at the table, I order meatballs and spaghetti, while Liv orders Lasagne and salad and Ben has Carbonara. I ask for a couple of extra servings of Garlic bread, my comfort food. If I was going to endure David with his wife, I was going to make sure I eat something that would make me feel happier, well that and a couple of bottles of wine.

"So, how was your day?" I ask Liv quietly.

"It was okay. I didn't have to kill anyone yet, so that was a positive. How was yours."

"Okay." I smile sadly. "I received a letter from mom, and it made me sad that I had missed twelve years of her being in my life. When I read it, I wasn't sure I wanted her back in mine or the boy's life but I think I might need her."

"Are you sure? It's not the alcohol talking is it?"

"I don't know. My father passed away last month or so, she says, and I think it would be nice to have a family involved in my life."

"I'm sorry Hannah, was that why you were upset in your office when I came to fetch you?"

I nod.

"Not so much about my father's passing, he was like Hitler. If you didn't do things his way, you were cut from his life, but my mom didn't have a say in how her life was run. She just toed the line, you know." they both nodded.

I took another gulp of wine as I heard his wife laugh at something David had said and I started to think that maybe things aren't as bad as he said they were. Had he just said that to get me to sleep with him. I wouldn't think so as he seemed like an honest man. I pull my eyes from them both.

197

"I don't know, I want her in my life, but it's been so long, we've both changed, who's to say we'd even get on. I just think this has come at the wrong time, I've got lots going on and I need to focus on myself," I let my eyes find David again and I see they are both in a discussion, his wife seems to be sucking on a lemon, as the waiters approach them with their food. I tear my eyes away, I need to trust him, like he asked me to do.

"So, Ben tell us about your date with Mr Dreamy, last weekend,"

"Oh, where do you want me to start?"

"The beginning is usually the best place, dude." Liv pulls his leg.

"Well as you know it was a blind date, I was so nervous, I nearly didn't show up. I couldn't get my hair to fall right, my jeans felt horrible and the shirt I was planning to wear just pulled wrong across my chest, so before I got there, I was one hundred percent stressed," he waved his hands around. "But I shit you not, once I walked in and introduced myself to Callum, I felt the tension leave my shoulders. He was perfect in every way."

"Did you bang him then, come on, don't hold out on me," Liv wiggled her eyebrow as Ben blushed.

"We didn't,"

"What?!?"

"I thought you said he was perfect in every way?" I exclaim.

"And that's why I won't be seeing him again."

"I don't understand, Ben,"

"I can't be with someone so perfect, Hannah. I would constantly be wondering if I am good enough."

My eyes drift over to David, and I wonder the same about myself, if I am good enough for him, I shake my head and return my eyes back to Ben.

"Ben, anyone who ends up with you would be extremely lucky."

"Ditto, Hannah." he stared at me with a raised eyebrow.

"It's totally different, Ben and you know it. You have no baggage or exes."

"That may be right, but your baggage is pretty amazing, don't you agree Liv?" Ben asks.

"Hannah, how many times do we need to talk about your baggage? Anyone would be a lucky man to have you and the boys."

I smile as I take another swig of my wine, willing my eyes not to search for David again, but they do, and I see them back in deep conversation. I wish I could see David's face and be able to lip read what he is saying.

The waiter's approach with our meal and starts placing the plates on the table, then leaves us to enjoy our food. We all start tucking in, I need some food to soak up the alcohol. I wouldn't normally drink this much or this fast.

I ask Liv how Matty was behaving at work, then continue to fill Ben in on my disaster of a date with Livvy's co-worker and how he was only interested in himself and talked about his crush on Liv. After we had finished laughing, eating and talking I glanced at the time and realised it was well past ten.

"I think it's time for me to make a move, I need to be up early in the morning, and I have to take Martha to a hospital appointment before I go into work. I'll just phone a taxi."

"No need," Liv said. "I've text Lenny to see if he was near about five minutes ago and he said he was just around the corner so he would pick us all up and drop us home,"

"That's so kind of him," I smile.

I hear the bell chime above the door, and it opens. I see Lenny stride in. He stands for a minute and looks around the restaurant before his eyes land on mine. I blush, as I see his smile widen, he must have known I was avoiding him because any time he messages to see if I have plans or wants to arrange something with the boys, I'm always busy. I didn't want it to be this way, but I don't want to lead him on. He marches past the hostess stand and heads straight for our table, I stand to grab my jacket but as I start to put it on, I feel him pull it from my hands and take over.

"Let me," he mumbles behind me.

Whether it's the alcohol, stress of the day or David sitting with his wife, I allow him to put my coat on and put his arm across my shoulders. I know I feel nothing for the man, but I also know he wants more and allowing him to put his arm across my shoulder will give him the wrong idea.

Once we've got everything, I watch Ben and Liv move towards the front of the restaurant, I glance in their direction as I let Lenny guide me to follow. Just as we reach the hostess, Livvy asks for the bill and starts laughing and joking with Ben, drawing the attention of all the customers in here. I close my eyes momentarily as I feel his eyes upon me, I'm frightened to open them because I know it's not going to end well. I try to step out from under Lenny's arm, but he grips me tighter, that is until I feel him ripped away from me as an angry, David seethes in front of us.

"What the fuck is going on here?" He bellows.

Lenny looks between us with a frown.

"What the fuck has it got to do with you, Arsehole?" Lenny squares up to David.

"David, you need to go back to your wife, you are making a scene." I step between them both.

"He's here with his wife?" Lenny repeats. "Man, if you would rather take your wife out than be completely with Hannah, you are seriously fucked up. For me Hannah would always be my priority." Lenny stares at David.

David looks down into my eyes. He grabbed my arm and marched me around the corner to the corridor that led to the toilets.

"I'm here to sort out our divorce. I thought I would try to end our marriage better than it started," he whispers. "I asked you to trust me. And now I see you're on a date without so much as a thought of me?"

I feel my cheeks flush.

"It's not a date," I whisper back. "Lenny has just picked us up. I came out with Liv and Ben, but I had too much to drink to drive, so Liv messaged Lenny to pick us up."

He raised his hands to my face and drops his lips to my mouth. The moment his mouth connects with mine, I feel today's stress drain away and my mind empties with nothing but thoughts of him. He enters my mouth with an urgency that tells me he needs me as much as I need him. Our tongues twist together as the kiss intensifies. I hear a sound behind me, but I don't want to lose this feeling. I can't explain how he makes everything alright with just one kiss.

"We are ready to go Hannah," I hear Liv behind me.

I want to tell her to leave without me, but I know it would be no use, his wife is still at the table and he needs to get her home. I slowly peel my lips from his as my heart begins to flutter. David rests his forehead against mine.

"I would have much preferred it to be you who was sitting in front of me tonight, but I need to do this properly, so that when I am finally free, you will be the centre of my world," he kissed my forehead and stood up straight.

I took a step back, steadying myself on my wobbly legs, was it just the alcohol, making me lightheaded or was it the kiss that sent my body into a frenzied need.

"I will call you later, to make sure you made it home okay," he nodded his head in the direction my friends were standing.

"I'll speak to you later," I say barely above a whisper.

I turn and walk towards Livvy who is standing just inside the door, as she grabs my arm to pull me through the door into the dark night air. I glance back and see David watching, I smile and leave through the door. I take a deep breath but as the fresh air hits my lungs, my head begins to spin.

Chapter Eighteen

David

I hated watching Hannah leave the office upset this afternoon, even though she tried to play it off, I wondered if her tears had been something to do with me. If I had not already emailed Gaynor, to ask her to have a meal with me tonight to try to end things, amicably I would have taken Hannah to my office. I wanted to put things in motion. I might not love the woman, but she too was a victim of circumstances and family expectations.

As I watch Ben comfort Hannah, I feel my heart splinter knowing I'm not the one she leant on. I was tempted to get on the elevator with them, but I could not put myself in the enclosed space and not touch her, so I allowed them to go ahead and waited for the lift to come back up.

As I walked to my car, my phone vibrated in my pocket, and I sighed. I did not want to talk to anyone, I just wanted to get through tonight and start looking to my future, hopefully with Hannah. I pull my phone out of my pocket and see my father's name on the screen. Nah, I groan to myself I am not dealing with that arsehole now, I need to keep my game head on tonight so I can get through a whole meal with Gaynor without making her angry.

I jump into my car, as I watch Hannah pull out of the carpark with Ben. I wonder where they are heading, but as I glance at the time, I know I don't have much time to over think it as I must pick Gaynor up and be at the restaurant before long. I pull out into the traffic as I listen to the radio, while I drive across town, I try not to think too much of what I am going to say to Gaynor. I just want to talk to her about how sad we both are and that her being with someone else will make her happy.

I pull up in front of the bungalow and see Gaynor waiting just outside the front door as I pull onto the drive, I see her wheeling herself towards the car. I get out of my side and walk around to open her door for her to get in, so I can put her chair into the car boot.

"You look nice," I smile.

"Thank you. It's just a shame you never said that before," she snipes.

I shake my head as I shut the passenger door, I can see how tonight's going to go but she can snipe all she likes, tonight I get my life back.

Once I shut the boot, I sit in my seat and put the car into reverse. The car is deathly silent as we make our way to the little Italian restaurant that was about half an hour from our house. I was going to ask if she had done anything today but thought better of it after the last time.

Once I have spoken to the hostess, we get settled at our table and I take my seat with my back to the restaurant because I do not want anyone to distract me while we have this talk.

The staff are so attentive and make a fuss over Gaynor. I wait to see if she will be irritated by their treatment but tonight, she eats it up. I smile as they take our drink order and then our food. When they walk away, I sense Gaynor's eyes on me.

"So" she says in her sarcastic voice.

"So," I repeat.

"What exactly are we doing here, David?"

"Don't mess around Gaynor," I smile.

"Why waste time beating around the bush?" She raises her eyebrows.

I see the bartender approaching the table with our drinks, so I pause while he places our drinks down.

"I thought it was about time we spoke about what we both want in our future,"

"Oh."

I watch her fidget in her chair and I sense she wants to say something, but she is holding back. I look her in the eyes.

"Is this how you want to continue your life? To be with someone that you do not really love?"

She drops her eyes to her wine glass as she contemplates my words.

"I know about Luke," I whisper as her eyes jolt to mine. "Don't worry, I'm not upset. I just wished you both would have come to me."

"How did you find out? We never meant to hurt you; we just couldn't help the attraction. We tried for so long to stay away from each other, but we couldn't fight it any longer."

"How long?"

"The first time was the night before the wedding, and we continued up until the accident. But recently I have started to see him again."

I nod my head and stare down at my fingers, trying to find the words for what I brought her here for.

"I want us to get divorced." I just rip the band aid off. I am not playing games again; it is now or never.

"Okay, but I don't understand why now."

"I've met someone, and I don't want to start something with her until I'm free to give her everything."

205

"Do I know her?" I shake my head. "She is one lucky woman. I know I've never appreciated who you were or what you did for me, but I will always be grateful to you, David."

I smile sadly as our food arrives.

"So, what happens now? Do you want me to move out?" She asks timidly.

"No, of course not, in fact I want to sign the house over to you," I hear the sharp intake of breath.

"What? I don't understand."

"In the divorce I get the business and you get the bungalow to do with what you want; I don't want it and it's perfect for you."

"I don't know what to say. In another life, another galaxy I would have been proud to have called you my husband,"

"Look, it is what it is, we were victims of circumstances and I think we should both find our happily ever after's," I smile.

"Thank you. So, tell me about this woman you've met."

"She's the one I've been waiting for all my life." I drop my eyes once again, feeling guilty that she would never mean that much to me. "Sorry, I shouldn't have said that."

"No don't be silly. We were never meant to be forever." she smiles caringly. "So, tell me all about her,"

"She is like a full moon on a dreary night breaking through the clouds. She's funny, loyal and free." I smile as I think of the most beautiful woman I have ever met. "She has two boys from a previous marriage, she helped me realise that I was unhappy even though I tried to do right by you."

"I'm sorry David, I know I haven't been easy to live with, but I've found it so hard to keep the hurt and anger away from all that I had to give up. I forgot you had to give up things too."

Just as we are finishing off our meal, I hear who I thought sounded like Liv being loud, laughing and joking around with someone who sounded like Ben and I was confused until I looked over my shoulder and saw them by the hostess, settling the bill.

As I look behind them, I see Hannah standing with a man's arm around her shoulders. I try to control the anger building inside me, before I know what I am doing, I march up to them and rip Hannah from under his arm.

"What the fuck is going on here?" I bellow.

The clown looks between us with a frown on his ugly mug.

"What the fuck has it got to do with you, Arsehole?" he squares up to me, I smile because he would stand no chance if I decided to punch his lights out.

"David, you need to go back to your wife, you are making a scene." Hannah steps between us.

"He's here with his wife?" Dick exclaims. "Man, if you would rather take your wife out than be completely with Hannah, you are seriously fucked up. For me, Hannah would always be my priority." Dickhead stares straight into my eyes, even though on the outside I look calm, I am seething on the inside.

How could she go out on a date with this clown, while I'm here finishing my marriage to be with her.

I look down into her eyes as I grab her arm and march her around the corner to the corridor that leads to the toilets.

"I'm here to sort out my divorce. I thought I would try to end my marriage better than it started," I whisper. "I asked you to trust me. And now I see you're on a date without so much as a thought of me?"

I see her cheeks flush.

"I'm not on a date David, who do you think I am?" She whispers back. "Lenny has just picked us up. I went out with Liv and Ben, but I've had too much drink to drive, so Liv messaged Lenny to pick us up."

I raise my hands to her face and drop my lips to hers. The moment my mouth connects with hers, I enter her mouth with an urgency that tells her, I need her as much as she needs me. As our tongues twist together, I feel the kiss intensify. I hear a sound behind me, but I need to try to make her understand that I am not going anywhere with just this kiss.

"We are ready to go Hannah," I hear Liv behind me.

I want to tell her to stay with me, but I know I cannot yet, because I need to get Gaynor home. I slowly peel my lips from her mouth as my heart slowly breaks. I rest my forehead against hers, I need to make her understand that she is the one and I will only ever want her.

"I would have much preferred it to be you who was sitting in front of me tonight, but I need to do this properly, so that when I am finally free, and you will be the centre of my world," I kiss her forehead and stand straight.

"I will call you later, to make sure you made it home okay," I nod my head in the direction of where her friends were standing.

"I'll speak to you later," she says barely above a whisper.

I watch her walk towards Livvy who is standing just inside the door, as she grabs her arm to pull her through the door, and I make my way back over to Gaynor.

"She's definitely a keeper," she winks.

"I need to leave. Are you ready?"

"Yeah, I'm ready. If she makes you happy, I wish you well David."

"She does, Gaynor. I've never felt like this before or ever will again."

"I'm happy for you."

I walk over to the hostess to get the bill; I pay with my card and meet Gaynor by the entrance. I rub my tired eyes and stifle a yawn, as I follow her back to my car.

After she is safe in her seat and the wheelchair is back in the boot, I start the car and make my way back home. My thoughts are running wild with images of that dicks arm around Hannah's shoulder.

"You have nothing to worry about, you know."

I flick my eyes over to Gaynor with a frown on my face.

"She only had eyes for you."

"What do you mean?"

"From the moment she saw us sitting down, I noticed she kept looking over to our table, but I thought it was because I was in a wheelchair but obviously it was because the love of her life was there with his wife," she winked.

I smiled.

"I thought it was strange that she kept looking towards us. She was obviously tracking her man."

"Gaynor, I need to say sorry."

"What for?" I see her watching me.

"If I could have swapped places with you and it had been me in that accident, I would have."

"David, it wasn't your fault."

"It was, I asked you to pick up my suit from the dry cleaners."

"I never told you before, because I always felt guilty, but it wasn't your fault. It was mine. I had been with Luke and didn't realize the time, when I noticed I rushed off and I didn't notice the lorry until it was too late. If I hadn't been distracted or thinking about Luke, I wouldn't have been in that accident."

I sit there, biting my lip, staring out the front of the car as I continued our journey home, trying to take in everything she had just said. I feel the anger building as I realized all these years, I felt guilty for the accident, all the time I had wished I could have swapped places and it was not my fault. I try to calm my breathing as I feel my emotions pushing to be released. I pull into the driveway and put the car into park, as I put my hand break on and rub my hands across my face as I try to stop the tears, I feel building from pouring down my face.

"David, say something." she whimpers.

I just sit there staring straight ahead, I try to understand everything that she had said. All these years I have blamed myself, all the times I have not been able to look in the mirror because of the hate I felt for myself and it was all for what?

I do not know how to react; I do not know what to say. I just sat and stared into the black sky. I open my door and lift out her chair from the boot. I need to get her out of the car and give myself some space.

"I need you to go in the house now?" I say quietly as I open the car door while I push her chair next to her.

"We need to talk about this David," she cries.

"NO!" I shout. "We've had plenty of time to talk about everything, but you chose to keep me in the dark and made me feel it was my fault,"

"I was trying to clear the air and be totally honest about everything."

"Four years too late, Love," I sigh. "Now go inside. I need some space."

I see her lift herself into her chair and wheel it to the front door, she pauses before she opens it.

"I am really sorry. I have wanted to say something for an awfully long time, but mum said it would make everything worse,"

"It couldn't have been any worse for me, Gaynor?" I say as I slam the car door, before walking back around the bonnet, then climbing into the driver's seat and reverse out of the drive.

I pull into the carpark, just outside the park I came with Hannah, Thomas, and Elliott. I turn off the engine and I stare at the area and smile at the memories we made. I cannot believe I wasted so much time feeling guilty about everything and put Gaynor's happiness before mine.

I must have twat tattooed on my forehead because that is exactly how she has made me feel, like a stupid twat. I glance at the time and I see its midnight, I did not realize I had been driving around so long.

I pull my phone from my pocket and pull up Hannah's number.

I hear the dialling tone ring twice before Hannah picks up.

"David, is that you?"

"It is. Are you home now?"

"I've been home for ages. Where are you?"

"I need some space, so I drove to the carpark by the park."

"Are you alone?"

"Who else is going to be here Hannah?" I sigh in frustration.

"I wasn't sure. Give me five minutes and I will be there."

"Hannah it's too...." the line went dead before I could finish.

I lie my head back and close my eyes as I think about the cluster fuck of an evening I've just had. Why can't my life be easy for once, instead of being such a mess. I must doze off because before I know it, there is a tap on the window, and I jump in fright.

"Fuck. Hannah." I slowly unlock my doors as Hannah runs round to get in the passenger side.

"Sorry, I didn't mean to make you jump."

"It's okay, I just wasn't expecting you yet."

She smiles and reaches for my hand as she threads her fingers through mine.

"So, how did it go?" She gives my hand a little squeeze.

"As good as it could." I sigh.

"So, what's next?"

I take my hand and place it delicately on her cheek, as I pull her face towards me, I place a kiss on her forehead.

"Next," I look into her eyes as she slightly nods her head. "Next, I kiss you until I can't work out where your lips start and mine ends." I lower my lips until they meet Hannah's in a rush of emotions, that stampede throughout my body, I am lost in everything that is her and I never want to be found.

As we sit in the car kissing, I feel my arousal growing, as the sexual tension builds between us.

I pull her over and into my lap as I run my hands through her hair, while I continue to kiss her mouth like I would die if she pulled away. She wraps me in her arms as I feel the stress of the evening fade. I drop my hand to her breasts and find her pebbled nipples under her top.

I feel myself start to lose control. She will never know how much I need her to survive, every breath I take when she is not with me, just seems a waste. She is the air that keeps me alive, she is the stars in my sky, the sunshine after a cloudy day and I need to feel her wrapped around my cock.

So, I drop my hand to her leg and start to push her skirt up her delectable legs, as I slowly raise it up her soft skin, I kiss along her jaw with my other hand on her neck to hold her in place.

As I reach the top of her thigh, I let my hand drift toward her centre, but as I get closer, I realize she has no underwear on. I pull back to look in her eyes as the smile on her face tells me she did this on purpose.

"I didn't want to waste any time," she blushes as she shrugs.

This woman right here, is everything and more to me. I drop a kiss to the corner of her mouth as my heart leaps in my chest.

"Do you have any idea what you do to me?"

She drops her eyes to my chest.

"Don't do that," I whisper as I place a finger under chin to bring her eyes back to mine. "Do not ever doubt how much I need you, Hannah. I thank God every day that I met you that night back in the club,"

"Me too," she hoarsely replies as she drops her hands to the button of my trousers. "I need you, David."

"Not as much as I need you, Baby."

I dip my finger into her centre and feel she is already wet, my mouth waters but in the limited space we have, I know I cannot feast on her at this moment. I feel Hannah's hand on my stiff cock as she grips and raises her hand to the tip, I pull her hand away because I know I will not last much longer if she carries on.

I pull her closer in my lap so my cock lines up with her entrance, I feel the heat of her pussy hovering over my tip, as the urge to impale her becomes too much.

"David, please." she pants as she tries to push down on me.

I thrust up, pausing as I enjoy the sensation. I love being inside Hannah, it is my most favourite place in the world, I have never felt at home anywhere else but when I am inside this beautiful woman, I know where I belong. I continue to kiss along her jaw, as I start to drive my cock in deeper and with fluid strokes. I feel Hannah's core tightening, so I know she is as close as I am.

"Where have you been all my life," I whisper as all my emotions wash over me like a tsunami, I am drowning in the love I feel for this woman.

"I was waiting for you," she puffed out as her orgasm took over and she squeezes me tightly, I feel myself falling off the edge as I came inside of her.

Every fear I had been holding onto had just been released with that orgasm, I now know that I am on the home straight and once I have my divorce filed, I can start to breathe properly and make plans to be with Hannah for the rest of my life. As we sit in the steamy car, with her in my arms I know that with Hannah beside me I can face anything.

As her head rests on my chest, with my arms encasing her, I thought she had fallen asleep but as I kiss her forehead, and whisper I love her, she lifts her head and looks into my eyes.

"Not as much as I love you, David." she leans forwards and connects with my lips.

I know this exactly where I am meant to be.

Chapter Nineteen

Hannah

"Hannah, we have a working lunch today, is that going to be a problem?" I hear from behind me by the door to my office.

"No, of course, not." I smile as I glance over my shoulder.

"Great, I've booked a table at The Buxton Inn, we will need to be there at twelve. I have the file, but you will need the laptop to make notes," David smiled.

"Sounds good to me. See you in a bit."

"Oh, and I'll drive no point having two cars going to the same place,"

"Yeah, okay," I replied as I glanced at my watch to see the time, and I noticed we need to be leaving in ten minutes. "Just give me two minutes to put everything together and I will meet you at the elevator."

"Perfect see you in a minute." I saw him rush from my office to pick up his things.

I had not been in the office long as I had to take Martha to a hospital appointment. I rubbed my tired eyes and sighed as I grabbed my coffee mug on my desk. I think I will need several of them today to get my arse moving. I did not leave David's car until two am this morning, as I did not want to leave the comfort of David's arms, but I knew I needed to get back and grab a few hours or I would be worthless today.

I pull open my top draw and spray some Jean Paul Gaultier on. If I am going to be in a car with David, I know I am going to start sweating with him being so close. Once I am sorted, I leave my office and head for the elevator, surprised to find David already there.

"You were quick?" I smiled.

"Yeah, when I know what I want I don't waste time." he winks.

The elevator arrives and David places his hand out in front of him, to allow me to walk on first. I love knowing he is watching me walk in, so I let my hips have a little more swagger than normal to make sure he enjoys the view. As we both stand side by side, I feel the energy building. Knowing David is leaving his wife, is making it hard to keep my distance and all the naughty things I want to do to him. I shake my head as I try to clear my dirty thoughts, but as I glance towards David. I see his sexy smirk.

"What are you smirking about," I ask as I crave his lips on mine.

"I was just thinking, I have about two hours to get through this afternoon and the kinds of thoughts I am having are not going to make this any easier."

The energy in the lift has my whole-body tense so much that I was praying David has the urge to push me up against the wall and kiss me. I hear the bell chime as the door opens. *Saved by the bell,* I think to myself, and I smile.

We walk out to the car in silence, as I try to put my game head on, I need to get my brain working so that I can make sure I take notes correctly.

When we reach the car, David opens the passenger door for me and I feel his eyes on my legs as I climb in and take a seat. He closes the door as I readjust myself on the chair and try to get comfortable. I watch David walk around the front of the car with purpose and quickly jump into his seat, then he leans over to

216

reach for my seat belt and clicks it in; to make sure it is on. As soon as I'm close enough to his neck, I inhale his gorgeous as hell scent, I know it goes beyond boss and employee guidelines, but I could not resist it.

"Did you just smell me?" he asks in a humorous voice.

"Hmm... I don't think so," I blush.

"I think you just smelt me," he grins.

I know it is no good denying it because he obviously heard me inhale.

"Would it make me weird if I said, I love your smell?"

"No but it might make me want to fuck you." He laughs. "I need to change the direction of this chat before my cock hardens and I have to pull over to have my wicked way."

I knew he would call me out, but the way he shook his head to clear his thoughts of us fucking, has me hornier than ever. I cross my legs to try to contain my desire; so, with a small smile, I look out of the window. David starts the car, reversing out of the space, and makes his way towards the Inn. The silence is unbearable, especially in this small space.

David must think the same because with the flick on the button on his steering wheel, music filled the car. I freeze as Lionel Richie starts to play; I was totally surprised he would listen to someone like this, then notice it is a CD so he must have put it on while he was on his drive into work today, as the sound of Three Times A Lady filled the car.

"Lionel Richie?" I raise my eyebrow, "I had you down more for a Rag'n'Bone Man, Man."

"Would it make me sound cool if I said, my mum loved Lionel?"

I was surprised that he wanted to talk about his mum, he never ever mentioned her before. I smile at him; I am happy that he feels comfortable to start to reveal parts of his past with me.

"To many women, probably would not but to me, I'd say, you've earned some brownie points and you are very cool."

I watch his shoulders drop as he starts to relax. I see him try to keep his eyes on the road but out of the corner of his eye, I see them drop to my skirt as it rides up my legs. I see his fingers tapping lightly on the steering wheel like his trying to fight the urge to touch my skin.

"Note one, Hannah likes Lionel."

"I wouldn't say I like him but it's cute that you listen to the music that your mum likes,"

He takes his eyes off the road for a second and glances over to me.

"Liked. She died when I was fourteen."

I take a heavy breath, as my heart drops through my stomach.

"I'm so sorry David, I didn't know."

"It's okay. It was a long time ago but sometimes I'll put her music on to feel close to her, you know."

I drop my hand onto his thigh to try to offer some comfort. I move in my seat, so I am slightly facing him as I take another deep breath.

"I do. My Mum isn't dead, but I haven't seen her since I was sixteen." I pause, I never really mention my family, in fact I hate talking about my parents, and my dad dying has really registered yet. "But when I miss my mum, I usually do some baking because it was our weekly thing and that helps me to feel close to what I don't have anymore."

"Do you want to talk about it?" He asks hesitantly.

218

"There's not much to say. When I met my ex-husband, my father did not agree with me dating him. Then I found out I was pregnant, six months after meeting Ian. My father told me to choose between my family and him, so I chose and haven't heard or spoken to them since."

He nods his head as I see him search for something to say.

"I'm sorry. That had to be hard, especially being so young and pregnant?"

"It was at first, as every girl needs their mum when they are pregnant, but I learnt to lean on myself and get on with it,"

"Were you close to your ex-husbands family?"

"Not really, his mum died giving birth to him, so it was always him and his dad, but his dad was always strange and had many sketchy deals going on in the garage he owned."

"Well, I think you are truly amazing and so strong too."

"Thank you, David, that means a lot. Especially after the last few years, I had started to doubt I could do the whole single parent deal." I smiled sadly.

"Let me tell you, Hannah, you are the best thing that ever happened to the boys." he pauses like he wanted to add something else but thought better of it.

I smile and turn back to look out of the window, just as David pulls into the carpark of The Buxton Inn and finds a space. He put the car into park and lifted the hand brake. We pause for a second as I tried to calm my rampant thoughts and not show him that I had noticed his hardened cock.

"Stay there, I'll come round and open your door," he says as he jumps from the car.

He rushes around, and opens my door, then offers me his hand as I take it, he helps me to get out of the car. Once I am on my feet, I bend back into the car to reach for my laptop and make

219

sure I give David an unobstructed view of my arse. I stand back up, I look down towards his hardened cock and see it straining against his suit trousers. I see David turn away and rearrange his pants.

"We need to get in there before I do something stupid and get arrested for indecent exposure in a public place, that would give Shawn years of pleasure." I hear him mumble.

When we walk through the door of the Inn, I notice that it is particularly quiet today and we are the only ones here. We walk over to the bar as David speaks to the bartender and tells him we were booked in for a business meeting lunch. He smiled and asked if we were all here as he eyed me, so I stepped closer to David and let my hand brush his. I could feel David step closer to me too as he told him we were waiting for the owner of Parkers Building Suppliers to arrive, so he asked us what we wanted to drink, while we waited for Mr. Norman to arrive.

We took a seat on the bar stools as the bartender sorted his lager and my wine.

"Do you think you'll ever speak again," David says aloud while I am lost in thought.

"Talk to who?" I glance over to him.

"You and your parents,"

"I always hoped they would come round, but they never got in contact, so neither did I. I feel a little hurt over the way I was treated, and I am also a little stubborn. If they did not want to be in my life or my children's then, I wouldn't beg them."

"I understand that." He smiles.

"Actually, when you asked yesterday why I was upset as I left my office, it was because I received a letter from my mum,"

"Oh," he frowns. "Are you going to write back?"

"I don't know." I sigh. "I miss my mum, obviously and in the letter my mum told me my father passed away last month but I don't know whether I want her in the boy's life, just in case she decides she doesn't want us again."

"I get that but what if she doesn't feel like that way anymore? What if she wants to be in your life and always has but because of your father she did not have any choice?"

"Maybe." I smile. I do not think making decisions on hardly any sleep will end well so I change the subject. "Do you get on with your dad?"

"That's another sad story." He frowns as the bartender places his drink in front of him.

"You don't have to tell me if you don't want to."

"No, it's not that. I do not have the best relationship with him. I never actually met him until I was fourteen," My eyes filled with surprise as my mouth formed an O. "I was the illegitimate child, my father met my mum while she was working for my grandfather, she was a trainee receptionist. She fell madly in love with him. They hid everything from my father's family but just before she found out she was expecting me, my father called it off, saying he was expected to marry his wife now Clara."

"Oh my, so what happened after that?" I look into his eyes. "Only if you want to tell me that is,"

"Of course, I do. My father married Clara, but then once they were married, he missed my mum, so he contacted her and apologised for the way my grandfather had treated her. She was nine months pregnant, and he promised her that once he gained the company from my grandfather, he would divorce Clara and then marry my mum, so they continued without his family knowledge. When I arrived, it made mum's life hard." He smiled sadly. "My father kept me secret from my grandfather, until my mum was ill with cancer."

"Wow."

"Yeah, I don't think it helped that my father's wife couldn't have children as she has medical issues. Mum always dreamed of my father choosing her, but it never happened, then she found out she had cancer just before my fourteenth birthday, after a short battle she passed away. Then I was packed up and hauled into their life. If it had not been for Joyce and Albert, I would have been probably in prison."

"The lady I met in my interview?"

He smiled as I referred to the day that changed my life.

"Yes, Mrs. Barkley. She was like my grandmother. Always there when I needed her and so was her husband, Albert."

"It's good that you had someone especially after losing your mum."

"It was. They were really supportive and helped me set up this business, just don't mention that to my father," He winked. "They were never blessed with children, and it was something that weighed heavily on Joyce for many years."

"My lips are sealed," I smiled. As he glanced at the time, and we realized we had been here for over forty-five minutes and Mr. Norman had not turned up yet.

David clicked open his Calendar on his phone and looked at the date of the meeting, I saw the look on his face and wondered what the matter was.

"You are not going to believe this,"

"What, what's happened?"

"I've got the wrong day,"

The laughter starts to roll from my lips, I cannot control my laughter.

"Really? I did think it was strange that I hadn't seen it when I checked the Calendar this morning,"

"I'm fucking stupid. It is not even this month. It's next."

"Oh well, nobody's dead," I wink.

"Well, we may as well have lunch. I mean, we are already here now." David smiles.

He waves his hand towards the bartender to catch his attention and tells him it will be just the two of us that will need a table. I should really be frustrated at the amount of work I have missed, but I can't be, because it allowed me to spend some quality time with David and if I was not hundred percent about how I felt about him before, well I am now.

As we are shown to our table, I cannot pull my eyes from David's face, I struggle to take the menu from the servers' hands as she passes it over.

"If you keep looking at me like that, we won't make it through this meal, Hannah." David continues to look at the menu.

"How do you know that I am looking at you," I frown in confusion as his eyes have not left the menu.

"I always know when your eyes are on me, Hannah. You set my skin on fire,"

I blush, biting my lip as his words wash over me, and lights my desire. I shift in my seat, trying to tighten my thighs to relieve some of the pressure. Before I know what is happening, I hear David's chair scrape across the wooden floor as he stands and pulls his wallet from his trouser pocket, he opens the clasp and fingers his notes as he chucks several on the table then reaches for my hand.

"Fuck, lunch," he grumbles, as he leads me from the table and towards the exit.

"I thought you were hungry,"

223

"I am, but not for food, well not that can be cooked in a kitchen, anyway." he winks, over his shoulder as he changes direction and heads for the Inn's reception desk.

"I thought we were leaving?"

"So, did I but I know I won't last until we get back. Do you have a room we can book?" he asks the receptionist.

I see her drop her eyes to the screen and flick her mouse across her desk.

"We have a double room with an en-suite available for the next three days, Sir."

"I just need the room for this afternoon," he replies as he chucks his credit card on the desk.

"Oh, okay." she replies as she busies herself to fill the online paperwork. I see David's foot tapping as the lady slowly takes his details.

"Okay, I have everything filled in. You will be in room Ten," she reaches behind her and pulls the key from the rack.

"Thank you," David replies quickly as he grabs my hand and dashes for the elevator. While we are waiting for it to arrive, he pulls me in front of him and pushes his hips forwards and I feel his arousal. I hiss as I feel his cock press in between my arse cheeks.

As the doors slide open, I am breathless as my desire continues to build. I feel the electricity sizzling between us, before we have even entered. We step on to the lift, as an older couple steps on after us, we both step back until we reach the back wall on the elevator to give them some room. I glance towards David out of the corner of my eyes and see him staring straight ahead as I start to fidget, I feel David fingers link with mine and I bite my lip.

I see the smirk on his beautiful full lips, and I know he is trying to hold in his laugh. Once we reach our floor, David pulls me along the corridor as he places the key in the lock, pushing me up against the wooden door, he cups the back of my neck as he brings my lips to his. I feel his tongue glide across my lips, asking for entrance, so I open my mouth and groan as I taste the lager on his tongue.

"We need to get into this bloody room, before I take you in this corridor."

I blush as I look up into his deep ocean blue eyes.

"As long as I feel you deeply, I'm not bothered where you do me." I wink.

"Are you trying to kill me?"

I shake my head as I feel his hand leave my hip and search for the door handle and open the door while I try not to fall on to my arse from the loss of the wood that was keeping me upright.

We stagger into the room, all hands and mouth, I feel his hands unbuttoning my blouse as I lean forwards to unbutton David's shirt. We both struggle to undress each other in between our heated kisses. I manage to take off my blouse and skirt by the time we reach the bed, I feel him push me back as I land on my back.

David pushes my legs open and kneels before me, then glides his nose along my groin until he reaches my black thong covering my pussy. I feel David slide the material to the side as he runs his tongue along my lips. I feel his breath blow across my skin as my skin starts to prickle. My head falls back on the mattress as I feel him pause to remove my panties, just when I think I'm going to scream from him taking too long.

The sensation of the first lick from his tongue on my clit has me jumping in surprise as he circles my little nub, and his

225

fingers continues to push into my core, pushing past my entrance and hitting my G-spot as I leap into the air. I feel David push down on my hips as he tries to control my movements so I can enjoy all he has to offer me.

I grip the material of the duvet in my fists as I know I will not last much longer. I start to feel the intense feeling of excitement as my orgasm starts to build, as I lie here in just my bra in front of the man, I want to spend the rest of my life with, I feel the spontaneous muscular spasms start at my toes and sense them building throughout me. I feel David increase the pressure on my clitoris with his tongue and fingers pump in and out of me faster. I can feel myself getting so close. I just need something a little more to push me over the edge, as I titter on the peak, David pushes his finger just inside my anus and I scream his name as I come like never before.

When people say they see stars, it is not an understatement, I was seeing stars in all pretty colours as I took flight and floated around the room. I struggle to catch my breath and feel myself panic as I try to control my breathing, David pulls himself up the bed until he is kissing my lips as he lines himself up at my entrance.

"I need to feel you, baby."

I put my arms around David's neck as I pull him closer to me, I wrap my legs around his waist, as I push the heels of my feet into his arse telling him I need to feel him as deep as he can go. With one smooth fluid thrust, David is so deep and it feels wonderful, I love the feeling of him inside of me. As I move to meet him thrust for thrust, I feel his balls slapping against my bum as we move in sync with each other, I sense David's impending orgasm as his breathing increases and sweat breaks from each pore on his soft pale skin.

226

"You better be close," he whispers in my ear.

I feel him slide his fingers between us as he glides down until he finds my clit, with one gentle touch I lose control. My body explodes as my walls tighten around his cock and he erupts deep inside me, we both start to slow down as we continue to kiss each other tenderly.

Once we stop, David rolls off and falls to his back, panting like he has been on a twenty-mile hike.

After we lay side by side silently for a few moments trying to calm our laboured breaths, I feel David reach for my hand. I turn onto my side, placing my hand under my head to support me so I am looking down at David, observing this gorgeous specimen lying beside me, I can't believe that soon he will be mine.

"You do know it's creepy watching someone while they have their eyes closed, right?"

I see the small smile dance on his lips, as he opens one eye to see me.

"I could lie here all day and watch you." I casually say. "Do you know I still don't know how old you are." I run my fingertips over his forehead, heading down his cheek, reaching for his lips, just as I reach them, he nips my fingertip.

"Does it really matter how old I am?" I shake my head as I look into his eyes.

"Not at all, I just wondered."

"I'm thirty-one."

"Still a spring chicken." I wink as I place my arm under my head as I close my eyes, feeling completely relaxed.

"How long before you have to fetch the boys?"

"A couple of hours,"

"Perfect." I squeal as he tosses me on top of him. "Plenty of time for round two and three,"

I smile down, I have never felt this free and desperate to be with someone.

"I think if we hurry, we could fit in a fourth," I laugh at his raised eyebrow.

"I believe I've created a monster,"

"No monster, just horny." I bite his lip as he rolls me back over until he is leaning over me, kissing me with as much passion as I feel when I am near him.

Chapter Twenty

David

It's been three weeks since I told Gaynor I wanted to get divorced, the time has flown by in the last couple of weeks. I can't believe that I have been seeing Hannah that long exclusively. We have been taking it slow, we didn't want to push the boys too hard, but we have taken them bowling and to the cinema a few times. Although I accept the boys are a big part of the package that comes with Hannah, I can't wait for our first official date tonight and then tomorrow I have planned with Joyce and Albert for them to meet Hannah, Thomas and Elliott.

I'm like a bag of nerves as I plan to sweep Ms. George off her feet, romance her and then drop her back home with a kiss on her cheek. This time around I want to do everything right and enjoy the journey of getting to know her as well as Thomas and Elliott. This is the first chance I have had to have something of my own, to make the decisions and pursue the love of my life without someone telling me how and when and I am not letting anyone destroy this for me.

I jumped into the shower as I drag my tired body from my bed, it was a late one yesterday, as I was at the new house, I'd bought from Mr. Wilson. It was supposed to be his retirement renovation, but he ran out of funds and couldn't afford to finish it, so after I spoke to him and had it valuated, we settled a decent price, so I bought it with the thoughts of Hannah and the boys moving in with me and now things with Gaynor are straightened out, I am one step closer to that dream.

I quickly washed my hair and body. I had plans to pick Thomas and Elliott up to take them to the site to show them around. I had forgotten I had said I would take them one weekend until Elliott reminded me at the cinema last week. After I agreed, I decided to take them out this afternoon for a few hours. I thought I could give Hannah some time to herself to get ready for tonight as we agreed to go out on our date. I loved that she trusted me already with the boys and I would get to spend some time with the duo, and really get to know them.

I dress as quickly as I can and rub my hands through my damp hair, before I make my way out to my car. Once I'm in the car, I start to pull off the drive and I put my foot down on the accelerator, with a feeling of excitement buzzing through my body as I rush over to Hannah's place to pick up the boys. Elliott is a dream, he's accepted me straight away and is my little shadow, but Thomas is still a little wary of me, which I expected but I'm sure over time I can win him over. He can be chatty one day and then the next he hardly says a word.

As soon as I pull up outside Hannah's house, the front door flies open as Elliott bounds out the door, he charges to the car and has my door open before I've even taken my seatbelt off.

"Hey, buddy, are we all ready?"

"Yeah, Thomas will be here in a minute,"

"Fantastic, jump in the back then,"

I open the backdoor as I watch him climb in and make sure he fastens his belt securely, I reach in just to check he has it on properly, the last thing I needed was him having an accident on our first outing. I wanted to show not just them but Hannah that I am in this one hundred per cent, for me to do that and win them over; I had to spend some time with them without Hannah. I stand straight as I feel Hannah's hand on my shoulder, I turn, and I take in her gorgeous face and sigh. I can't believe how I got so lucky.

"Hey, Beautiful," I kiss her cheek.

"Hey, David," she smiles. "I have warned them both to behave, so hopefully they won't cause you too much trouble."

"No need to worry, I've got this, I promise. Now go get ready for later."

I watch her back away, as she smiles, wishing I was following her and we'd end up in bed, but I know we need to do this properly.

As I pull up at the site, I'm sure Elliott has nearly wet himself, he is so excited. The drive over he was a buzz of excitement. Thomas on the other hand, didn't really say much, but Elliott kept me entertained with little stories about his friends at school.

"Oh, wow! Can we climb to the top of that scaffolding, David?" Elliott enquires with amazement as he stares up at the scaffolding erected around the house.

"Not today mate, but when you're older, you definitely can. The last thing I need to do is take you back to mum, with broken bones." I wink, "Come on, I'll show you both around and we can see what Shawn is doing,"

They follow me out of the car and across to the site office. As we reach the office, I grab them both hard hats.

"Safety first," I smile. "When you enter a building site, you need to always have a hard hat on, it helps protect that perfect head of yours." I tell them both.

"Can I keep mine?" Elliott askes.

"Of course, buddy," I glance towards Thomas as he puts his on. "I think Shawn said he was plastering today, maybe you both would like to have a go?"

"Can we?" Elliott sings.

"We can go and check it out, come on." I smile. "Stay close boy's, I don't want you getting lost or hurt."

We make our way into the house through the patio doors on the back, as we walk into the space that will eventually be the living room, Shawn has the plaster in his bucket as he plasters the far wall. We walk further in, Elliott shouts for Shawn's attention. He spins on the spot as the plaster on his trowel, drops and lands on his work boots. I laugh.

"Hey, you frightened me, you little rascal." He winks at him.

Elliott giggles and I smile.

"How about we help you?" I suggest as I need to get them involved and although there is an art to plastering, it seems probably the safest thing to do.

"Well only if you think you can all handle it." he winks.

"Let's show him boys how good we are," I smile towards Thomas, hoping this might lighten his mood.

We mix some more plaster up in the buckets in the corner of the room, I pass one to Shawn and I carry the other. Shawn calls Joe and asks him to bring over three more trowels from the lock up. Just as we have the boys set up with their own piece of wall, Joe arrives with the trowels and leaves to fetch the boys some drinks and a burger.

"So, are we ready Thomas?" I say over his shoulder as I stand behind him.

I am working with Thomas, while Shawn's with Elliott.

"Yeah," he smiles.

"Now there's an art to getting the plaster to flatten to the walls." he nods as he listens to me. "So firstly, load the trowel with plaster, we need quite a bit at first, we are going to apply it at an angle, moving with the leading edge of the trowel. We are going to use a long motion to gradually flatten the plaster to the wall. The first coat is more important to get the plaster flat and even without bulges," I say. "Did you understand that?"

"Yes, load the trowel, use the leading edge at an angle, with long motions to get the plaster to stick to the wall."

"Go on then, give it a go."

I watch in amazement at his first attempt. For eleven he did really well, there was a good amount of plaster attached to the walls and it was mostly flat without many bulges.

"Well done, Thomas, that's brilliant on your first attempt, I'm proud of you mate," I see him drop his eyes to his feet.

"I just followed what you told me to do,"

"You did, but that is brilliant. When you are older, you can join my team any day." I beamed as I watch Thomas smile and I notice his shoulders relax.

He tries a few more times and each time is slightly better than the one before. When I glance at my watch, I find it hard to believe we have been at it for the last three hours, with just a small break for the boys to eat their burgers. Just as I think to call it a day, I feel a sharp pain in my shoulder and see Shawn lobbing plaster at me, like it was snow. That bastard, I dip my hand into our bucket and lob some back, before long we are all covered in fresh plaster and look like we've bathed in it.

I should have known he would act like a child; I smile as I hear Thomas and Elliott rolling with laughter, that is until I turn around to see the state of them. The colour drains from my face as

I see them covered in plaster. Hannah is going to kill me, and my poor car is going to be destroyed.

I place some tarpaulin all over my seats as I take them back home to Hannah, hoping she sees the funny side of the state of the boys. As soon as I let the boys out, the front door flies open. When Hannah sees the state of us, she starts to laugh.

"I gather you've all had a good afternoon?" She enquires.

"We had the best time," Thomas smiles. Hannah lifts her eyebrow as I smile with pride that Thomas has enjoyed himself.

"That's brilliant, but I think you both need to jump into the shower, before you do anything else."

I step back to my car as Hannah follows.

"I'm so sorry I returned them in a mess," I apologize.

"There's no need to be sorry, David, they've enjoyed it, so that's all that matters,"

I lean forward and cup her face as I pull her towards me, bringing her lips to mine. I quickly peck a kiss to her supple lips and pull back.

"I will see you in a few hours,"

"You will. Are you still not telling me where we are going?"

"Nope."

She rolls her eyes as she steps back from the car.

"Okay, I will see you later." she says as she walks back towards the house. "Oh, and David."

I look up.

"I don't think I'll bother with panties later." I hear the growl leave my lips before I feel my chest expand as I watch her close the door behind her. If I wasn't being such a gentleman, I would make her pay for that.

The last few hours have dragged on as I wait for the time to collect Hannah, but as I pull up outside her house for the third time that day, my nerves start to get the better of me.

It's the first date, as in a date of my choice, I've ever had and to say I'm shitting myself would be an understatement. I just hope I don't mess this up because when I'm with Hannah and the boys, I feel like I've won the lottery.

I sit in the car for a few minutes trying to calm my heartbeat before I decide to go and knock on the door but as I'm pulling myself together, I hear a tap on the car window.

I look up and I nearly swallow my tongue at the vision on the other side of the glass. I close my eyes as I feel the familiar feeling of my cock stirring. Oh God, please let me get through the night without me making a prat of myself. I send a silent prayer up to the heavens.

I push open my door and smile. I give Hannah a once over and I think how stunning she is, the way she looks; makes me want to eat her and my mouth waters. She is standing there, dressed in a plum fitted dress, that stops mid-thigh.

"You haven't changed your mind, have you?" I hear the uncertainty in Hannah's voice.

"Of course not, why would you think that?"

"Well, you've been sitting in your car for the last twenty minutes and I thought that perhaps you'd changed your mind."

I glanced down at my watch as I noticed the time and she's right, I had been sitting out here the last twenty minutes but not for the reasons she thought. I pulled her into my arms as I proceeded to kiss her forehead.

"I could never change my mind, Baby." I look deep into her eyes because I need her to understand how much she means to me and how much I love her. "I was waiting in my seat, because I am nervous of what I have in mind for tonight, but that has nothing to do with you, Angel." I see her release a steady breath like she had been holding it in.

"David, we could be having sandwiches sitting in your car and it would be perfect for me." she beams.

"You could have told me that earlier," I winked.

I feel her hand on my chest as she tries to push me away, but I hold on tighter, not ever wanting to let her go.

"Come on let's get you into the car," I take her hand and walk her around to her side. "I need to blindfold you," I see the look of shock on her face. "You have nothing to worry about, I have a surprise for you, but I want it to stay that way, and I don't want you to see it, until I am ready."

"Okay."

"It's not far, so you won't have it on long." I kissed her lips as I placed the blindfold over her eyes.

After I have helped her into her seat, making sure she doesn't injure herself. I rush around to myside then climb into mine, as I quickly shoot off a text to Shawn to let him know we are on our way. I'm so grateful to him for all his help to make sure everything was perfect for Hannah. I start the car as Can I Be Him by James Arthur starts to fill the warm space. We drive in silence, and I get the feeling Hannah is listening to this song as she hums along. She seems to be intently listening to the words, and I couldn't have thought of a better song that says what I want to say to this beautiful woman. I touch her leg as I feel the words down deep inside my soul, I want to be the one and the only one for the rest of our lives. She's it for me, no one else would do.

236

I feel her jump a little at the touch of my hand as I had forgotten she had the blindfold on. As the song ends, I rub my thumb in circles on her leg. I watch as her skin prickles and the goosebumps appear. It's good to know I affect her the way she affects me.

"We are nearly there, Baby,"

She turned her head in the direction of my words and smiled with a small nod. The nearer we get to our destination the more I start to think I have made the wrong decision. Maybe I should leave this a little longer before showing her my plans for the future that I hope she wants to be a part of.

I hear my phone vibrate and see Shawn has messaged me to say everything is ready for our night. As I pull up outside, I pause, and I stare at where I'm taking Hannah and pray that I have made the right choice. I turn off the car and unclick my seatbelt.

"We are here."

"Can I take off my blindfold?" Hannah whispers, sounding a little nervous.

"Not yet," I hold back, trying to think of the best way to proceed. "I need you to trust me and let me guide you, can you do that?"

"Of course, I will follow you anywhere, you know that."

I jump from the car and walk around to open her door as I take her hand and help her stand from her seat. I kiss her gently on her cheek as I take her hand, guiding her around the car to the garden path, then I lead her around the back, I feel my heart beating out of my chest.

When I reach the gate, I have an awful feeling that I have fucked this up and I might have jumped in before she was ready. Whilst I held my breath, I opened the gate and guided her to the pavers with my hand on her back, just before we reached the decking, I stopped her and stood behind her. I braced my hands on her shoulders, as I tried to gather my thoughts. I need to get this spot on, I need to sell her the whole idea and make her understand that if this isn't what she wants that we can find something together.

"I am going to remove your blindfold in a second, but I just want to say before I do that," I pause not sure what words I needed to say.

"David just tell me, you make me nervous when you pause."

I close my eyes, before leaning forward until my lips hover over her ear.

"I don't know what to say, so I'll show you instead," I said at the same time I dropped her blindfold, I hear a loud intake of breath as her eyes take in her surroundings.

"Oh my God!!" she whips around until her eyes meet mine with shock. "You brought me to your house where your soon to be ex-wife lives?"

"WHAT??" I step back. "Of course not. Why would you think that?"

"Well, the last I heard you still lived with her, and I don't know of any other houses you own." She shrilled and I could see the tears forming in her eyes.

"Hannah, if you had let me explain, I want this to be ours. I bought it a few weeks ago after a client couldn't afford to carry on with the renovation." I see the moment when everything becomes clear to her, she blushes as the words I have just said flit through her mind.

She spins back around to look at the beautifully decorated oak tree with twinkling lights, beside it a gorgeous black wrought iron garden set, table and chairs sitting on the decking.

At the back of the garden is a stunning swimming pool that I had installed for the boys to have somewhere to swim when they eventually move in.

"Say something." I whispered.

Her eyes connect with mine over her shoulder, as I see the tears dancing in her delicious brown eyes.

"I don't know what to say. I am speechless."

"Hannah.... What I feel for you, I have never felt for anyone else before you and I won't feel that way about anyone else after." I run my finger down her cheek. "I want to spend every second with you and the boys. Now I know it's too soon for you and the boys to move in with me, I'm not expecting you to do that right now, but I want to make my intentions clear. You are it for me. Trust me there is no one else I want to spend the rest of my life with." I step forward and pull her into my arms. "Please don't cry,"

"They aren't sad tears," I wipe the tears from her cheeks. "David, I have never felt this way about anyone, not like I do when I am with you. You are it for me too, trust me." she winks.

She wraps her arms around my neck and kisses me like I'm her last meal. Even though I don't want it to end, I pull back and rest my forehead to hers as I close my eyes trying to catch my breath.

"Come on, let's sit down and I will pour you some wine. Then after I have fed you, I can show you around."

"I love you," she whispers, and my heart rate speeds up. I have never felt the way I have when I hear those three words from her mouth. If I died at this very moment, I would die a very happy man.

"I love you, more," I replied.

I take her hand as she follows me over to her chair, I pull it out as she sits down. Once I've poured her wine, I head off into the kitchen, I pull the steak, chips and onion rings from the oven that I had asked Shawn to put in. The smell was making my belly rumble, I headed back outside and saw Hannah watching the lights twinkle in the tree.

"Penny for your thoughts," I whisper behind her causing her to leap a little. "Sorry I didn't mean to make you jump,"

"No, you didn't, I was just watching the lights and thinking I could spend the rest of my life watching them,"

"Well, you can if you decide you want to move in." I smile.

"Are you sure that's what you want?"

I place her plate of food in front of her, as I put mine down too.

"Hannah, talk to me, please. I'm worried you're having second thoughts about us."

She sighs as she drops her eyes to the plate.

"I'm not having second thoughts about us, but I just want to be sure that you want to take us all on. It's a lot to take on two boys too."

"You have nothing to worry about, Hannah. Those boys are a credit to you, and I want to be a part of their life as much as yours." I smile down. "Look let's talk while we eat, we don't want the food getting cold,"

She nods her head as I decide to take the seat next to her, rather than the one opposite. I see her looking at the house.

"Do you like it?" I ask first.

"I love it," she smiles as she cuts her steak and places it in her mouth. I watch her lips chewing on the piece of meat and I wish that her lips were wrapped around my cock. "It's my dream home, David,"

I smile as I follow suit and try to eat my meal as thoughts of her gorgeous mouth has my cock hardening.

I told her about the way I acquired the house, then we talked about my ideas and asked if she had any thoughts while we continued to finish our meal. As we both place our knives and forks down on our plates, I reach over and tuck her soft as silk hair behind her ears, while I look into her eyes.

"Do you want a tour of the house?"

"Can I? I'm so desperate to see it," she replies with excitement in her voice.

"Come on." I stand.

We walk hand in hand, heading for the patio doors. As we reach the threshold, I pull on Hannah's hand to stop her before she enters.

"We can decorate it any way you like, I mean when you feel it's time. There's no rush, I know the boys still need to get to know me better, but I think knowing the house is all ready for you, will help with that. We can show them their rooms and they can decorate them how they want……"

I feel Hannah's lips hit mine as I tried to ramble on, she kisses me so tenderly and I feel my cock harden as I get the urge to push her up against the glass window and fuck her harder than I've ever fucked before. I let her control the kiss as I'm terrified that I'll overstep the line and take her, when I'm trying to be a gentleman. I really want to drag her to the master room and show her all the ways I love her, but I am desperate to do this the right way. I want to treasure the woman before me and take our time.

Chapter Twenty-one

Hannah

I don't really know how to explain how I feel at this moment but if my lips were attached to David's for the rest of my life, I know I would always be happy. I was nervous about our first official date as it had been years since I'd had one, unless I count the disastrous evening with Matty. I had forgotten what to do or expect, but so far tonight has out done anything I had experienced before David; he has totally blown me away.

When he first arrived at the house, and I watched him through the kitchen window just sitting there, making no attempt to come in, I had a moment of dread. I thought spending time with the boys this afternoon had changed his mind on the whole being together situation.

After twenty minutes, I couldn't wait any longer. I took a deep breath before I grabbed my clutch and opened the front door before I changed my mind. I watched him staring up at the sky and wondered what he was doing. I followed his eyes to the sky to see if I could see what he was looking at; but found nothing.

So, I took one step forward, marching to the car and tapped on his window. I saw him jump, so he must have been miles away but once his eyes connected with mine through the window. I study his face as the surprise crosses his profile. Then as he closes his eyes, a feeling of dread starts to form in the pit of my stomach. I watch David push open his door and smile.

"You haven't changed your mind, have you?" I ask as the uncertainty leaks into my voice.

"Of course not, why would you think that?"

"Well, you've been sitting in your car for the last twenty minutes and I thought that perhaps you'd changed your mind."

He glanced down at his watch and noticed the time, as he realised, I was right; before he pulled me into his arms as he proceeded to kiss my forehead.

"I could never change my mind, Baby." he looked deep into my eyes, "I was waiting in my seat, because I am nervous of what I have in mind for tonight. But that has nothing to do with you, Angel."

I release a steady breath at his words.

"David, we could be having sandwiches sitting in your car and it would be perfect for me." I beam at him.

"You could have told me that earlier," he winked.

I push his chest and try to push him away, but he holds on tighter.

"Come on, let's get you into the car," He takes my hand and walks me around to my side. "I need to blindfold you,"

I raise my eyebrows in complete shock, what the fuck does he want to do to me and why am I slightly turned on by the thought?

"You have nothing to worry about, I have a surprise for you, but I want it to stay that way, and I don't want you to see it, until I am ready."

Hmm I am hoping the surprise is between his legs, but I don't think that's what he means, but a girl can hope.

"Okay."

"It's not far, so you won't have it on long." He kisses my lips as he places the blindfold over my eyes.

I blink a few times as I try to get my bearings; I have never had a blindfold on before and as strange as it feels, I feel the moisture collect between my legs.

I was only joking this afternoon when I told David I wouldn't be wearing panties tonight but as I started to get dressed in my tight-fitted plum dress, I decided I would go without but now I am regretting my decision as I can feel the dampness.

As David starts the car, I hear the radio flick on, and Can I Be Him by James Arthur fills the car while we drive to wherever he is taking me.

While we drive in silence, I listen to the song, I hum along to the words, it is one of my favourites. I feel the heat of David's hand as he touches my leg, I jump slightly at the touch of his fingers as I have the blindfold on, so I didn't see him move. As his skin touches mine, I feel my skin prickle and goosebumps rise.

The words flow through my mind, and I pray for him to be the one for me and we get to spend the rest of our lives together. As the song ends, I feel his thumb rubbing in circles on my thigh and the sensation shoots straight to my core.

"We are nearly there, Baby,"

I turn my head in the direction of the sound of his voice and smile with a small nod of my head, acknowledging I had heard his words. The longer the drive the more I wonder where we are heading and what we were going to do.

I sense the nervous energy coming from David and wonder why he is so on edge. I try to listen to any clues on where we might be heading but nothing sticks out, only the sound of his phone vibrating.

I feel the car come to a stop, and I hold my breath as I wait for David to make a move as the little butterflies start to take flight in my tummy at the thought of what the rest of the night might hold.

I hear the click of David's seatbelt and I wait for him to remove my blindfold.

"We are here."

"Can I take off my blindfold?" I ask breathlessly as my excitement builds, though I feel a little nervous.

"Not yet," he tells me like he is trying to hold back. "I need you to trust me and let me guide you, can you do that?"

"Of course, I will follow you anywhere, you know that."

I hear David open his car door as he jumps from his seat and walks around to open mine. He takes my hand and helps me climb from the car. I feel his lips gently on my cheek as he holds on tightly to my hand while he guides me around the car and onto some kind of concrete path; I have no idea where we are.

I feel like my heart is beating out of my chest as I feel David's other hand on my lower back when I hear a click of a latch. I feel the slight shake on David's hand and my nerves return, I hear the gate open, I am guided further in, but I still have no idea where I am.

David stops me, I feel the heat from his body against my back as stands behind me. I feel his warm hands brace my shoulders, as I listen to his breathing.

"I am going to remove your blindfold in a second, but I just want to say before I do that," He pauses like he's unsure of what he is going to say next.

"David just tell me, you make me nervous when you pause."

I sense him lean forward until his breath hoovers over my ear.

"I don't know what to say, so I'll show you instead," he said at the same time I felt my blindfold falls from my face. I wait a second before opening my eyes as they adjust to the light.

I take loud intake of breath as my eyes take in my surroundings and I am shocked.

I cannot believe he would bring me here for our first date. Why would he think I would want our date to be at the same place he has lived the last six or seven years with his wife?

"Oh my God!!" I whip around as I fight the feeling, I have to smack his face as my eyes meet his. "You brought me to your house where your soon to be ex-wife lives?"

"WHAT?" he steps back. "Of course not. Why would you think that?"

"Well, the last I heard you still lived with her, and I don't know of any other houses you own."

I can feel my anger rising, as a look of realisation covers his face.

"Hannah, if you had let me explain, I want this to be ours. I bought it a few weeks ago after a client couldn't afford to carry on with the renovation." I frown as I listen to everything, he just told me, I blush as David tries to explain I have the wrong idea. I feel so stupid.

I spin back around to look at the beautifully decorated oak tree, my eyes fill with tears as I watch the twinkling lights. I look down beside the long branches that hang over the decking area and see a gorgeous black wrought iron garden set. The table and chairs sitting on the freshly painted decking. I lift my eyes to the far side of the garden and see a stunning swimming pool that I know for a fact Thomas will adore, he had dreams of swimming for his local swimming team but had to give up his swimming lessons due to lack of funds after Ian left.

246

I am speechless, I honestly do not know what to say.

"Say something." He whispered.

I turn my head as my eyes connect with his over my shoulder, I feel the tears teetering on the edge of my lashes.

"I don't know what to say. I am speechless."

"Hannah..... What I feel for you, I have never felt for anyone else before you and I won't feel that way about anyone else after." David stops and runs his finger down my cheek. "I want to spend every second with you and the boys. Now I know it is too soon for you and the boys to move in with me, I am not expecting you to do that right now, but I want to make my intentions clear. You are it for me. Trust me there is no one else I want to spend the rest of my life with." he steps forward and pulls me into his arms. "Please don't cry,"

"They aren't sad tears," David wipes the tears from my cheeks. "David, I have never felt this way about anyone, not like I do when I am with you. You are it for me too, trust me." I wink.

I wrap my arms around his neck and kiss him like he is my last meal. I do not ever want it to end, I feel him pull back and rest his forehead to mine as he closes his eyes trying to catch his breath.

"Come on, let's sit down and I will pour you some wine. Then after I have fed you, I can show you around."

"I love you," I whispered, and I felt his heart beating next to mine. I didn't mean to let those words fall from my lips so soon but no matter what I tried; I could not hold them back any longer.

"I love you, more." he smiles.

He takes my hand as I follow him over to a chair, as he pulls it out for me to sit down. Once he has poured the wine, he heads off into the kitchen. While he is busy sorting the food, I sit

247

and drop my head back to watch the twinkling lights in the tree, as the breeze softly blows through the branches.

"Penny for your thoughts," I hear David whisper from behind me as I jump a little. "Sorry I didn't mean to make you jump,"

"No, you didn't, I was just watching the lights and thinking I could spend the rest of my life watching them,"

"Well, you can if you decide you want move in." He smiles.

"Are you sure that's what you want?" I need to be sure that he wants this as much as me.

He places my plate in front of me, as he puts his down too.

"Hannah, talk to me, please. I'm worried you're having second thoughts about us."

I sigh as I drop my eyes to the plate.

"I'm not having second thoughts about us, David, but I just want to be sure that you want to take us all on. It's a lot to take on two boys too."

"You have nothing to worry about, Hannah. Those boys are a credit to you, and I want to be a part of their life as much as yours." He smiles down. "Look, let's talk while we eat, we don't want the food getting cold,"

I nod my head as he takes the seat next to me, rather the one opposite. My eyes keep drifting back towards the house as I take in the spectacular design.

"Do you like it?" He asks as he watched me.

"I love it," I smile as I cut my steak and place it in my mouth.

I bring my eye back towards David and watch him put his steak into his mouth with a smirk. As I watch him chew his food, all my thoughts of what his stunning mouth can do has my desire building. I listened to him tell me all about the way he acquired this house, and he asked me what my thoughts were as I tried to concentrate on finishing our meal.

When we both place our knives and forks down on our plates, he reaches over and tucks some of my soft hair behind my ears and he gazes into my eyes.

"Do you want a tour of the house?"

"Can I? I'm so desperate to see it," I reply with excitement running through my veins.

"Come on." He stands.

We walk hand in hand, heading for the patio doors, but as we reach the threshold, I feel a pull on my hand to stop me before we enter. I lift my eyes to him in confusion.

"We can decorate it any way you like, I mean when you feel it's time. There is no rush, I know the boys still need to get to know me better, but I think knowing the house is all ready for you, will help with that. We can show them their rooms and they can decorate them how they want……"

I stop him dead as I lean forward and plant my lips to his as he rambles on, I start the kiss tenderly, but my desire has me deepening the kiss within seconds. I wrap my arms around his neck as I feel his harden cock push into my tummy, I just wished he would push me up against the cold glass and fuck me.

I feel David letting me take control as I push my tongue inside his mouth, I moan as my core tightens, I just wished David weren't trying to be a gentleman.

The urge I feel has me desperate for him to fuck me. David tries to step back as I feel his lips leaving mine, but I grab his shirt and pull him back towards me.

I'm not ready to stop just yet and I know I can tempt him into fucking me with a few soft rubs in the right area, but David steps back out of my reach with a sexy glint in his eyes.

"I know what you are doing Hannah, and no."

I pout and give him my best puppy eyes, with no luck.

"Come on, I want to show you the house, before you have me lose my mind completely and do something I shouldn't."

I know I'm not going to win this one right at this moment, so I play along.

"Okay, I'll be good," I bat my eyes at him.

"Yeah, that will be a first," he swats my arse as I walk in the door, while he follows.

I turn my head back to look at him over my shoulder and smile at the look on his face.

"Watch where you are going, Baby. There's still things lying about, and I don't want you falling or hurting yourself,"

I turn back to see where I was walking, when I see a trail of some beautiful tea lights lighting the way through the room and disappear into what I assume is the hallway.

When I take another step in, I notice a magnificent looking leather suite and two bucket chairs, with an enormous tv hanging above the fire surround on the wall above the large wood burner. I look to the far wall and see a large bay window that is dressed in gorgeous, grey curtains and the room feels warm and cosy. I feel David's hand at the centre of my lower back, as he tries to guide me on, but I just want to stand and observe this luscious room. I have never seen a room that makes me want to sit down, kick off my shoes and relax.

Even in the house with Ian it never looked this good, we could never afford the finer things in life and this room shouts money. I feel a little intimidated by how gorgeous it looks.

250

I start to move forward and let David guide me on. We walk into the hallway and head straight for the door in front of us.

As David opens the door, I see the most, spacious kitchen I have ever seen. I walk in further to look at this glorious space, I smile as I glide my finger across the worktop, the kitchen cupboards are solid oak wood, and the worktops are grey speckled. I look to the left and see the most gorgeous range cooker and hood, it reminds me of the one I had when I lived at home, as the vision of me and my mum baking filled my mind. With every room, I fall in love with the house.

"What do you think so far?" David asks cautiously behind me.

"I love it, David." I turn to see his face; I walk up to him and pull him close. "And I can't wait to christen every surface with you." I whisper.

"Come on, there's still upstairs to see and I think you might like the bathroom, especially the en-suite," he winks.

I follow him out the kitchen and up the stairs as we walk along the landing, my heartbeat increases.

"On the left here is Thomas's room and next to his is Elliott's." I glance in each room as he points them out, as we reach the end of the hallway.

David opens the door to the bathroom and my heart stops at the sight of the old-fashioned freestanding bath sitting below a double window facing the view of the fields that stretch for miles. I walk over and run my hand across the traditional indulgent bath and imagine sitting in here after a hard day in the office with lots of bubbles and a large glass of wine. I think I'm sold.

I feel David's presence behind me, and I feel his breath down my neck as we both stand to watch the view of the sun setting in the distance, I want to be able to do this every day for the rest of my life.

"There's also a small shower, so it will be easier for the boys to use,"

"Oh, David, I love it," I spin on the spot and face him.

"You've not seen our room yet,"

I can feel my excitement mount at the mention of our room.

"Show me," I whisper with my eyes holding his.

He smiles as he reaches for my hand, before he brings it to his mouth and places a gentle kiss on the top.

"Your wish is my command."

I feel a gentle tug as he pulls me out of the family bathroom and back along the landing until we reach the lever, I frown as I look at David, but he smiles at my confusion. I see him pull on the lever as he pulls me out of the way and the loft cover drops down and some ladders slowly fall.

"These are only temporary," he smiles. "I plan to have some stairs fitted but I will need to have plans drawn up to be able to fit them properly."

I watch as I see him straighten the ladders and hold his hand out for me to go first and I blush as I remember my no pantie situation.

"What are you blushing for, Baby," he leans forward and whispers.

"No reason," I wink as I place my foot on the first step and start to climb up.

I am so glad I've only had one glass of wine because anymore and I wouldn't be able to make it up here.

As I reach the top, I feel David coming up behind me, so step off and into the master room and my eyes bulge. I have never seen a bedroom look so serene, decorated in olive green and

252

silver, it just feels so calm. I walk to the four-poster bed as I run my finger across the silk fitted covers.

David wraps his arms around me as he pulls me into his embrace.

"I wanted us to have our own private nook, somewhere we can have our own space and we can relax." he says as he rests his chin on my shoulder.

"David, I'm speechless. I love everything about this house and so will the boys."

"The en-suite is by the fitted wardrobes," he spins me around to show me the doors. "I wanted you to know I am one hundred per cent in this with you all, the house isn't exactly finished but hopefully by the time you're all ready, it will be completed."

I turn in his arms so I can see his gorgeous eyes.

"I love you." I wrap my arms around his and pull his head towards mine. As our lips collide my desire spikes and I need him more than my next breath. Just as I feel the air changing around us, David steps back.

"Come on, I need to get you home," he winks as I growl. I am so turned on; I think I could kill someone.

"Really?"

"Really,"

"But David, I need you."

"I need you too, but I promised myself I would take you home after our first date and that's what I'm doing,"

"So, you are going to send me home wet and needy?"

"What do you think I am? I don't have sex on my first date," he laughs.

I huff in frustration; I have never needed someone like I have needed David now.

"I didn't put panties on," I say like a child who doesn't get her own way, all I needed to add was stamping my feet and you would think I was a toddler. I run my finger along his jaw and down his neck until I reach the top of his shirt, to try to persuade him to fuck me before I go back home but he just shakes his head and smirks as he moves back to the ladder.

If I wasn't so desperate, I would go on a sex strike until he is begging me for a fuck, but I know he has more will power than I'll ever have; so I know that wouldn't work. I would just be punishing myself for nothing.

I follow David back down the ladders as he moves back through the house turning off the lights, blowing the candles out. I offer to blow them out too, to show him how good my blow is but he shakes his head and smirks. As we reach the car, I am nearly on my knees with desire.

He pushes me until my backs connected with the cold car door.

"Do you know how hard you have made me tonight, Hannah?"

I shake my head as he takes my hand and places it on his stiff cock.

"Very hard." he closes his eyes as my hand touches his length. "If I wasn't trying to be a gentleman and show you how committed to you, I am. I would push you up against this car and fuck you right here,"

"I wouldn't say no," I say as I flutter my lashes at him.

"I knew you would be a pain in my arse, the second my eyes met yours. Now get in the car, so I can get you home."

I pout as I step out of the way and David opens my door. I take my seat as I watch David skip around to his side and he gets in.

"Thank you," I whisper as I lean over and kiss his cheek.

He smiles and starts the car as we start in the direction of my house. As we drive all the rooms at the new house flit through my mind as I'm excited for the future we are starting to build. I lie my head back as I try to stay awake but before we reach the main road, I've nodded off.

Chapter Twenty-two

David

Sitting in my bedroom, with boxes all around me, I look at my stuff scattered all around the room. It has been two weeks since my first official date with Hannah and everything is going perfectly. I could not be any happier if I tried.

I take a sip of coffee from my mug as I try to think of the best way to organize the boxes.

I have finally got the paperwork in order for my divorce, and we have arranged for my lawyer to come out to the house on Monday evening to sign over the bungalow to Gaynor. So, I plan on spending Monday moving all my stuff over to the house and start working on plans to put in the stairs to mine and Hannah's bedroom in.

After I showed Hannah the house, the next day we spoke about them all moving in and we have decided to leave it until it is fully completed. We don't want to risk the boys getting hurt or having people in and out the house with them there. The plan is, I'm moving in and Hannah and the boys will move in at a later date. I just don't feel comfortable living here with Gaynor when my heart belongs to Hannah.

I look up at the time, to see I have an hour and half until we must be at Joyce's and Bert's. I have arranged for us to visit the other two main people in my life, so I rush through my shower routine and quickly slip on my favourite jeans and t-shirt. I grab my mug and walk into the kitchen, as I reach the door, I see Gaynor flicking on the kettle.

"Hey," I say as I walk to put my mug into the sink.

"Hi," I see her glance my way. "Are you off out?"

"I am. I'm off to pick Hannah and the boys up."

"Have a good afternoon." she smiles sadly.

"I will," I backed out of the kitchen as I headed for the car.

I pull open my door but hover and look back towards the house before I continue to get in the car. I really feel bad leaving while Gaynor obviously is feeling down but if I went back, what could I say? Every time in the past I have tried to say something to make things better, she snapped my head off. So, I take a deep breath and start the car, before reversing off the drive and heading towards Hannah's, but I decide to make a little stop on the way to get two bouquets of flowers, one for the love of my life, the other for Joyce.

Once I pull up outside Hannah's house, I jump from my seat and pull the red rose bouquet from the boot. But before I can knock on the door, it swings open with a stunning Hannah standing there looking sexy as fuck. I swallow back my urge to push her up against the wall, then fucking her hard and fast.

"Hey, Baby." I smile as I pass the bouquet over to her.

"Oh my God, these are gorgeous, David."

"Only the best for you, Beautiful,"

"Thank you," Hannah whispers against my lips as I hear gagging in the background.

I pull my head back and see Thomas and Elliott watching.

"Hey, boys. Are you ready?"

"Yes," Elliott replies.

"Good. Go and get in the car, the doors open,"

I smile as they both run straight out to the door.

257

"I'm not sure if they are happy to go out in the car or just to get away from us kissing but I have never seen them run that fast." I laugh as I look back towards Hannah.

"I think it's the kissing," she pecks my lips. "Let me go put these in some water and get my bag, then I'm ready."

"Okay, I'll go and wait with the boys,"

I leave the hallway and make my way towards the car as I see them both sitting in the back with their seatbelts fastened. I smile because when they first started getting into my car, they never put their seatbelts on, I always had to remind them but know they do it without me saying anything.

I start the engine as I watch Hannah walk down the drive and jump in the passenger side, next to me. I smile as I pull away from the curb, I love the feeling of being with my family. It takes us about forty minutes to get to Joyce's and the boys are on top form, Elliott loves winding Thomas up about a girl he has been seen walking around the playground with, but Hannah warns them to behave and not to show her up.

As we pull up in front of the garage attached to Joyce's house, I see her standing on the front step, I know she has been excited to meet the boys, she loves a busy home and the sound of kids messing around, but it has been a few years since she has been in the presence of any children.

I pull open Hannah's door, as the boys jump out too, but Hannah pauses as she bites her bottom lip. I crouch down beside her and take her hand in mine.

"Hey, what's up?"

"What if they don't like us?"

I frown, because there is no way they would not fall head over heels for them all.

"Hannah, what are you talking about?"

"I was thinking on the way over, what if they don't accept us. I don't want you to have to choose,"

"There is no choice to be made, beautiful, they will love you just as much as I do, I promise."

She looks up and into my eyes, and I see the sadness seeping through.

"Come on, the boys are chomping at the bit to play in the garden," I smile as I offer her my hand.

I watch the internal battle play out on her gorgeous face but eventually she puts her hand in mine and I help her from her seat. I pull her to the back of the car as I open the boot and pull the yellow bouquet I bought for Joyce from the back. I hand them to Hannah as she carries them up the garden path, Joyce comes down to greet them and beams as she greets Hannah.

"Hannah, it's so lovely to see you again."

"You too, Mrs. Barkley,"

"Ah, enough of Mrs. Barkley, call me Joyce, dear." she smiles as she hugs Hannah before pulling back and looking towards the boys. "And who are these handsome young boys?"

"I'm Elliott," Elliott steps forward, "And that's Thomas," he directs over his shoulder before leaning forward like he is going to tell Joyce a big secret. "He's got a girlfriend, but he doesn't want to admit it." He grins.

We all start laughing as Thomas' face turns a lovely shade of red, I feel bad for him, so I walk over and put my arm around him, then I walk him up and into the house. I hear Hannah, Joyce and Elliott following us indoors. As I reach the kitchen, I see Albert gluing some matchsticks onto the WW2 plane he is working on.

"Hey, Bert." I watch as he delicately places the piece in his hands before lifting his eyes to mine and smiles.

"Hey, son, I didn't realize the time, I'll just put this away before Joy has my balls." I laugh because I know Joyce loves to bust his balls, but she loves that he has got a hobby. Especially since his accident he had to retire and now has nothing to keep him occupied while she is out at work, apart from his garden and his aircrafts.

"What are you doing?" Thomas enquires.

"I'm building a WW2 aircraft from match sticks," Bert smiles. "Would you like to have a go, Son?"

I see Thomas hesitant smile, as he shakes his head.

"I don't want to break it,"

"You could never break it son, and if you do, we can build it again. Come and sit by me and I will show you how to do it."

I watch as Thomas sits down beside Bert and they talk about the glue he uses and the best way to apply the match sticks, after a few minutes you would have thought they had known each other all their life.

I smile as I make my way towards the living room where Hannah and Elliott are talking with Joyce. As I reach the door, I lean on the door frame as I see them all sitting down and chatting about Joyce's garden. I knew they would all feel at home here, just as I had all those years ago.

"What are you all talking about," I push from the door frame and take a seat next to Hannah.

"Joyce is just telling us about her garden," Hannah smiles but as she looks behind me, she frowns. "Where's Thomas?"

"He's helping Bert with his WW2 aircraft."

"I hope he doesn't break it," Hannah frets.

"He will be fine, Dear," Joyce says. "Bert loves a little company when he makes his crafts, but he doesn't get it very often. Now David has grown up, he doesn't get any help at all. It will do them both good." she smiles.

I see Hannah's shoulders relax, as she glances back towards Joyce.

"How about I take you both to see the back garden," Joyce asks Elliott and Hannah.

"Can we?" Elliott jumps with excitement at the thought of being outside in the fresh air.

"I'll go and help Thomas and Bert, and while I'm there I will put the kettle on," I beam as I watch them walk through the patio doors onto the luxurious garden.

As I walk back towards the kitchen, I hear Thomas chatting with Bert. It is the most I have ever heard him talk, normally it is the odd word here and there but nothing to write home about.

"What are you two talking about?" I ask as I plop down on the other side of the table.

"I was just telling Thomas about our first aircraft we worked on,"

"Ah, the Hawker Demon, from 1931," I smile as I reminisce.

"It took months for us to finish," he smiles as he tells Thomas the story of how we nearly got to the end and I accidentally knocked it off the side and it smashed to a thousand pieces. I remember being so distraught, I barely slept for days as we tried to put all the bits back together.

I loved that time I spent with Bert, it was not long after my mom had died, and I thought the world was against me. But spending time with Bert, his match sticks, and his glue; I realized that there still were people who cared about me.

Thomas' eyes shone with a light I had not seen before, he smiled as he placed a piece on the wing of the plane and beamed when he saw it starting to take shape.

"Well done, Son. You've got a steady hand,"

"He was really good with the plastering a few weeks ago on the site, too," I smile proudly.

"Get him an apprenticeship quickly, before someone snaps him up," Bert winks at Thomas.

"He's definitely got a job with me if he wants one when he is older." I rub his head as I get up to fill the kettle. Just as I flick it on I hear Joyce, Hannah and Elliott walking down the hallway towards the kitchen.

"What are you three doing?" Joyce asks when Elliott's eyes light up when his eyes land on the plane.

"Wow," Elliott moves closer to look. "That's amazing. Can we do one like that David?"

"I'm sure we can, buddy," I smile as I look up to meet Hannah's eyes. It is nice to see the sadness has left her face.

"Who wants a drink then?" I ask.

"You, sit down. I'll do the drinks." Joyce insists.

"Okay but let me help."

"There's no need David, you go and sit down,"

I do as I am told because there is no way to win with Joyce. She likes to take care of the people she loves, and she is not happy unless she is looking after someone else. I take a seat at the dining room table as Hannah joins me, I place my hand on her thigh as we both watch the boys with their excited voices asking Albert lots of questions.

"Is a roast okay for dinner," Joyce asks.

"Of course, Joyce, but let me help you," Hannah stands to walk to where Joyce was ready to put the meat in.

I sit and watch Hannah talking to Joyce as she peels the potatoes and they both share a mutual joke and I smile as I watch them laugh. I'm happy because everyone in this room are the most important people in my life. I turn my eyes back to the table and see Elliott sitting on Bert's lap as he watches Thomas putting glue on the matchstick and finding the right place to put it. They are all so engrossed in what they are doing they pay no mind to me watching.

As I look back up towards where Hannah and Joyce are busy, Joyce catches my eye and smiles and I know she approves of my choice. I jump up and help carry the hot drinks over to the table, then I go into the living room to collect the special dinner service as I know Joyce will want to use it.

I carry the set through and start to place all the cutlery and plates in their correct places. I smile to myself as I hear all the noise and chatter, I cannot wait until we are living together, and this will be a nightly affair. I never really put much thought into how much I was missing out on but the more time I spend with Hannah and the boys, the more I know that I could have really missed out on something good.

I feel a hand on the middle of my back, and I am pulled from my thoughts as I glance to see Hannah.

"What are you doing over here on your own?"

"I was just thinking how lucky I am to have you in my life," I smile as I turn and pull her into my arms.

"Not as lucky as I am,"

"Do you want to bet on that?" I wink.

She smiles and shakes her head.

"Thank you," I whisper.

"What are you thanking me for?"

"For making all my dreams come true," I pause. "I never knew what I was missing until you came along, but now, you have answered all my prayers." I run my finger down her cheek. I see her skin prickle and her breathing increase.

"If only we were on our own," I peck her forehead, but I step back and adjust my hardened cock as thoughts of Hannah naked on the dining room table fills my head.

I see Hannah glance in the direction of Bert, Thomas and Elliott, as the embarrassment takes over. I glance over in the direction of Joyce and see her observing us as she smiles.

"How about we all head outside while we wait for the meat to finish?" Joyce announces.

"I'll clear the table, you guys go ahead," I volunteer.

"Are you sure, I can do it if you want to go with the others," Joyce interjects.

"No, don't be stupid. I'll clean it up, you go and enjoy the pleasant weather with the boys." I reply, not really needing to clean up but to wait for my stiff length to soften again.

"If you're sure," she kisses my cheek as she follows the others out.

"I'm sure," I smile.

Once I have the table cleared, checked the meat, and turned on the potatoes and vegetables, then I head for the patio door. As I reach them, I stand by the door frame as I watch Hannah, playing snatch with the boys. I smile as I see them all running around and laughing.

"You know, I knew you two were a perfect match," I jump as I hear Joyce speak from behind me.

"Really? I thought you thought I was thinking with the wrong head," I smile.

"Oh, you were, my dear boy, but I have never seen anyone switch on a light in your eyes the way Hannah does to yours."

I smile as I turn back to watch them running and playing.

"She's the one," I whisper, as I watch on with love.

"I can see that." Joyce says. "Have you spoken to your dad?"

"Nope. I don't plan on talking to him either," I say as my good mood changes.

"I know you don't get on, but I'm sure If he saw you with Hannah and those gorgeous boys, he'd change his mind."

"I don't need him to change his mind, Joy. I have come to realize I don't need to please him; I need to please myself and for the first time in forever I am doing exactly that."

"I know, and I am proud of you, David," she squeezes my shoulder as she walks out past me onto the grass to play catch with the boys.

All my life I have wanted to hear those five little words, I am proud of you. But now I realize I don't need to hear those words from someone else, I just need to believe in myself and be proud of who I am.

I wander back into the kitchen to make another drink as I hear Hannah's shoes follow behind me.

"Why are you hiding out here?" She smiles.

"I'm not hiding out; I was just going to make a drink before dinner." I smirk. "Are you enjoying yourself?"

"I love them. Joyce and Albert remind me of my grandparents,"

"Are they still alive?"

"No. My grandfather died when I was eleven and my grandmother passed just before I was disowned,"

I smile sadly, she really was like me, on her own.

265

"Have you decided whether to speak to your mum yet?"

"I think I want to try; I miss having her around and I think it will be good for the boys too."

"I agree."

I pull Hannah into my arms and wrap her up in a cuddle. I cup the back of her head and bring her lips to mine; I've been dying to kiss her properly since I picked them up earlier.

"Eww... You and mum are always kissing." Elliott shouts his disgust.

I step back and look over Hannah's shoulder to see everyone standing just outside the kitchen door watching us. I look towards the boys who have a look, like they are sucking a lemon and then to Joyce and Bert who are beaming with pride.

"We've just come to dish dinner up." Bert winks.

This time I blush as well as Hannah. It feels like we've been caught by parents doing something we shouldn't.

"I was just making us drinks."

"Is that what they call it nowadays?" Bert laughs.

I shake my head as I laugh. Bert always loved to pull my leg and some things never change.

We all muck in and help sort the food then place it on the table. As we all sit down, Joyce asks the boys about school and what they love to do. Thomas rambles on for ages about his love for swimming and woodwork, while Elliott tells them about his art and how he loves to draw. We all tuck in and the roast beef is to die for. Joyce has done her famous Yorkshire puddings too, and they are perfect.

Bert asks me about any latest projects we have going on and I tell them that we have never been busier. Shawn takes on the new builds and Joe oversees the renovations. When I look up, I see Joyce and Hannah deep in conversation, it's like they have been friends all their lives and it warms my heart. Gaynor wouldn't accept Joyce or Bert, and every time they met, she would be pleasant but never friendly.

"You know," Bert whispers so only I can hear. "You've got a good one there and these boys are priceless."

I smile as I move my eyes away from the direction of Hannah.

"I know, I have found my place in the world."

"I believe you have, Son, I believe you have."

I feel Bert's hand gently squeeze my shoulder as my eyes connect with Hannah's and she smiles in my direction. All I ever wanted was to feel part of something and sitting here that is exactly how I feel now with her.

Chapter Twenty-three

Hannah

I yawned as I pulled the car into the drive, my stomach felt a little tender, I helped Martha out of the car, and we took a steady walk around to her house.

"What's made you so tired today, missy." Martha asks.

"Oh, no reason, Martha. We went to meet David's friends yesterday and I think I'm still recovering," I laugh.

"Did you have a fun time?" She asked as I helped her into her chair. I can't believe how fail she is looking the last few weeks.

"I loved them. They were so lovely, and they loved the boys."

"Who couldn't love those two," she smiled. "You have done a wonderful job bringing them up, Dear, you should be very proud."

"Thank you, Martha, that means a lot."

"Have you spoken to your mum yet?"

I smile sadly because I haven't built up enough courage to call her, but I knew it was more to do with, I was worried she would turn her back on me again.

"I haven't yet. I was going to try in the week, but we'll see."

"Take the step, beautiful. She obviously wants to be in your life. Why else would she have written to you? It took a lot of guts for her to do that."

I knew Martha was right but putting myself out there again with the woman who was supposed to love me unconditionally is hard.

"I will, I promise. Is there anything else you need before I go?"

"No, I'm okay Hannah. Thank you for going with me today."

"Martha, you only have to ask, and I will always be here. You mean the world to me and the boys, you know that." I kiss her forehead as I move towards the door but pause. "Martha."

"Yes, Dear."

"I just wanted to say, thank you for being here when I needed someone over the last few years. Without you I wouldn't have managed,"

"You never have to thank me, Hannah, I have loved every moment," she smiles.

I nod my head, before I turn and make my way back home.

❧❦❧

I hear the banging on the door, as I jump from the shower. I am so glad David dropped the boys at school, or else this morning would have been a nightmare. Not only because I feel a little under the weather, but also because it takes Martha a little longer to get to places now.

I grab a bath sheet and wrap it around my body as I make my way downstairs, water dripping everywhere as I walk towards the door. I bet David has forgotten something or has left something behind. He is moving his boxes today, so no doubt he wants to drop something off or pick something up.

"I really need to get you a key cut," I start but the words die on my lips when I open the door and see who is on the other side.

"Well, that would be helpful," Ian grins at me as he takes in the towel around my body.

"What do you want?" I stutter as I take in my ex.

"I was hoping for a better reception than that, beautiful."

"Ian, what do you want?"

"I came back to see my wife and boys."

"Where the fuck have you been?" I demand.

"I had to work away, I told you that."

"Maybe you have lost some marbles over the years, but you never once told me you were working away," I mutter bitterly.

"Are you not going to invite me in, Beautiful?"

"No,"

"Why? Worried your little plaything will find out I'm back." He looks at me with a raised eyebrow.

"If I'm being honest, I couldn't give a fuck. I'm not the one who left you high and dry with nothing to your name and expected you to take care of our sons with nothing but bills." I spit back as I try to push the door closed.

"Oh, I don't think so princess. We need to talk."

Ian pushes his way into the hallway and slams the door behind him. I stumble back and land on the bottom step of the stairs. I can't believe he has decided to turn up now.

"I suggest you go and get some clothes on before I take it as an invite and rip that flimsy towel off you and fuck you right where you are." His eyes leer at my uncovered legs.

I scramble to my feet and take the stairs two at a time heading straight for my bedroom door. Once I shut it behind me, I make sure it's secure. I turn until my back hits the wood as I sag into the door, then slide down until my bum lands on the floor. I

270

try to calm my breathing as my heart rate goes mad. I can't believe it after all this time, he decides now to come back.

After a few minutes, I raise myself off the floor and search for some leggings and a baggy t-shirt. There's no point in getting ready for work because I need to find out what he wants and get him to leave before the boys return home from school.

I rush around my room, trying to get dressed as fast as possible. I decide to just run a brush through my hair. I don't bother doing anything else with it but grabbing it and tying it back.

As I reach the bottom of the stairs, I walk towards the living room and see Ian looking at all the pictures hanging on the wall of the boys in the last few years. He reaches out and runs his finger over the picture of me and the boys taken by Liv on our day out earlier in the year.

I watch as he stands in his old worn jeans and old tattered trainers. His hair looks a little longer than it had been since I last saw him, but it had been nearly three years since the day he walked away. I wished when I saw him, I felt something more than hate. I hate what he did to us and how he left us in the lurch. I know we need to talk but I hope he'll say his peace and then fucks back off.

"What do you want, Ian?"

I see him freeze when he hears my voice but doesn't remove his finger.

"I came back for my family, I miss them."

"You lost your family as soon as you walked out that door and didn't look back." I replied in a matter-of-fact way, I tried to keep my voice even. I don't have the energy or heart to care about anything he has to say anymore.

"I was keeping you safe," his voice strains with emotion.

"Oh, I suppose the younger model was your way to protect us too." I raise my eyebrow.

"There was no younger model or baby," he hollers disdainfully. "I told my dad that so you wouldn't come looking for me," he sighs.

I frown, I am trying my best not to punch him in the face.

"What the fuck is going on, Ian? No bullshit."

"Are you not going to offer me a drink, before I spill my shit."

"No, I'm not. Get on with it, I have a job I need to get too,"

"Where's the kitchen? I will do myself one then." he walked past me and knocked my shoulder as I followed him into my kitchen.

He flicks on the kettle, as I pace the kitchen floor, I don't know what to do next. I hear the cupboards being opened and shut as it pulls me from my thoughts.

"What are you doing?" I ask.

"I'm looking for a mug," he replies sarcastically.

I push past him and reach into the one with the mugs in, as I pull two down and start making two coffees. Just as I finish pouring in the boiling water into both mugs, I feel Ian slide in closer to my body and place his hands on my hips. His fingers slide under my t-shirt as I feel his finger rub along my skin; I shudder and not in a good way, his touch makes me feel repulsed.

"I've missed you, Baby."

I jump as I hear him whisper those words in my ear.

"Yep. Well, I haven't missed you."

I step out of his hands and walk over to the table, before sitting down, trying to calm my racing heart. I see the frown dance on Ian's face as he turns towards the table, walking over and then sits on the opposite side.

"Start talking."

I hear him sigh.

"No, small talk first?"

"No. I have a life I have to get back too." I raise my brow as my patience wavers.

"Ouch. That didn't hurt much."

"Well usually when someone walks from your life, they give up all rights to the person they left behind."

"I didn't walk away," he shakes his head.

I laugh.

"So, remind me where have you been for the last two and half years?"

"I...."

"Exactly, Ian. While you've been off doing, God knows what, I have had to hold down a job, look after the boys and do a night course. All on my own..." my chest pants as I feel the anger building. "You do not get to walk back in here and demand anything or think we can go back to what we were."

I watch him as he takes in my words.

"I left to protect you and the boys." He mumbles.

"Really? Well, you can protect me some more and fuck off!"

He shakes his head in frustration.

"Hannah, please let me explain."

As I sit here listening to his voice, I find it extremely hard to see what I loved about this man, he is not how I remembered him.

"What's there to explain, Ian?" I say his name with venom in my voice. "You walked out of our lives without so much as a word. You emptied our bank account, you left ME to deal with all the red-letter bills and I was in so much debt that I lost the house because you hadn't been paying anything for months." I shout as I stand to walk over to the sink. I see Ian follow me from the corner of my eye as I look out of the window wishing this was over already.

"If I could go back..." He starts.

I felt the energy drain from my body, he wished we could go back. It's ironic because for six months after he left, if he had come back then, I would have jumped at the chance to take him back but now....

"Well, I am glad we can't." I stop him dead. "I thought what we had was everything but what I have now is so much more,"

He scoffs as a laugh leaves his lips.

"I bet. A shag and a good salary, what more could a girl want."

I turn on the spot and slap him across his cheek. How dare he come into my house and make me feel cheap. There is nothing cheap about my relationship with David.

"How dare you? You have no idea what I have now. He is more of a man than you will ever be."

"I'm sure he is but you are still my wife, and those boys still have my genes, so you are still MY family," he grunts out.

"Ian you can beat your chest all you want but I don't love you anymore. I don't want to be with you. I am not going to beat around the bush, I want a divorce."

"WHAT!"

I see him draw a breath. The look of shock on his face is evident. I think he thought he could walk back in here and everything would go back to normal. There was a time he only had to click his fingers and I would jump, but those days are long gone.

"You heard me; but I am glad you have come back," I see his eyes light in hope, but as I continue, I see the light fade. "Because it saves me trying to find you. I had been thinking for the last month or so, about contacting your dad to see if he knew where you were."

He takes a step back and shakes his head in disbelief.

"A man leaves for a while and comes back to find his wife shacked up with another man and playing happy families."

I couldn't believe the words spewing from his mouth. The resentment I felt for this man was close to boiling over.

"It wasn't a while, Ian! It is NEARLY THREE FUCKING YEARS!!" I seethe.

"It doesn't matter, years, months, days. You belong to me."

I stand for a second trying to control the loathing I am currently feeling. How dare he say I belong to him!

"I belong to no one, Ian. It may have taken me years to work that out, but I know who I am and who I want to be." I calmly say.

"You wear my ring," I see him glance down to my finger.

"I haven't worn your ring in two years. Why would I want a constant reminder that my husband didn't give two shits about me or my boys?"

I see him trying to control his temper as he stands still staring at my hand.

"I did what I thought was best." He mutters. "I did something stupid, got involved with something dodgy and I had a few men after me. They knew where I worked but not where I lived but it would have only taken them a few weeks to find out and I would have put you all in danger."

"Ian, I don't care." I say as I look deep into his eyes, I need him to realize I have moved on. "I have gone well past the caring

275

stage. I had spent enough nights crying and wishing you'd come back..."

Ian rushes around the table, then pulls me into his arms and kisses me before I can finish what I was saying. The kiss was hard and felt foreign on my lips, I pushed hard on his chest as our lips sprung apart. I cringed as I realized he had kissed me.

"You don't have to cry anymore, I'm back and back for good." He smiles as he rests his head against my forehead.

I step left, to remove him from my space.

"If you had let me finish," I whisper. "I was going to saying, I have spent enough nights crying and wishing you would come back, but after I pulled my big girl pants up, I realized I didn't need a man to make me complete anymore or take care of me. So, I moved on and built a life for me and the boys."

"We could be a family again,"

I shake my head in disbelief, was he ever going to get it into his thick head? I've moved on and I don't want to be with him anymore.

"No, we couldn't. I don't love you anymore, Ian. I love that you gave me two gorgeous boys, but I don't love you as a partner."

"You don't mean that."

"I really do. And I think if I am being honest, I stayed with you because you were a security blanket. If things had been different, we wouldn't have lasted anyway. I think we have run our course and we need to start being honest about who we were."

"We were perfect together,"

I used to think the same, until I met David and my perspective changed on everything that happened before him.

"Perfect because you controlled the money, our life and me. I am not the same person I was back then; I won't be controlled again."

"I never wanted to control you, Hannah." He sniped. "You never challenged me, what I said went, that was your way not mine."

I pause for a moment as I let his words flow through my head, was he right? Did I just let him do what he wanted to do?

He was right, I never challenged him but not because I didn't want to, but because I didn't feel confident enough. But with David, he asks for my opinion, he never takes my feelings and thoughts for granted, so I never feel I need to challenge him. We work as a team.

"That may be so, but I do not love you, Ian. I love who I am now and who I am with."

He sighs in defeat.

"What will happen with the boys?"

"I would never stop you from seeing them, but it would be gradual as they haven't seen you for such a long time."

It's quiet in the kitchen for a few minutes and I think he's finally seeing the light.

"Can we try counselling?" He asks out of nowhere.

I try to keep my emotions out of my voice as my annoyance is starting to bubble.

"Counselling? What for?"

"I've heard it can work to make relationships better."

"Yes, if you are in a relationship, but we aren't Ian, and never will be again."

He steps towards me, as I step back, and I'm backed up against the kitchen work top.

"Isn't it worth a try?" He asks as I shake my head, "Not even for the boys?"

"They deserve something better than two parents that aren't fully committed,"

"But I am."

"Yes, but I'm not."

He runs his fingertip gently down my cheek as he leans forward, and his breath blows across my face.

"But you could be, I mean we were good once, we could be again."

I smile sadly as I watch the wrinkles appear on his forehead as he frowns.

"We couldn't be, I am not the same person, and neither are you."

"So that's it? I don't get a say, I don't get a choice?"

"You had a choice and chose to leave me with all that debt and the boys and no food." I move from out of his space and stand by the kitchen table, while I turn and make sure he is listening. "Now I am making the choice, and that doesn't involve you."

"I'm not letting you go,"

"It's not your choice," I sigh sadly.

"There has to be some way we can make this work. Maybe we could move away, just the four of us, build a new life?"

I hear the desperation in his voice, but it still doesn't change my mind.

"Ian, it won't work. I love my life now, I love my job, my freedom and I have someone who wants to support my dreams, not just expect me to follow theirs."

He walks back over and drops back down into the chair at the table with his head in his hands. I do feel kind of sad for him, but he made his bed and now he needs to lie in it.

"Ian, you will meet someone, one day that will make you so happy, but I'm not her, well not anymore."

"Well, I disagree, Hannah."

"You can't force someone to love you, Ian." I say sadly. "I really wished things were different, but they aren't. I'm sorry but I think a divorce is the only way for us both to move forward."

Ian stands abruptly knocking the chair, making it fall to the floor, I jump back up and as I lift my eyes up to meet his.

"Is that really what you want?" He hoarsely asks. "And I mean, really what you want?"

I take a seat back on my side of the table, I want to try to calm the situation down, I can feel the anger coming from Ian as the energy changes in the room.

"Yes." I whisper.

"And there's nothing I can say to change your mind?"

"No," I shake my head as I study my nails nervously.

"I came back with the perfect idea I would pick up from where I'd left off, but it's not going to happen is it."

"I'm sorry Ian, it's not. I don't want that life now. I am the happiest I've ever been or felt."

"Fine," he storms through the hallway, towards the front door and slams it behind him.

I sit there stunned for a moment not sure what just happened. I try to process what has transpired over the last couple of hours and my brain struggles to make sense of everything. The only good thing that had happened was I had made my intentions clear to Ian and explained that I wanted a divorce.

As I sit here staring into the distance, I hear a knock on the front door again and freeze. What if Ian has come back? Do I really want to see him again?

I slowly stand and walk to the front door; I rest my head on the cold wood as I try to force myself to open it.

"Who is it?" I hesitantly ask through the door.

"It's me." I hear David reply without any warmth in his voice. I don't want David to find out about Ian being back like this.

I unlock the door, and I pull it open. Once the door is unlocked, I'm greeted with David's angry face as my stomach drops, I know this isn't going to end well.

"What the fuck is going on?" David shouts at me.

"Wwhattt do you mean?"

I try to play today off. If I need to tell him anything about not going to work, I'll say I've been poorly because after this morning I am starting to feel really sick.

"Hannah, drop the act, I saw you kiss him, and I watched him leave. What the fuck is going on?" He demands as he pushes his way into the hallway.

I take a step back as if he's just slapped me across my face, does he really think I would get back with my ex? Especially after the last few months together.

"What the fuck do think happened, David?"

I feel my anger building and my body stiffens.

"That's what I'm asking you?" He shouts.

"Do you know what, get out."

I really can't deal with his attitude after what I've just been through this morning. I just need him out of here, so I can get some peace and time to process everything.

"What."

"I said, GET OUT!" I scream in his face as I try to hold back my tears.

"You aren't going to tell me what's going on?" He asks in shock.

"No. I. Am. Not."

"Do I not deserve an explanation?"

"I'm too tired for this David, just get the fuck out."

"Did you fuck him?" he demands to know.

"What does it matter? You've made your mind up, with or without me saying so."

"I need to know Hannah; DID YOU FUCK HIM?"

"NO!" I bellowed. "I did not fuck him. If you had asked me properly, I would have told you that it was Ian."

"What?"

"Yes, my delightful ex turned up, wanting us to be a family again but I sent him packing."

I feel myself losing my resolve to be strong, I just want to go to bed and forget this day ever happened.

"Hannah, I'm sorry. I saw him kiss you and thought. Actually, I don't know what I thought."

"I don't care, David. Just get out, NOW."

"Please Hannah,"

I see the hurt on David's face, but I have too much to deal with my own feelings without having to deal with his too.

"NO, Get Out,"

I feel my heartbreak as my world comes crashing down around me, the tears I had been trying to hold back are now streaming down my face and my energy has all but gone. I feel David try to step forward and embrace me, but I was just too angry to have him anywhere near me, so I pushed on his chest as hard as I could, and he stumbled back.

"David, just go. I don't want you here." I turn on the spot and make my way back into the kitchen and shut the door behind me. I walk to the kitchen table and plonk myself down on the chair, as I rest my head in my hands, as a sob escapes me. Just when I thought I had started to create the life I've always wanted, my floor falls out from underneath me.

Chapter Twenty-four

David

After I dropped the boys off at school, I decided to pop into the office to see if Shawn was busy or whether he wanted to grab breakfast and help me move my boxes to the new house, with the two of us it shouldn't take long.

As I rush through the reception, I see Ben from the corner of my eye and give him a wave.

"Is Hannah, okay?" He asks.

"Yeah, she is fine, why?"

"Oh, she hasn't arrived yet and Hannah is always on time."

"Ah, she is taking Martha to a doctor's appointment this morning so she will be in late."

"Okay, have all your phone calls diverted to the main desk and I'll take your messages,"

"Thanks, Ben, I really appreciate it."

I pat his shoulder as I make my way over to the elevator's and call for the lift.

As I leave the elevator, I notice the difference in the atmosphere not having Hannah already here. Usually, we have the light orchestra playing in the background but today it is silent. I walk past Hannah's office and glance in like I always do. I sigh when I see it empty, I hadn't realized how much Hannah had become the centre of my world. Just as I reach my office, I lean over my desk to get the house keys from the top draw.

"Hey what are you doing here?" I hear Shawn say behind me.

"Just picking up the keys, while I came to see if you wanted to grab some breakfast and if you were free to help me move my boxes?"

"I'm free and if you're buying, I'm definitely up for breakfast."

"I should have known the mention of food and you'd be there," I laugh as we make our way back to the elevator and back out to my car.

After we have finished our food, we make our way over to the bungalow. As we pull up, I see my father's car in the driveway, just what I needed. As I place my key in the lock of the front door, I take a deep breath and push the door open.

"Oh, he still lives then," my father spits as I walk through the hallway.

"Pleased to see you too," I say sarcastically as Shawn follows me through and heads to my room.

"When were you going to tell me?" He demands.

"Tell you what?"

"You're leaving your wife for your secretary?"

"I'm not leaving my wife for anyone, Father. I am moving out because I don't love Gaynor and she doesn't love me. We both deserve more." I say as I pass by him.

"And as for my secretary, double standards? What was my mum?"

"Don't bring her into this, Son."

"Well stay out of my business. I have nothing to prove to you or anyone else. I'm finally doing something for myself and not you or anyone else is going to destroy it." I slam my bedroom door.

He is the last thing I need at the moment. He always seemed to have this sixth sense of when I'm starting to feel happy

284

or things are working out, and he somehow destroys it. I help Shawn lift some boxes onto the bed, as my bedroom door flies open, here we go round two. My father isn't one to back down or to let someone else win.

"You do realise how bad this looks?"

I stand straight and draw a breath as my anger starts to build.

"What are you talking about?" I grit my teeth as I ask.

"Well now that you ask, I will tell you. Not only are you leaving your wife for another woman but your disabled wife at that,"

"Dad, if I really cared about your opinion, I would have asked you before now, but I don't." I shake my head. "How about you go and ask Gaynor about her affair with my so-called good friend, Luke?"

"It still looks bad on our family name. Why don't you stay here but carry on your fling with this woman in private?"

"Because she deserves better than a fuck, couple of times a week." I shout. "She deserves the world, and I'm going to give her that, not that you'll understand."

"That is uncalled for! I gave your mother all that I could. She never complained."

"No, she probably didn't, but you didn't have to listen to her night after night, crying herself to sleep, wishing and waiting for something that was never going to happen. She spent her whole adult life waiting for something she was never going to get and then died before she had a chance to experience real love. I am not going to be like my mother." I struggle to control my breathing as my anger for my mum builds. "I have never asked you for anything and I'm not going to start now, but what I will say is." I pause as I know what I need to do. "I don't want you to

285

be part of my life anymore. I have always wanted you to be proud of me, to love me for me, but now I realise I don't need your approval. So, get out of here and do not bother me or my family again. If you are that bothered about appearances, you fucking move in with Gaynor and live a lie."

I turn on the spot, pick up the nearest box and walk out of the bedroom door, as my stunned dad just stood there frozen to the spot, and I felt a moment of relief that I have never felt before. I am finally free to do what I need to do and I think now is the time to make Hannah and the boys my family officially. As I place the box in the boot of my car, I feel Shawn walking up behind and placing his box in there too.

"It's about fucking time," he says as he stands back up.

I frown as I try to work out what he's referring to.

"You, telling your dad to fuck off,"

I smile and nod my head. It does feel good knowing all my ducks are finally lining up and I can finally have the family I have been dreaming of. As we rearrange the boxes to make sure we can fit more in, I hear my father's car start up and reverse off the drive and speed down the road. I hope that's the last time I ever see him, but I very much doubt it will be.

While Shawn runs in to fetch another box, I text James to see if he is free and has the paperwork to the bungalow ready to sign. I know we were meeting tonight to sign it over, but now I have nearly tied up all my loose ends. The last one is signing over the bungalow and I want it done now, so when I put the last box in the car. I am free to walk away with nothing hanging over me. As I reach my old bedroom, James texts to say he's on his way and I feel the end is nigh.

Just as we put the last box into the boot and shut it down, James pulls into the driveway. I smile as he steps from his car, with the paperwork in his hand.

"Hey James, I'm sorry to drag you over early,"

"Not a problem, David. Let's get this done. It should take us less than an hour,"

As we stepped into the hallway, I knocked on Gaynor's bedroom door and shouted we'd meet her in the kitchen. Once I reached the kitchen, I filled the kettle for what would be my last time and pulled four mugs down from the cupboard.

"I thought we were signing the papers tonight?" Gaynor asks from the door.

"We were, but I just thought it would be easier to do it now."

"Oh, okay." She wheeled herself up to the kitchen island as I continued to make our drinks. As I was busy, I could hear James talking her through all the legal jargon and making sure she understood that once she signed, she was sole owner of the property, and any repairs would need to be carried out by her.

"I will help with repairs, so you have nothing to worry about," I smiled as I placed their drinks in front of them.

"Thank you," Gaynor smiled.

"David had the bungalow valued and at this current time it is valued at one hundred and thirty thousand pounds,"

I see Gaynor's eyes widen.

"Wow, that is a lot of money," she smiles.

"It is, but if you sign the paperwork, you wouldn't get anything else from the divorce. I need you to understand that Gaynor. David is signing the house over to you as your divorce settlement."

"I understand,"

287

"You are free to sell it or keep it." I smile. "It's yours to do what you want with."

"Thank you, David,"

"No, need to thank me Gaynor."

"So where do I sign? We might as well just get on with it."

"I need four signatures," James replies as he show's her where to sign.

At the last signature, I took my key off my keyring and gently lay it on the worktop as I won't be needing it ever again.

"I'll just run through my room to see if I have forgotten anything," I say as I walk towards my old bedroom. After I have checked the bathroom, bedroom and walked in the wardrobe I see there's nothing left so I make my way to the front door.

"David," I hear Gaynor call me from the kitchen, so I make my way back.

"Hey, what's up?" I smile.

"I am really sorry, you know."

I frown, not really understanding what she really meant.

"I should have been honest with you about Luke from the start."

"Forget about it, what's done is done," I smile, I don't feel anything negative towards Gaynor. Circumstances were at play here, nothing more.

I turn and make my way outside and see James and Shawn chatting away.

"Are you all done?" Shawn asks.

"Yep," I smile.

"No, last fuck or anything?" He winks as James laughs.

"There was never any fucking involved," I smirk.

"Man, how have you lived this long as a priest? Have you checked to see if little man still works?"

288

"Oh, he works perfectly fine, thank you very much and he's no way little."

"I'll get you some Viagra, just in case," he laughs at me as James joins in.

"Twat's." I move past them both and head for my car.

"Are you coming or not," I shout over my shoulder as I reach my door.

"I've been coming for years, it's you I'm worried about."

I throw my middle finger in Shawn's direction as I open my car door. Once he stopped laughing, he made his way over and jumped in. I start up the engine and wait for James to reverse off the drive, with one last look, I make my way to my new life and hope that the woman I love will move in with me.

I breathe a sigh of relief once the last box has been placed in the living room, I glance at the time and see it's just past one. Shawn has gone back to shut the boot and is waiting for me to drop him back at the office to get his car. So, I thought I would run and see if Hannah has eaten, if not I will fetch her some lunch. As we pull in the car park, I notice Hannah's cars not here, but think nothing of it as she had said it had been playing up for the last couple of days, so maybe she got a taxi in.

As I reach our floor with Shawn, I know Hannah's not here because there's no music and the floor feels empty.

"I wonder where Hannah is?" Shawn asks.

"I'll go and check her house," I frown as a cold sensation settles over me. "Maybe Martha isn't well, and she's decided to stay with her, I know she had a doctor's appointment this morning."

"That's probably it," Shawn agrees. "I'll catch you later, I need to get out on site."

"Okay, mate. Speak to you later."

I climb back into the elevator, then head for my car as I make my way over to Hannah's. Just as I round the corner, I slow down as I see a banged up blue fiesta sitting in the driveway. Confused, I pull up to the other side of the road opposite Martha's, while I'm deciding what to do next. I look towards Hannah's kitchen window and see her standing by the sink with her back towards me and standing in front of her is a short man. As I watch I see what looks like them to be talking and then I see him pull her into his arms and kiss her.

I close my eyes as my heart aches, I can't understand what I have just witnessed. I let my head drop to the steering wheel as I try to process my thoughts. Surely, she isn't seeing someone else, she can't be. When she's not with me at the office she is at home with the boys, unless she is out with me and the boys at the cinema or bowling. I sit here for what feels like forever as the tears fill my eyes. I thought that I had everything tied up, so we could move forward with our lives together but now...

I slam my hands down on the wheel, as I feel my anger building. Was she just stringing me along all this time? Did she really love me?

I look up and see the man leaving the house as the door slammed shut behind him. I wait as I watch his car pull off the drive and tear down the street at top speed. I don't know what to do. I watch for a few minutes to see if she follows or if she is staying where she is and after five minutes there's no movement, I decide I need to find out, what the fuck is going on.

I jump from my car and glance towards the house as I start to make my way across the street. I stop in the middle of the road. I'm not sure if I want to find out. Do I really want to know if she is with someone else, or do I just disappear? I thought we were happy, I thought we were building a life together. I was going to ask her to marry me next month. I wanted to spend the rest of my life with her.

I hear the beeping of a horn and realize I'm standing in the road. I turn on the spot and head back towards my car but think better of it as I need to know what is going on.

As I reach the front door, I rest my forehead upon the wood as I try to listen for any sound inside and I hear nothing. I knock on the wood and wait for her to open. It takes a while before I hear movement from behind the door. Then I hear someone approach from the other side.

"Who is it?" I hear weakly through the door.

"It's me." I reply without any warmth in my voice, I have dealt with enough shit today without finding the woman I love with another man.

I hear the lock on the door open, then she pulls open the door, and I see Hannah's sad face as my heart aches to hold her but I'm too angry to console her.

"What the fuck is going on?" I question sternly.

"Wwhattt do you mean?"

She tries to play dumb.

"Hannah, drop the act, I saw you kiss him, and I watched him leave. What the fuck is going on?" I demand as I push my way into the hallway.

She takes a step back as if I've slapped her as a shocked look takes her face.

"What the fuck do think happened, David?"

I can see the anger building in her body as she stands stiffly.

"That's what I'm asking you?" I shout.

"Do you know what, get out."

I jumped back in surprise at her throwing me out.

"What."

"I said, GET OUT!" she screams in my face as she tries to hold in her tears.

"You aren't going to tell me what's going on?" I ask in shock.

"No. I. Am. Not."

"Do I not deserve an explanation?"

"I'm too tired for this David, just get the fuck out."

"Did you fuck him?" I needed to know.

"What does it matter? You've made your mind up, with or without me saying so."

"I need to know Hannah; DID YOU FUCK HIM?"

"NO!" she bellowed. "I did not fuck him. If you had asked me properly, I would have told you that it was Ian."

"What?"

"Yes, my delightful ex turned up, wanting us to be a family again but I sent him packing."

"Hannah, I'm sorry. I saw him kiss you and thought. Actually, I don't know what I thought."

"I don't care, David. Just get out, NOW."

"Please Hannah,"

"NO, Get Out,"

I feel my heart sink as I see the tears streaming down her face. I try to step forward to embrace her and try to wipe her tears away, but she pushes hard on my chest, and I stumble back.

"David, just go. I don't want you here." She turns her back and walks towards the kitchen shutting the door behind her.

I stumble back and lean against the hall wall. *What the fuck just happened;* I think to myself. I really want to go in there and talk to her until I make her see what a fool I am and that I need her more than life, but as I hear her sobbing. I know the best thing to do was to text Liv to come around and comfort her, while I give her some space and work out what I'm going to do to win her back because there is no way I'm letting her go.

As I make my way across the street to reach my car, I open the door and slump in my seat. I try to steady my breathing as I open my phone to text Liv to ask her to go to Hannah and then I drop Shawn a text message to ask him to lock up later. Then I start my car and head home, but it's not home anymore, it's just a house. As I pull up to the curb, I look up at the house I'm supposed to spend the rest of my life with Hannah in. I don't know how I've got to this point. This morning I had the world at my feet and the woman I love by my side. What the hell happened?

Chapter Twenty-five

Hannah

I do not know how long it has been since I heard the front door close behind David and if you asked me how long it had been since I sat down, I could not tell you that either. Time just seems to have stood still. I really thought I had it all worked out, I thought my life was perfect now, but how wrong can you be? I was so hurt David thought I had been seeing someone behind his back. How could he seriously think I would do something like that to him? I love him more than life.

I rub my tired eyes as my head starts to hurt. I stand as I move to the sink and look out the window as I notice the dark clouds start rolling in. I know how the sky feels when darkness overtakes me. I do not know how to sort this. I know I should have told David about what happened with Ian but when he accused me of fucking him, I lost it and threw him out.

Another deep sob wracked my body and I want to curl up into a ball. I walk into the living room and take a seat on the sofa as I roll backwards until I am lying down. I reach over the settee and pull the crocheted cover off the back and drape it over me. I just want to go to sleep and hope it eases the ache in my temples.

Just as I am drifting off, I hear a knock on the door, I try to open my eyes, but they feel too heavy. I just want to sleep. I hear the knock again and drag myself off towards the door. As I open the door slightly, Liv is standing on the other side, as soon my eyes connect with hers, she pulls me into her embrace and the tears fall again.

"Oh, Hannah. Come with me."

"What are you doing here?" I ask as I cry on her shoulder.

"David text me and said he was worried about you and asked if I would come over to see that you were okay,"

Just hearing his name made me want to cry more, I have really fucked up.

"Come on, let's get you in bed and I will go and collect the boys."

I let Livvy help me to bed, as I crawl in and snuggle down into my blankets, and I submit to sleep.

As I start to stir, I feel stiff as I roll over in my bed and suddenly feel cold. I do not know how long I have been asleep but I notice it's dark outside so it must be quite late. The house is silent, and I wonder where the boys are. When I stand from the bed, the room begins to spin, so I grab onto the bedstead as I try to walk towards the bathroom because I need a wee. I just manage to make it in time before I weed myself.

Once I have finished, I leant up onto the sink to steady myself as I washed my hands. I must be coming down with something because I feel worse than before. I try to stand while I try to make my way downstairs; I pause as I suddenly feel sick. I just manage to reach the toilet as I lean in and empty my already empty stomach.

Once I finish being sick, I wash my mouth out with mouthwash, then I crawl downstairs slowly to see where everyone is. Taking each step on my bum because every time I try to stand, I feel my head begin to spin. When I reach the bottom, I hear the television on low but there is no sign of the boys. I want to cry; it is the first time I have ever wished my mum were here to take care of me. I suddenly miss her so much and wished I had not left it this long to contact her. I try to stand again but the sickness returns so I crawl into the living room to find Liv on the sofa, half asleep.

"Hannah, what are you doing?" she jumps up.

"I don't feel well,"

"You don't look it, sweets." She helps me onto the sofa. "Come on, let me help you back to bed and then I will fetch you a drink,"

"Where are the boys?" I ask weakly.

"They are in bed, exactly where you should be."

Liv helps me stagger back up the stairs as I hold onto her for dear life.

"You need a doctor, Hannah. You are burning up!"

"I just need to sleep, I'll be fine, we had a busy weekend and I'm just tired, mentally and physically too."

"I have never seen you this ill. Are you sure I cannot get a doctor? I really think you need one."

"I'll be fine, I promise, I just need to sleep it off. I could do with a drink of water though," I try to smile but I felt too fragile to smile properly.

I lie down on the bed as I watch Liv walk from my room and my head is still spinning. While I am waiting for the water, I start to shake uncontrollably as the ague takes over my body from my high temperature. I keep my eyes closed as I hear Liv walk back into the room.

"Here, try to drink some of this," I try to pull myself up but only manage halfway as I take a small sip of the cool fluid, I don't even open my eyes as the room still spins. "I've brought up the bowl, so if you feel sick again you don't have to leave the bed," she gently lifts my hair off my forehead.

296

"Thank you," I whisper.

"Let's lie you down, I just need to fetch something from downstairs and then I'll be back to lie down here, so I can keep my eye on you."

I listen to her make her way out of my bedroom and across the landing as the burning in my stomach starts again. I lean over the side of the bed; in the direction I think the bowl is and I am sick repeatedly. Just as I am being sick the last time, Liv rushes back in and she is on the phone, but I feel too ill to care who she is talking to.

"Okay, hurry. She might listen to you, but she needs to see someone. I'll leave the door on the latch." I hear her mumble.

Liv comes over to sit on the edge of my bed, while she helps me back onto my pillow and tenderly rubs a cool face cloth over my head and neck as I drift off to sleep.

Just the touch of his hand and I know everything will be okay. I feel his touch as he gently strokes my cheek. I don't even have to open my eyes to know David is here, which is a good job because I feel too feeble to open my eyelids.

"Hey, Baby, I'm here." I hear him whisper as his lips touch my forehead. I try to smile but I do not have the energy, but I do move slightly into his touch. "Hannah, you have a feverish temperature. I'm taking you to the hospital."

I want to tell him he is being ridiculous, but I know it is no use.

I feel him put his one arm around my neck and the other under my legs as he lifts me into his arms and carries me down the stairs and into the back of his car.

I must have drifted off in the car as we drove to the Uckfield hospital because the next thing I know, David is carrying me through the main reception, and I am being lifted

297

onto a bed. I try to open my eyes, but the lights hurt my pupils as we are directed into a cubicle.

I hear David explaining that I kept being sick, with a temperature, but complaining I am feeling cold and when I try to stand, I am dizzy. I feel something being pushed into my ear as I try to move my head out of the way and a small prick in my arm. If I had the energy to complain I would demand to know what they are doing but I just shut off my brain and fall back to sleep.

⁓⁓⁓⁓⁓⁓

I try to turn over in my bed, but something feels strange, I cannot remember my bed feeling this hard. I move my arm, but I feel someone grab my hand and stroke my face.

"Careful Hannah, you have a drip in your arm," I hear David whisper. I frown, I do not remember David coming around last night and what does he mean I have a drip in my arm. I slowly let my eyes drift open as my eyes connect to his.

"Good morning, baby." He smiles timidly.

I glance around the room and notice we are not in my bedroom.

"Morning. Where am I?" I croak.

David holds my hands tighter as he lowers his lips to mine. After a quick peck, he lifts himself back up until he can see my eyes.

"You are at the hospital. Can you not remember?"

I try to rack my brains as the last thing I remember was being sick in bed.

"No, I don't think so. I know I was ill, and Liv was looking after me."

"Well, you got worse, and Liv called me worried, so I brought you in here."

298

"There was no need David, I could have just slept it off."

"There was no way you could have slept that off, Hannah. You were seriously dehydrated."

Just as I was going to reply, the curtain pulled open as a doctor and nurse walked.

"Good to see you awake, Ms. George. How are you feeling now?"

I pause as I had not really had time to think about it as I was too busy chewing David out over bringing me in.

"Surprisingly better," I smile at the Doctor.

"I'm glad. I'm Dr Richards." he introduced himself and I smiled. "When you arrived at the hospital you were seriously dehydrated, so we put you on a drip, with fluids and gave you an anti-sickness injection to calm the sickness down." He smiled as he looked down at my notes. "We also took some blood to see what was going on." He paused and then looked at David before returning to me.

"I have to ask before we proceed, I have the tests back, but do you want me to ask," he looked down at the file once more. "Mr. Shepard to leave before I give you your results." He flicked his eyes across to David once more.

"No, of course, not. We are to...." I paused because our argument flashed back into my head, and I had kicked him out.

David stepped in as he held my hand.

"We are together, Doctor. We have been dating a while now."

"Perfect," the doctor replied. "Okay, so we had your results from your bloods back and there were a few things showing up."

I looked at David at the same time David looked at me and with a timid smile, he squeezed my hand. All sorts of things start running through my mind, Cancer being the main one, I am not

299

ready to leave David or the boys. Our life is just starting and there are so many things we want to do.

I look back towards the doctor as I wait for the dreaded news that something is seriously wrong.

"The test first picked up an UTI, which can easily be treated with a course of antibiotics." he smiled.

"Okay."

"And the second thing that was picked up was a hormone called HCG, it can only be detected when you are pregnant."

I see his mouth moving but nothing goes in, I saw this in a movie once but had never thought it could happen in real life. He continues talking but all my brain can register is the pregnancy hormone and what does that mean.

"Can I stop you there?" I say out of nowhere. "What do you mean 'pregnancy hormone'?"

"I mean you are pregnant."

"I can't be. I have the birth control injection every three months and it's due...."

I stop talking because I cannot remember the last time, I had it. In fact, I think I should have had it two months ago. That can't be right. I never forget things. I drop my eyes to the hospital sheet as I realize I have fucked up. David is going to think I have trapped him, and I am going to end up bringing the baby up on my own.

"You can still get pregnant on any form of birth control, Ms. George. Nothing is one hundred percent."

I nod but say nothing else because what can I say? I fucked up. David will leave me, and I will have two boys and a newborn to look after. I am so lost in thought that I don't see David lean forward and grab my face as he brings his lips to mine and kisses me tenderly.

"I'm going to be a dad," he whispers against my lips.

I blush, I can't believe he has kissed me so tenderly in front of the doctor but then as I look over David's shoulder, I see the Doctor is nowhere to be seen.

"David, I'm so sorry, I fucked up." I feel the tears escape my eyes.

"What are you on about, Baby?"

"I forgot to have my last injection; I don't want you to think I tried to trap you."

"I don't care, Hannah, you have given me the best gift ever." He beams. "I'm sorry for flying off the handle yesterday when I saw Ian at the house. I shouldn't have done that, but I'd had to deal with my father and then I saw him kiss you and jumped off the deep end."

"So, you don't want to leave me?"

"Of course not, woman, but I do want you all to move in with me now."

I sigh in relief as the doctor returns.

"I have booked you at nine to have a scan to determine how far along you are." he smiles. "And I will get the nurse to give you your next lot of antibiotics."

"Thank you." David stands and shakes the doctor's hand.

"Someone will be down at eight-fifty to take you for your scan and if everything's okay, you will be discharged to bed rest for the next few days to allow your body, time to recover."

"Thank you, Dr. Richards." I smile as I lie back down and I yawn.

"Get a little nap," David says as he kisses my forehead. "We have a couple of hours before you have your scan,"

"Thank you for being you, David. I love you so much."

"I love you, more, Baby."

It doesn't take long for the sleep to pull me under as I dream of a little boy just like his father running around our new home. I feel happy as I dream of the life we are going to have as a family. I feel myself being pulled from the best dream ever with David's lips upon mine.

I slowly open my eyes and meet David's.

"It's time," he whispers as his eyes light up.

"Okay." I try to sit up.

"It's okay, Ms. George, we'll wheel you up, so you just stay where you are." the porter smiled.

As he took the breaks off, I had a warm feeling take over at the thought of seeing our baby for the first time. As we enter the elevator, I feel David grab my hand as we ride up to the next level. I look up and see him smiling like he's won the lottery. When we reached the maternity ward, we were wheeled into the sonogram room as the sonographer entered through the door at the back of the room. Once the porter has put the brakes on, he retreats back into the corridor.

"Good morning, Ms. George. I'm Caitlan, your sonographer today. Let's get everything set up and we'll see how far along you have gone."

She offers David a seat next to my bed, and turns to switch on the machine, while she sets everything up, David holds my hand. I could feel the nervousness coming off him in droves. I gave his hand a squeeze.

"Can you pull down the blanket and lift up the hospital gown, please Ms. George, and we can get started." Caitlan asked, pulling me from my thoughts.

"Of course," I do as she asked.

"Right, because we don't know how far along you are we might not be able to see anything, so if nothing show's up, please don't panic," she smiles warmly.

I nod my head as I feel the cold liquid land onto my belly, I shiver as it touches my skin.

I feel the probe glide across my tummy as a swirling sound comes through on the monitor, as Caitlan moves it around. I hold my breath as I wait for the sound of the heartbeat. After a few moments I hear a light beating as she finds the baby.

"Ah, there we are. I just need to take the measurements and check everything is okay, then I will turn the screen around."

I hold my breath as I feel David's hand tighten on mine. We waited for Caitlan to turn the screen for us to see.

As the screen moved, my eyes watch the movement on the screen and gasped. There on the monitor was our little baby, nothing more than a tiny little jellybean.

"From the measurements, I would say you are eight weeks gone. Everything looks perfect and where it should be." She smiled.

I turned to look at David as the tears danced along my lids, but when I saw David tears flowing down his cheeks, mine followed suit.

"We made that," he whispered. "We made our baby; I can't believe it. The baby's perfect, just like it's mum," he turned his eyes to mine.

"I love you, Hannah. You've made my life complete."

David turned to Caitlan and smiled.

"Can we have a couple of print outs of our baby?"

"Of course. You might just make out baby, but it won't be very clear because it's quite little. The next scan will be much clearer."

"Thank you," David smiles as he turns to me and leans over to kiss my lips. "You are going to be the sexiest mum there has ever been."

"We'll see if you're still saying that at forty weeks gone," I laugh.

"You will always be sexy to me, woman, and when you're better, I will show you," he wiggles his eyebrows as I try not to laugh.

After Caitlan had passed me some blue roll to clear the gel from my tummy, she popped out of the room to fetch the scan pictures she had printed off. When she returned, she passed David the pictures before wishing us well, then the porter returned to take us back to my room.

I was itching to get back home, I hated hospitals at the best of times but now I just want to be back in my own bedroom. Once the Doctor had the notes back from the sonographer, he was happy to release me on complete rest for the next few days, though I knew I would struggle to follow his instructions when there's so many things I need to sort, especially if we are going to be moving in with David.

Once I had my discharge papers and the midwifery number to make an appointment for next week to get a check-up. David wheeled me in the hospital wheelchair to the front, even though I had told him I was more than capable of walking myself, but he refused to let me. He said I needed to rest and to build up my energy. If it meant getting out of here quicker, I would have agreed to anything, but I was still sulking, even though I know his concern is warranted.

As we pull onto the drive, the front door springs open as a worried Liv comes bounding out straight for my door, before I could draw breath, she had pulled me into her arms.

"I am so glad to see your ugly mush," She whispers. "I have never seen you look that ill, ever."

"I'm absolutely fine, Liv. Well, I will be once I can breathe," I laugh as Liv loosens her hold on me.

"Oops sorry. Come on, let's get you comfortable,"

Liv moves out of the way, as David reaches in and lifts me from the car.

"I can walk you know," I say in a low voice. "I've not lost the use of my legs,"

"I know, but I want to look after you, Baby," He kisses my cheek.

As we reach the living room, Liv has got me a blanket ready as David puts me down on the settee, as Liv continues to cover my legs.

"So, what did the hospital say?" Liv asks.

I freeze and look straight at David; we hadn't said if we were telling people or whether to keep it secret a little while longer. I see the slight shake of his head and I nod in agreement, but a moment of guilt hits my stomach. Liv is my best friend; we tell each other everything and I'm feeling awful keeping this from her.

I sigh, ask her for a glass of water before I fill her in. As she disappears out the room, I know I need to be quick because she'll be back before I know it.

"David, I need to tell Livvy. We don't keep secrets." I pause waiting for him to disagree but to my surprise, he kisses my lips.

"If it will make you happy, then tell Liv, tell the world; as long as I have you, I'm not too worried about the rest."

I wrap my arms around his neck and pull him closer, as my lips connect with his I feel his tongue brush against mine. I groan with desire as I hear Liv clear her throat behind us. I blush and pull back.

"Sorry," David laughs.

"It's okay, big man. I thought you were giving her mouth to mouth," she winked as she passed me my water.

"Thank you, Liv." I smile as David blushes.

"So, what did they say?"

"I had bloodwork done and two things have shown up, so I'm on bed rest for a few days, to allow my body to recover."

"What was it that has shown up? You're okay, aren't you?"

"I'm absolutely fine," I look over to David before I proceed. "They found I have a water infection and a foreign object growing in my abdomen,"

"Oh my God, what are they going to do? Operate?"

"I hope not," David replies. "I want my baby to last the whole nine months, thank you," he winks at me.

"Ekkkkk… You're pregnant? I'm going to be an auntie again?"

"You are," I reply as Livvy jumps up and down and wraps me in her embrace.

"So, the old man works then?"

"You spend too much time with Shawn," David smiles as he shakes his head.

As I sit here listening to the two most important people in my life laughing and joking, I feel the luckiest person in the world. I never thought I'd get a second chance at love again, but destiny had other ideas for us both.

Epilogue

Hannah

The weather is so warm today, lying here in the sun is the best way to spend my maternity leave. In the distance I hear Thomas and Elliott playing in the pool, and I feel great, huge, but great.

The last seven months have been a dream since I found out about baby bump. The weekend after the hospital, I took the courage to visit my mum. To say it was emotional was an understatement. I couldn't believe how much I had missed her, but as soon as she wrapped her arms around me, it just felt right. I cried solidly for over an hour, I blamed the hormones, but David and I knew it was more than that. I never truly admitted to anyone, but David knew how much I really missed my mum. It killed me a little more every day I didn't see her. It was even worse the weekend after when she met the boys, she cried for a solid hour this time, she couldn't apologise enough for not being there and was sad that she had missed them growing up.

We didn't tell anyone apart from Liv and Shawn about the baby until I was fourteen weeks pregnant, we didn't want to jinx it. I was still trying to talk David into speaking to his dad, but he wasn't budging. He didn't want him to have any part in his grandchild's life, so I respected his decision, but I just need to be sure.

Two weeks after our first scan, we moved into the house, the boys were ecstatic with their bedrooms and adored the pool, we barely got them out of it. Especially Thomas, he lived in the pool and would bring his friends back to swim. The first really good weekend of weather, we decided to have a Barbeque and invited Mum, Joyce, Bert, Martha, Liv and Shawn around to celebrate the new house. It was perfect. Mum, Joyce and Martha hit it off straight away. I heard Mum thanking Martha for being there for me and the boys, while she couldn't be, and I heard Martha say it was her pleasure. Shawn kept the boys entertained in the pool.

When we had all eaten, I looked at David and nodded. I knew it was the time to tell everyone about the bump, not that I really had one, I didn't really start showing until I was five months with the boys, so hopefully this one will be the same.

David stood and tapped the side of his mug to draw the attention to him. I watched as I saw the love and admiration there was around the table for my man.

"I just want to make a little speech and then you can all get back to what you were doing," I see him lift his eyes to mine. "I just wanted to thank you all for being a part of my life. Without each and every one of you sitting around the table I wouldn't have reached this point. I couldn't explain how happy I am, and what the woman in front of me means to me. Since the first time I laid eyes on my beautiful Hannah I knew I was in trouble, and I was right."

We all laugh as I shake my head. David kept his eyes glued to mine as he continued to talk.

"I never knew love until I met you. I never knew life until you entered mine." He takes another breath as my smile beams. "We wanted you all here tonight, not just to show you our home, but to tell you our good news. Hannah is carrying my baby. She is making all my dreams come true."

The cheer erupted around the table as I felt my mum's arms around me.

"Those better be happy tears," she pulls back and wipes them away.

I giggle as I look up in David's direction again.

"They are, Mum. I have never been this happy."

"I'm glad, sweetheart. And I'm going to be a grandma." She beams.

"You are." I reply as she kisses my forehead before stepping back to let Joyce give me a cuddle.

Once everyone congratulated us, Liv put the music on and said it was time to really get the party started. I sat in my chair on the decking watching everyone enjoying themselves, as I felt a little tired. While I watched everyone having a good time, a feeling of warmth came over me as I realised how much these people mean to me. My eyes were blinking as the tiredness started to take over, I think I was overwhelmed by the whole day and it had taken it out of me.

"What are you doing over here?" I hear from behind me as David arms engulf me from behind.

"Nothing, I am just enjoying watching everyone have a good time," I smile. "What are you doing?"

"I was just thinking we should kick everyone out and let me finish what we started earlier in the shower,"

I squirm in my seat as the memories of our sexipade in the shower this morning runs through my mind.

"I see my woman is horny." he winks.

"Shh. We have guests David."

"One word and they can be gone."

"No. It's the first time we've all been together as a family, so you will have to wait to get your dick out." I say as I look over my shoulder.

I see David pout and I laugh, he's like a child when doesn't get his own way.

"Go and see if we have any red velvet cake left and then we will see,"

I watch as he makes his way all the way down to the kitchen as my eyes eat him up. I really can't believe how lucky I am, from six weeks ago, thinking everything had been destroyed when Ian turned up and I kicked David out; to sitting here in this beautiful house with my beautiful family, I don't think anything could top this. Well at least until bump arrives and then our family will be complete.

David

I stand in the kitchen as I wash the dishes watching Hannah lying on the sun lounger. I love seeing her belly swollen with my child. We had talked about only having one but seeing her as gorgeous as she is now, one will never be enough. I am thinking about a football team, I just need to convince my beautiful woman but I'm sure with the power of my tongue I can get her to agree.

As I dry my hands on the hand towel, I walk upstairs and push open the nursery door. I can't believe in the next week or so we will have a little baby lying in its crib. Hannah only has six days until her due date, even though I think she's wishing it was now.

The past seven months have been a dream, the boys settled in straight away without many issues.

Hannah has been amazing, the sex is exceptional, I have never known someone as horny as my woman. Twenty-four, seven, she is ready and waiting, whether it's at home or work, if she's needed it, I've given it, she's never had to ask. Although it has had us in some sticky situations with both Ben and Shawn, I smile as I remember how many times they've walked in and caught us up to something. Hannah has made them both knock before entering either of our offices to make sure we aren't up to something.

When we first told the family about bump, we had a few ropey days with Elliott, he didn't want a younger brother or sister, but I had a man-to-man chat. It turned out he was worried we wouldn't love him anymore because he wouldn't be the baby but when I explained he would always be my favourite, he came around and now he's looking forward to meeting his new sibling. We decided at the twenty-week scan, we wouldn't find out what sex the baby was as we didn't want it to ruin the surprise, but now the weeks are dragging I'm kind of regretting it. I just wish he or she would make her entrance into the world.

The one thing I have loved watching over the last six months is Hannah and her Mum, Imogen's bond grow. They are barely apart now, and we see her every other day, either she comes here, or we go to hers. It has been truly magical seeing them both together. I know Hannah always felt like there was something missing from her life, but she couldn't quite put her finger on it but now, she's the happiest I have ever seen her. Thomas has really taken to his nan too, but Elliott is Bert's little helper. Every Sunday we go over for dinner with Joyce and Bert and while we are there Elliott follows Bert everywhere. He's even calling him Grandad, which I find adorable. We have Martha over

311

twice a week too, well when she's up to it, she's getting really frail.

As I walk over to pick the teddy up, where it must have fallen off the chest of drawers on to the floor overnight. I hear a noise downstairs.

"DAVID!" I hear Hannah groan.

I rush from the room with my heart in my mouth, taking the stairs two at a time to get to her, she must have fallen or hurt herself because she sounds in pain. As I turn the corner, I see Hannah leaning scrunched up against the kitchen side, holding on for dear life.

"Hey, Baby. What's the matter?" I ask calmly, trying to feel calmer than I was feeling.

Hannah turned her head and scowled at me.

"What do you think is wrong with me, David? My waters broke and my contractions are strong," I hear her pant.

"Okay," I stroke her back, gently. "What do we do? I forgot what we said."

Taking in a deep long breath Hannah starts to pant.

"Phone my Mum and Liv, I need to get the boys sorted."

I rush into the living room and pick up my phone as I walk towards the kitchen as I hear another scream come from Hannah's mouth. First, I dial her mum telling her Hannah is in labour and then Liv asking her to make her way to the house and then I call the midwife, before I help Hannah into the living room, then calmly take her to the car.

Once I make sure she's settled in the seat, I run back through the house to collect her bag. As I run through the back garden, Liv is standing by the car and talking to Hannah.

"David, we really need to move," she pants. "I have the feeling to push."

312

"Do not push, Hannah, whatever you do." I feel the panic bubble up.

We wave goodbye to Liv as we pull away from the house, as we approach the town on the way to the hospital, the traffic is at a standstill. OMG, if Hannah starts to push, there is no way I could deliver the baby, I wouldn't have a clue.

"What the fuck is hold us uppppp..." Hannah screams as another contraction takes over her abdomen.

"Just hold on a little longer Baby, I can't see us being too much longer,"

"David, call an ambulance, I can't hold on. I can feel it coming."

"Just close your legs, Hannah, keep them crossed. We shouldn't be too long."

"DAVID, for the love of god. PULL THE FUCKING CAR OVER AND CALL AN AMBULANCE, the baby is coming now. You dick!"

I pulled the car over, helping Hannah into the back of the car as I spoke to the control room as we waited for the ambulance.

As the operator asks me questions, I start to clam up. I hear them talking to me, but it feels like they are speaking to me in the wrong language, until I hear Hannah squeal in agony as the contractions build.

"How long has Hannah been having contractions for?" the operator asks.

"Hannah, how long have you been having contractions?"

AHHHHH..... Hannah squeals as another one arrives.

"They," pant, "Started," pant, "This," pant, "Morning," pant.

"Why the fuck didn't you say anything?" I ask annoyed.

"Because I thought they were Braxton hicks, DAVID." She says through gritted teeth.

I lean back, because the look I'm getting is telling me she is ready to chop off my dick and feed it to me.

"How close are the contractions?" the operator asks.

"How close are they, Baby?

"Do. Not. Baby. Me." Hannah grunts. "I don't fucking know; I haven't got a bloody watch on." As another contraction takes over.

"David, I need you to check to see if you can see the baby's head,"

"And where will I find that?" I screech.

"You will need to remove any underwear and look into her vagina."

"Are you mad? You can't see the look I'm getting from Hannah. If I go down there, she will probably kill me."

"We'll deal with that after," I hear the slight chuckle from the other side of the phone.

Taking a deep breath and giving Hannah my sexiest smile.

"Hey, darling. I need to remove your pants and look down there, to see if I can see the baby, is that okay?"

"David, you better hope this baby is out soon, or otherwise you will never have sex again." She grunts as another contraction starts.

I slowly peel her underwear off and gently open her legs. I take a deep breath as I lower my head.

"You need to describe to us what you can see David."

"Oh, okay. I can see hair, lots of hair."

"For," pant, "Fuck," pant, "Sake," pant, "David," pant, "She wants to know if you can see the baby, not my muff hair," she screams.

314

"Oh, yeah, right. Lift your bum for me, baby," I help Hannah slide down more so I can see between her legs properly in the cramped space. "OH. MY. GOD, I can see the head,"

I start to feel lightheaded; I can see the top of my baby's head.

"Okay, I am going to talk you through the next stage, David, I need you to do as I say as the ambulance is five minutes away, so it should be with you soon."

"Okay, but I'm not sure I can do this," I start to stutter.

"You can David, but I need you to concentrate,"

I take a deep as I see Hannah preparing to push.

"I am going to put you on speakerphone," I say.

"Okay, I need you both to work together," I hear through the phone. "Hannah, I need you to pant as you feel your next contraction, I need you to push, David, I need you to watch and guide the baby."

Hannah takes a deep breath and grits her teeth as she pushes through her contraction.

I cup my hands at the edge of her vagina as the baby's head starts to move down the birth canal. I feel the tears building in my eyes, my baby is coming and I'm the one to catch it. I hear Hannah scream again as another contraction takes hold.

"Push, Hannah, push,"

"I'm pushing, dumb-twat," she grits her teeth as she pushes with all she has.

I hold my breath as the baby's head arrives.

"OH, we have a head," I shout excitedly.

"Well done, Hannah, the ambulance is two minutes away, but we need you to push again."

I look up and my eyes connect with Hannah's as my heart fills with so much love for this woman.

"Come on, Baby. You can do this."

With an almighty last push, Hannah delivers a perfect little girl, and my baby girl has some lungs on her, just like her mum.

Lifting the baby up, I place her onto Hannah's chest, and kiss my woman on the lips.

"Thank you,"

"What for?" Hannah whispers.

"For making my life complete,"

"I love you," she cups the back of my head and pulls me back to her lips.

When I pulled back, I knew it was now or never.

"Marry me?"

"What?"

"Marry me and make me the happiest man on the planet,"

"Yes,"

"Really,"

"Yes, really. I love you David and all that you have given me."

"Not as much as l love you." I look down at our beautiful baby girl.

"Estelle Imogen." Hannah says out of nowhere.

"What?"

"Estelle Imogen, is perfect for our little angel."

I couldn't agree more. Not only was my baby named after my mum, but she carried two strong ladies' names. Just as I wiped the tears away, the ambulance arrived, so I moved out of the way to allow them to help Hannah get checked and wrapped Estelle in a blanket. I can't believe how lucky I am. Not only have I got the woman of my dreams, but I helped bring my daughter into the world and as long as I breathe, I will always make sure they are both as happy as they make me......

THE END

Thank You! Thank you! Thank you! Thank you! Thank you, to each and every one of you!
Without your support, none of this would be possible.
Thank you for all the love, support, and friendship. It means more to me than you'll ever know.
Each book I write is a journey I immensely love and I hope you enjoyed this one.
With all my love!

Amii xoxo

Made in the USA
Las Vegas, NV
27 August 2021